Another Person

KANG HWAGIL is one of South Korea's new group of 'young feminists'. Her writing has received numerous accolades, most recently the 2020 Munhakdongne Young Writers' Award for her short story 'Eumbok'. She has published two short story collections, *A Decent Person* (2016) and *White Horse* (2020), as well as two novels, *Another Person* (2017), which won the Hankyoreh Literary Award the same year, and *The Haunting of Daebul Hotel* (2021).

CLARE RICHARDS is an editor and translator from Korean, with a key interest in feminist literary fiction. She is the recipient of grants and awards from the National Centre for Writing, Literature Translation Institute of Korea and The Korea Times, amongst others. Her translation of Kang Hwagil's prize-winning short story *The Lake* was published by The Massachusetts Review in 2022. *Another Person* is Clare's debut novel translation. @clarehannahmary

Kang Hwagil

Another Person

TRANSLATED FROM
THE KOREAN BY
CLARE RICHARDS

PUSHKIN PRESS

Pushkin Press

Somerset House, Strand,

London WC2R ILA

Original text © Kang Hwagil 2017

First published in Korean language by Hankyoreh En Co., Ltd. in 2017.

English translation © Clare Richards 2023

First published by Pushkin Press in 2023

1 3 5 7 9 8 6 4 2

ISBN 13: 978-1-78227-935-8

This book is published with the support of the Literature
Translation Institute of Korea (LTI Korea)

Quotation from *We Were the Mulvaneys* by Joyce Carol Oates reprinted by
permission of HarperCollins Publishers Ltd. © 1996 Joyce Carol Oates

Designed and typeset by Tetragon, London

Printed and bound by Clays Ltd, Elcograf S.p.A.

www.pushkinpress.com

Contents

PART 1

Jina

MY MIND EMPTIES when I think back to that day. What happened to me? Which memories still remain?

There was a small lake. Its odour was thick and deep. When it rained, the dark stench spread throughout the whole neighbourhood. Its stickiness seeped in from all directions; the air, heavy with moisture, trembled in the rain. I tramped down on the blades of grass as I drifted along the roadside.

You want to know what happened? What I did?

I wasn't satisfied until the smell of fresh green grass permeated every inch of my soles. I wasn't at ease until the edges of my trainers were smeared dark green. Until the smell of mangled grass shot through me like a sharp cry, I couldn't forget. Forget what was coming for me. Forget that my body was already sodden with the stench of the water, emitting its stale tang.

For a long time I couldn't remember. But it's sharp and vivid now, like it were only yesterday. And feels, too, like an echo from the distant past.

The voice calling my name.

Jina-ya? Jina-ya?

There was a rice field. The field was vast—so vast I thought my heart would burst. At dusk the world was coloured every warm shade of red. The air breathed in the last heat of the day, radiating the gentle scent of the afternoon sunlight. The sun trembled as I stretched out my hand. I filled my lungs with the breeze and ran to the end of the levee. The crimson-dyed evening was tender, a smile brimming with love.

Jina-ya? Jina-ya?

That day, someone called my name. I didn't look back. Looking straight into the faraway, setting sun, I walked and walked. It was the only thing before me, all that was coming for me. I forgot the smell of the voice that clung to my body.

Wait.

The sun lighting my path never existed.

I haven't left my flat in three months.

Stupid woman.

Today, too, people hated me. I was spending today, like every other day, alone at home, reading articles and comments written about me. The subject this time was 'stupidity'. The pattern in which the disputes unfolded was generally similar. Someone called me stupid, and then the responses followed: she's not stupid, just afraid. No, she wasn't stupid or afraid, she was just a hopeless case to begin with. Then came another rebuttal. Look, let me explain to you what 'stupid' means. Haven't you heard the story? The girl dancing in the red shoes. Beanpole legs limping as she walks. The girl who couldn't stop dancing, in shoes she should never have worn. She shouldn't have longed for what didn't suit her to begin with. Should've known the shoes were bad. She had no clue the shoes weren't right for her—you think she would have known her two legs would spread up in the air?

That's what stupid is.

These people I'd never met knew me better than I knew myself.

My ringtone pierced the air. Like a disobedient child caught in the act, I blinked and directed my gaze down at the white flashing screen. It was Tana. I looked at the phone for a brief moment before turning back towards the monitor. I didn't pick up.

I knew what Tana would say. She'd tell me to stop looking at what I was reading. It was obvious. At first she'd say she'd phoned out of boredom—it was only when the conversation neared its end that she'd bring up what she really wanted to talk about.

Jina-ya, don't pay attention to any of that bullshit.

I always responded that I wouldn't. Then, as soon as we hung up, I'd type my name, 'Kim Jina', into the search engine.

I was aware that what people were saying was bullshit. How could I not be? I just couldn't stop reading. Tana knew my obsession with what other people were saying. That must be why she made a habit of stressing the same thing every time.

'Most of them are on your side. You know that, right?'

But today I wasn't having any of it. I ignored the phone. It continued to ring. Once. And again. And again. Then silence.

I burst out laughing. I was actually disappointed. I mean,

really? I'd deliberately avoided the call, but the moment the ringing stopped, the disappointment I felt was unbelievable. Then came a violent rush of loneliness, a sickness in the pit of my stomach. I'm this predictable, this dull.

Like on that day last summer.

My boyfriend grabbed me by the neck.

Right. It's a stupid story.

Lately I'm most envious of the people who think my story is pointless. I, too, want to look at myself and think, 'I just don't *get* her.' To see myself in that same way. To become another person. A person totally distinct from this someone I can't understand, don't want to understand. I want to heave a deep sigh and call out my own name.

Jina-ya, come on. Why would you do that?

I wish emotions were something you could choose to feel. The fear that someone might leave me, discarded, without value—I hate that feeling. People have realized the hold these thoughts have over me, and treat me in whatever way they please. I want to stop consoling myself, to stop telling myself that despite all this I'm still okay. I want to harden. To not feel anything at all. What I need is to lay my body on a bone-dry mound of hay. To breathe in the parched, stiff scent of the grass. To have every drop of moisture sucked from me. And then, one day, looking at the dampened heart of another, draw a long breath and ask,

Come on, why would you do that?

Why didn't you end things?

*

He was my senior at work, and it was the fifth time he'd assaulted me.

That day, I reported him.

I've thought enough.

I shot up from my chair and put some water on the stove. For tea. Or coffee. But inside my head the thoughts continued to unravel like balls of yarn, one after another, disordered and entangled.

Like Tana said, not everyone was bad-mouthing me. Some said I was brave, some offered help. I was thankful, but their words weren't enough to rid me of my shame and embarrassment. Sometimes what was more crushing was not what he did to me, but the fact everyone knew.

Click. I extinguish the flame the moment it ignites. Taking a bottle of water from the fridge, a gulping noise sings out as the cold liquid slides down my throat. I still want tea or coffee, but it feels like a hassle. I don't want to do anything that requires attention or exertion.

What's the point?

My psychiatrist advised me to do something for myself. Eat your favourite food, tidy up, exercise, talk to friends. I went to three sessions before giving up. It felt like the psychiatrist wasn't simply listening to me, but doing me a *favour* by listening to me. The last time I went, I was handed a questionnaire to fill out, but each and every checkbox was a struggle. These kinds of things: do you often feel lonely? Do you ever feel insignificant? Are you often unable to control your emotions? I felt I might as well be taking one of those online psychology tests. The last question was something like this:

Do you feel like the world is out to get you?

I didn't go back after that. I didn't follow a single one of the doctor's recommendations. Especially not today. The bin is full to the brim with junk-food packaging. Clumps of dust and hair balled up on the floor. As long as it's not for anything in particular—and by that, I mean occasionally getting up to take out the overflowing rubbish—I don't leave the flat at all. Inside the flat, I barely move, either. I order food over the internet, and anything I can't get online, I don't eat.

Three months of this. Since leaving my job, this has been my life.

I'm the living record of a terrible mistake.

'This isn't your fault,' Tana would say whenever I put myself down.

I know. That's why I miss Tana, and why I don't want to listen to her. I want to feel her affection, but hate feeling how I've become someone requiring constant encouragement. Just because she's a friend, it doesn't make it any less embarrassing to bare myself in front of her each and every time we speak. And whenever I talk to Tana, I have to do my best to hide my brokenness—I don't want her to know I've been ruined to an extent beyond what she can handle. I'm afraid of seeing the look in Tana's eyes that says she's had enough. But concealing my teeming anxiety is exhausting. Just the fact that I need to exert myself irritates me. I don't want to lose Tana, but I also don't want to work to keep her. Just the fact I have this mindset makes me a terrible human being.

I'm suddenly overcome by the most awful thought. That's right. I *am* that kind of person.

That's why he hit me.

I hurriedly pull out the cold water again and drink from the bottle. I try to push the thought away, but in the end I can hear his voice once more, distinctly. He said the same thing every time he hit me.

'Don't think this is over.'

At the end of the trial, he was fined three million won for assault.

My chest freezes solid.

If anyone were to meet me as I am now, they'd likely think me weak—but I haven't always been this way. I *became* weak.

I thought if the police investigated him, he'd be put under house arrest, surveillance, something—but none of that happened. I knew nothing about the legal system. I'd likewise thought there'd be protective measures put in place for the victim. I could of course apply for a restraining order. But that took time. I needed evidence as to why he shouldn't be allowed contact with me, and then that evidence needed to be approved. I didn't know the laws. I didn't know the trial would take so long. Believing he would at some point be punished, I waited. Then five months passed.

I know. I should have informed the company and requested to be reassigned departments, or instead asked for him to be moved to another team. But I was more afraid of other people knowing than I was of seeing him. So the whole year we were dating, I didn't make a single friend at work. I kept my colleagues at a distance. At first my shyness had been the problem, but later it was the fear our relationship would be found out. As time went on, I didn't want anyone knowing what had happened to me. And when I started exceeding my performance targets again and again, I became a complete outcast. It was immediately clear I was first and foremost a competitor. Owning up to these people and asking for their help was unimaginable. I didn't feel there'd be a single person on my side.

After I told my story, someone actually said this to me: I would never have expected it from you. You didn't look like the type of girl this kind of thing happens to.

What exactly should a woman who's beaten by the man she loves look like? And what about him, the man who hit me, who as he beat his girlfriend, whispered he was going to kill me? What does Lee Jinsub look like?

I can say one thing for certain. He was a good-looking man. I still remember it all clearly. His height clearing 180 centimetres, deep-set eyes, sharp nose—features that would arrest your gaze from far away. But, how should I put it? He didn't have much of a personality, and so despite his good looks, left somewhat of a vague impression. Because of that, ironically, I felt less nervous around bigger guys when I was with him. He didn't assert himself aggressively, nor did he do anything to flaunt his presence. Even if he had, his vagueness meant it never felt that way. In fact, it was only as he looked down at me, hands squeezed around my neck, that I felt his presence distinctly. Forced down against the floor, unable to breathe, I could see him clearly. There, in the centre of my blurring field of vision, was the distinct image of his face.

He knew very well how he came across to people. He told me once. That there was a time a different girl would confess her feelings for him almost every day. And he said this too. That he'd never dated a short girl with darker skin like me. He felt very certain of what his type was, and made sure to emphasize it. I like girls with soft, porcelain skin. He said that was the kind of girl who suited him. We look perfect together. But he said there weren't many girls like that, and that it took a *lot* for him to tell a girl she was beautiful. I couldn't be angry at him, though. After all, he whispered this to me as I shrunk away—*but I don't care about any of that when it comes to you.*

His words were like looking into an upside-down mirror. My face inverted inside of it. As soon as his certainty faded, I would become nothing—it was clear. Yet I, upside down, always smiled. I looked prettier that way.

One of the online comments said this: women who lose themselves over words like that are pathetic.

I hope they all continue to live with such certainty.

And then, when something unexpected comes their way, they'll crumble to pieces all the easier.

He took for granted that he'd been the one to choose me—but he never considered that *I* could have chosen him. He was wrong, of course. I chose him. And I was certain, too. Red shoes? Didn't know I'd be dancing forever? No, that was wrong as well. I hadn't even realized I was dancing. I believed those two flailing legs were not my own, and so I was certain. That I would never love a man like him.

It was summer then, too. I'd recently moved jobs from another company. He was the manager of the department I was assigned to. The first day I worked late, I went out to get something to eat. When I came back, he called me over. He slid across a few papers, seemingly trying to avoid the gaze of our colleagues. They were documents outlining the work's contents and procedures. And he passed me a coffee. It smelt good.

That wasn't enough, though. That was useless by itself.

It wasn't just that he was good-looking—I knew all sorts of things about him. That he was good at his job. That he had an excellent reputation. That the female employees enjoyed talking with him. That he was the son of a rich family. That he was related to one of the directors. That everyone envied him. That he'd never once doubted he was a 'good guy'.

As he handed me the coffee, his fingertips brushed mine.

'If you're struggling with anything, let me know. I'll give you a hand.'

I didn't misunderstand the situation that day. Instead I ignored the old flat, crumpled circle rising sharply in my mind.

It was emotion; it was memory.

I was nineteen, and would turn twenty the following year. Before moving to study in Seoul, I went to high school, and then university, in the small city of Anjin, North Jeolla Province. It took around an hour by bus from my home town of Palhyun. Anjin was filled with the stark colonial leftovers of red brick buildings and homes with bright blue tiled roofs. There was a small lake in the city. On rainy days the smell of damp would seep right into your hair. At sixteen I arrived in Anjin, and at twenty I left.

Before I met Hyeongyu sunbae, I thought good-looking, rich, smart guys were liked only by women. But that wasn't true. The guys liked him even more. Being close with Ryu Hyeongyu was something to be proud of. It felt like being on a level with him. If level and position are determined by who you associate with, he resembled a kind of unachievable dream.

So I dreamt, too. I liked him. It was *my* dream, and I wanted to cherish it, secretly, quietly. It would have stayed a pleasant memory to this day—if only his girlfriend hadn't found out.

She was in my year, and different from me in every way. Standing next to her, I felt even plainer. Still carrying my highschool weight; tanned skin; grades a complete mess, unable to adjust to university life. Above all, I was a loner. I didn't fit in anywhere. Fiddling awkwardly with my still-wet hair, stealing glances at the people around me. Couldn't they have shown just a little compassion? I heard people talking behind my back—*Who does she think she is?* Rumours started that I was following Hyeongyu sunbae around. Then other rumours, other gossip continued the knotted trail and stuck—though I can't say this was the deciding factor, I transferred to a university in Seoul at the end of my second year. I was determined not to let the same thing happen twice.

I had no intention of making a complete mess of myself—for nothing other than to see his lovely face one more time—all over again. I felt confident.

But the coffee he handed me smelt so good. The swelling circle. The slowly expanding sharp curve. The whole time I sipped the coffee, I could still feel the warmth where his fingertips had brushed mine. Not long afterwards, he bought me coffee again. The next time it was snacks. He texted me asking if I'd got home safely. He asked what I got up to on the weekends. Was this important? It was important. The feeling of being important to someone. The twinkling light invading the worn-out empty home that was my heart. These things were important. I was dancing.

Around the end of summer, he asked me on a date.

He said he wanted to see me again. He said he wanted to keep seeing me. He said he was happy.

I remembered that feeling every time he gripped me like a wrinkled mound of clothes. He clearly loved me. He'd just changed a little. Surely he can change again? Surely he can go back to how he was before? Maybe he's just tired. Maybe he's a bit depressed, finding it difficult to cope with the stress. Could I have made him feel lonely? Then maybe it's my fault. I didn't read the situation; I didn't pick up on it at first—it's my fault. I'll try harder. If I treat him better, if I remind him of how he used to feel about me, we can go back to being happy, like we were at the beginning.

'I'm an affectionate person. You're just not bringing it out in me. Can't you help me show my affectionate side?'

The resolutions I'd made really were important. I didn't want to die, however—it was only after the fifth time his hands had almost squeezed the last breath out of me that I realized what was more important was survival. That's why I was able to report him.

*

Once I'd decided to end it with him, the things I used to want lost all their meaning. I didn't want to earn his approval and I didn't want to earn his love. Was it really this simple? This easy? Had these things really been so worthless? Enduring him, holding on while my body was crushed—these things were so, so hard. He was probably taken aback. He'd been used to me putting up quietly with it all.

I refused to come to an agreement with him, and wouldn't accept his apology. I asked that he leave the company. I told him he needed to be punished by law. I remember the expression on his face. He would have hit me if he could. The trial lasted five months. But it's really funny—in the end he was proved right.

'Don't think this is over.'

I wasn't a weak person. I didn't want to become a weak person. I didn't want him to remember me as a weak person.

But a mere three million won—really?

I was forced to see him every day. The man who threatened to kill me. Would he really leave me alone? Even if privately he let me be, would he really play fair at work? Wouldn't he punish me? Or treat me unjustly? Spread weird rumours? I was overwhelmed by every kind of anxiety, I was angry, it wasn't fair. It was then that I pulled myself together completely. The problem wasn't people finding out—what I needed was protection.

After agonizing a long while, I posted my story online.

It was a film review message board, but I uploaded it there anyway. The number of times he hit me, the violent language he used, the extent of my injuries, the medical certificate and photos, the judge's ruling—I posted everything. Of all the message boards I knew, it was the one that got the most traffic. Film critics and magazine journalists were registered too—I thought I could get some help from the press.

When the first snow fell, my post was published in a news article. He was sent on paid leave.

I had no idea this would only be the beginning.

2

You need to grow up

I KNOW YOU'RE UPSET with us, Jina-ssi. But listen to our side of the story for a minute. To be honest, I really don't think I need to justify myself at this point. We're both a laughing stock now that the press has picked it up. But let's be honest, the company looks so bad. We need to be able to plan ahead. Our employees should be able to trust us. To be confident we'll deal with any issue, whatever it is. You think the company can trust you lot now? Dating—whatever you call it—why did you have to bring the company into it? Why post it online? You should have come to me. I had no idea. After all, Jina-ssi, you never looked like that kind of girl. You really should've come to me first. What were you thinking? Both your name and the company's are out there now. Jina-ssi, image is everything for us. We're a travel company. As the director, should I really have to be calling you in for this? Jina-ssi, do you know how irresponsible you've been? You've done colossal damage to our revenue.

You wrote it yourself. That you couldn't trust the company would handle it properly, and that's why you asked for help online. Do you know how much you've lowered employee morale? You realize the company could hold you legally liable. Why are you so shocked? You didn't know? You're saying you never thought you'd have to take responsibility for something like this? Did you ever once ask for our help? Did we refuse? That's why you posted it online? That wasn't it, was it? When you said you couldn't trust we'd handle it properly, you were lying, weren't you? It was a lie. You lied.

You know Manager Lee is like a son to me, right? It was me who asked him to take time off. What he did was wrong. Guess I'm a feminist too. I teach our youngest properly. My son's nine, and I always tell him—girls need protecting. If another lad breaks your nose, you go and punch him right back—but girls are a different matter. Our son would never, ever hit a girl, even as a joke. And he doesn't tease them then do a runner, or pull pranks to make them cry. He's a decent kid. But sometimes girls hit him. Young girls are too cocky these days. Our boy is so restrained the girls think they're winning by their own strength. They chase him and kick him, punch him in the stomach—it's unbelievable. They seem to get some kind of joy out of beating up the boys. They've got no idea my lad is just letting them off the hook. If you ask me, their parents need to get their acts together. Boy, girl, what does it matter? Isn't it the punching that's the issue? If a girl takes a swing at a boy, she needs a bollocking.

We tell lads to control their anger—just in case they don't know their own strength and end up causing proper harm. But letting girls run around punching and kicking whoever they like—does that make any sense to you? Those kinds of girls, they're unattractive. I can't speak when it comes to you, but those girls, they act up to get the lads' attention. Either that, or they really just hate losing. I've worked a good number of years now, and girls like that grow up exactly the same. They don't listen. They're obstinate. They're unattractive. I don't want to generalize, but those kinds of girls, their faces are stuck like that forever. The lads are just the same. There are always the ones that don't listen to a word you say. No manners. They think they've come this far because they're God's gift or something. They're so arrogant. Men shouldn't be able to get away with it. I've gotten off topic, but what I'm saying is—I'm on your side, Jina-ssi.

It really never crossed my mind that Miyoung-ssi would post screenshots of the employee chat room to go against what you said. The other staff didn't see it coming either. I guess we all trusted her. The conversations we had weren't criticizing you, Jina-ssi. We were just onlookers sharing how bad we felt about the whole situation.

Look, it was within that context that I said you'd 'ruined a good man's life'. Jina-ssi, every story has a context. You need to take that into consideration.

Manager Lee made a mistake. He was wrong. I'm not siding with him. Miyoung-ssi probably wasn't either. I suppose she just felt bad for Manager Lee and wanted to tell the story from a different angle. She wanted people to know he was someone we trusted, and that's why she wanted them to see our conversation. Of course, that was just how Miyoung-ssi saw it—I'm not saying that's how it actually was.

And all hell broke loose when you posted it online, didn't it? Everyone was tearing into Manager Lee and slagging off the company. Miyoung-ssi must've thought we needed some balance. I don't know her exact reasoning. Maybe the rumours she had feelings for him were true, and maybe she'd just misunderstood you as a person. Anyway, I feel really bad seeing you hurt like this.

But Jina-ssi, it's like I said. Listen to the context, Jina-ssi.

I heard you hardly ever picked up the tab at dinner? All right, I know. Just listen to what I have to say first. What I want to say is—it was about a year ago. Manager Lee looked like there was new life in him—I knew he must've started seeing someone. I can tell right away. Young lads give it away immediately. But it wasn't long before his face changed. His mind seemed elsewhere. So I went for a drink with him.

Manager Lee doesn't give things away easily. He never once mentioned your name.

My girlfriend doesn't pay for anything. That's what he said to me. I know, I know. It wasn't like you spent nothing at all. After all, you're earning, too. But apparently he almost always paid for dinner? And the drinks, too? Yeah, all right. You bought the coffee, Jina-ssi, and the cinema tickets. I know, I know. Presents? All right. I didn't know about that. I can't know each and every transaction between the two of you. I'm sure you took good care of him in your own way, Jina-ssi. But presents weren't what was important to him.

You knew Manager Lee is all front, right, Jina-ssi? He looks like he's from a rich family, when actually they're drowning in debt. You were aware of this, right? Once he's sent money home each month, made the loan payments, and taken out his living costs, the guy has nothing left. There were even rumours going around that he's related to one of the directors, but none of it's true. The lad's proud and refuses to show any weakness—that's all it is. His whole life he's hardly ever been able to spend a thing on himself. On the surface he looks like someone with a decent job living off a good wage. Naturally it's the man's bravado that's to blame. He wanted people to think he was well-off.

Honestly, I reckon you must've found that front attractive at the beginning, Jina-ssi. I'm right, aren't I? Let's be upfront. Manager Lee is out of your league, isn't he? I'm not being sexist here. That's just the reality. But in the end you found out everything about his situation. And you kept seeing him? Because you loved him? And about love. Love lets us put up with just about anything. But listen, Jina-ssi. I heard you like high-end restaurants? And on holiday you refused to stay in motels—insisted he book a hotel instead? And once when he came back from a business trip to China, you sulked that he hadn't bought you a gift from the duty-free store?

All right, I know. Manager Lee probably said he was okay with it all. That's what I'd expect. I'm sure you had your own reasons, too, Jina-ssi. But just listen to everything I have to say, Jina-ssi. When it comes to me—look, maybe it's because I'm a bit older than your generation—you lot will probably find me conservative. I don't think men spending money on women is such a big deal. My woman's worth every penny. Of course I'd spend money on her. She's my woman, after all. When I was first dating my wife, I spent money without even thinking. I wanted to do everything I could for her. That's love. I know about love too, you know. But what I'm saying is this. It's also because my wife gave her all to me too. She was the one who filled our fridge with banchan. She always knew what I needed right away. How could I not be thankful? And my wife had the sense to know when to say no. I was so grateful for that. Jina-ssi, do you think people always mean it when they offer to do something for you? You should've known to refuse. I had no idea you had so little sense, Jina-ssi.

I'm not taking sides here. I'm just saying I understand the context. Context, all right? Those things were always suffocating him, dragging him near to explosion. His family were asking him for money, the bank was chasing him too. He just wanted a bit of encouragement from his girlfriend, but then you'd just stare at him expecting him to do something for you—honestly who wouldn't be messed up after that?

What Miyoung-ssi did was wrong. I know. She took things too far. But that's not what's important. It's that part she wrote. When she said you'd got what you wanted from him and then even labelled him a violent offender—that part. I think there was a misunderstanding on her side, too. The important thing is to look at the context of why that misunderstanding happened in the first place.

I know you're good at your job, Jina-ssi. You read the article so you'll know already, but I didn't say a thing about this particular issue. Society runs on competition, Jina-ssi.

You kept getting better results, so of course everyone was on guard. You need to be careful in those situations. Even if you get good results off your own back, people will get jealous. But who's going to accept you did that all on your own, if you go and get help from Manager Lee? You remember the time you stayed late to work on that presentation, don't you? Apparently you carried a mountain of paperwork over to his desk and screamed at him to find something useful in it? No? Okay, all right. All right, but the important thing is that's what people think. The way you acted caused a misunderstanding, Jina-ssi. It's not what you say, but how you say it. I'm not saying you lied, I'm saying rumours were going round the company saying you were taking advantage of Manager Lee. That's what's important.

It's absurd that Miyoung-ssi's post was turned into a news article. It's not like this is some kind of celebrity scandal. We're wallowing in mud now. I'll say it again, but I don't want to take sides here. I don't want to talk about why Miyoung-ssi took things so far, or what her feelings behind it were. An individual's privacy needs to be protected. I'm not saying what you did was wrong, Jina-ssi, I'm saying that's how it looked. People have the right to their own opinion. Once you'd bled Manager Lee dry, he couldn't take it anymore and let it out through his fists—some people might see it that way.

Anyway, it's true that you provoked him that day, Jina-ssi, isn't it? So why exactly did you post it to begin with? If you really had to post it, you should have at least been objective and explained how you were unfair to him, too. Then the staff would have understood your position. Did you expect them to side with you after you wrote that the company had no interest in these things, and that you couldn't trust your colleagues? How could you be so immature? You need to grow up, Jina-ssi, grow up.

Apparently that day you'd asked him to buy you a designer handbag? When he refused, you called him a waste of space? That was what really pissed him off, am I right?

3

Jina

I HAD SO MANY ANSWERS within me. For you, my dear.
And again, my dear, for you. For you, my friend. And
again, my friend, for you.

There was plenty I could have said. I could've brought them
all before me and told them everything I'd been through. I
could've explained my issue—the one you think you understand
better than me, my dear—in great detail. I never questioned
Kim Miyoung; about how she, my closest friend at work (at
least that's what I thought), could post about me online and
call me a cheap slag like that. Or the way she published contents of that work group chat, where they all gossiped about
me, as 'evidence' of my reputation. How once my name
had been leaked, even my parents found out. How those
anonymous individuals who'd once taken my side turned
their backs and treated me like dirt overnight. How as the
news scandal unfolded, my parents started getting calls at
home, and soon everyone I knew had found out my business.
I didn't say a thing.

*

Even now I sometimes get calls to my mobile. Snickering voices. Unprovoked curses seething with rage. I hear those words spoken by people I've never met:

You bitch. Go die.

Why does everyone tell me to go die like that?

I could've sued Kim Miyoung. I could've searched out the internet trolls and reported them one by one. I could've done anything if I'd wanted to. But I didn't do a thing.

I lost the will to fight. And then I locked myself up at home.

Thoughts slosh like water in a cup full to the brim. My head swims. I crane my neck back and stare at the ceiling. Diagonal lines on the wall pour over my face like rain. There's no way to prevent the growing damp. My phone buzzes again. A text this time. Tana, of course.

'Whatever you're reading right now, stop looking at it.'

I smiled. She seemed pretty worried. I sent a reply.

'I'm not reading anything.'

I'd been reading until just a moment ago, but I wasn't look-ing at anything right then, so it wasn't exactly a lie. I thought it was a reasonable response. Her reply was instant.

'Then what are you doing?'

'Nothing.'

This time there was a gap. The absence of an immediate response made me fret unnecessarily. Feeling left with nothing to do, I repeatedly picked up the phone and set it back down again. I turned my head surreptitiously towards the monitor, but my phone vibrated once more and a message appeared on the screen.

'I told you, if you've got nothing to do, come to Anjin.'

I didn't respond.

Tana believed Seoul was making me unwell. She wasn't necessarily wrong. Seoul was unfamiliar, I had no friends, and the guy I'd been seeing had hit me and got off with just a fine. I handed in my resignation, but I might as well have been fired. My savings had run dry, too.

Lately I've been wondering why I'm still trying to tough it out alone in this city.

Why? Why am I going to all this effort?

But even so, I don't miss Anjin.

Tana sees Anjin as our home town, but to me, home is the tiny village in Palhyun County where my parents live. It was never my choice to be in Anjin. I was only there because of my parents' pestering. I needed to study in at least a largish city to get into a good university, they said. It was all right at first. I was young, and a city like Anjin was better than the countryside. That was how I ended up in Anjin, like a 1970s country boy chosen as the family breadwinner, sent to the city to study. My parents wanted me to go to teacher-training university in Anjin. Though it might not seem like much of a goal, to my parents, who ran a tiny supermarket and farmed off rented land, it was pretty ambitious. They hoped I'd settle down in Anjin. What I thought would be easy to achieve soon became difficult. Though my grades were decent, they weren't good enough for teacher-training university, and as I lost confidence, my marks plummeted even further. It would've been better if I'd just given up on it all, but I'd never been that sort of person. I began to wake up more and more in the middle of the night. Each day I was tortured by thoughts of becoming a nobody who'd never amount to anything. At first, I would cry sometimes, but later even that stopped. I just slept. It became more difficult for my body to grow tired. With the grades I had, I was able to get into Anjin University's Eurasia Cultural Content department. It was a new department, with a goal of creating and developing Anjin's cultural exports; the city had gotten some attention at the time as a 'modern cultural tourist destination'. Though slightly grandiose, the course taught management of bibliographical information, and I applied upon hearing you could get a job straight after graduating. There are a few things I remember from classes. 'The relics of modern culture and their tourism value'; 'The value of archival management contributing to the cultural export business'; 'Information session on the preservation of Anjin's traditional culture—with a focus on recording traditional folk music sung during rice planting'; 'Conference on the records of Anjin Pansori'; 'Exhibition of Japanese Colonial Period local activist archival material'. And yet, in one class we read *Jane Eyre* in English. This was apparently for the creation of worldwide-reaching cultural exports, but everyone knew it was simply the only thing that particular English department lecturer was able to teach. And there were yet other classes where they made us write novels, or poetry, claiming it was content creation or whatever. The department made no sense.

I really hated Anjin. And I even hated that girl who pushed her way through every difficult situation towards happiness. 'Jane Eyre'.

I no longer have anywhere else to go.

My phone rang again. Not a text this time, but a picture.

A lake blanketed in wet fog. Not far from our high school, it was somewhere Tana and I often went as students. Our teachers, fearful of accidents, threatened the pupils not to set foot near the lake, but we of course paid no notice. We often saw other students chatting by the water. It was an all-girls' school. Though we all wore the same uniforms, with the same shoulder-length hair, we could instantly tell who was who. But bringing to mind that time, the faces of those girls—now nothing more than an after-image—all look the same. Even Tana's and mine.

Gazing at the lake and its throng of fog, little different from all that time ago, I was hit with something like nostalgia. No matter how much I'd hated the place, I couldn't prevent the memories piling up. Part of me was already plugged with that watery mud dug up from Anjin. It neither hardens nor dries.

No matter how you try, memories are difficult to ignore.

Should I go down to Anjin to see Tana at least?

No. I don't want to. I leant my head back again and closed my eyes. If nothing else, I didn't want to go like this, not in this state.

I strained to remember how I'd felt when I left Anjin. How humiliated, tormented. I don't want to trigger that old feeling of trying to stick it out somewhere I'd never belonged. Then, is Seoul not the same? I've never felt welcome in this city. I have no clue how to live like other people. Things seemingly second nature for everyone else—getting a job at a good company, watching films and reading books at the weekend, then finding a decent partner and going on dates and days out, marrying, having kids... How do they do it? How does finding happiness come so naturally to them? For me, the only thing that comes naturally is self-pity.

I'm not going back. I opened my eyes and deleted the photo of the lake. Else I'll keep looking at it, and my resolve will weaken. I know that much by now. I'm the kind of person to do stupid things when I lose resolve. I mustn't let that happen.

Just then, another message arrived: a photo of Tana and me in front of the lake. It'd been taken on a visit to Anjin, when I was around twenty-four. It was after Tana passed the postal civil servant exam. Tana and I had happened to be in the same department at university. Nothing unusual. It was a small city, and at the time the department was new and had been extremely popular. Whoever you spoke to would know someone you knew. But Tana rarely came to classes. She poured all her hours into part-time jobs, and whenever she'd saved a bit of money, would go off on a trip. I'd thought she'd always live her life like that, when one day she suddenly announced that she wanted to be responsible for post sent all across the world, and started studying for the civil service exam. Two years later, she'd passed. That was when we took the photo. I'd also just secured my first job. Maybe that's why we both look relaxed. We were so young, enjoying our lives; you can sense our expectation and positivity for the future. There'd been a time like that.

I'd once never dreamt such a time would come for me. My friendship with Tana was the one and only relationship I hadn't messed up. It gave me courage to believe I could form a similar connection with others, too. And so, I thought—if I leave Anjin, I'll be able to find another friend like Tana, right?

I had no friends in Palhyun, either. The adult world is simply an extension of childhood. I struggled to make friends with the owner's and caretaker's children at the place my parents rented. They knew no one would call them out on it if they bullied or pulled horrible pranks on other kids at school. We were friends, but we weren't equals. Those children could pick on me whenever they liked, and they did exactly that. When they were kind to me, it was occasionally well-intentioned; but when I was kind to them, I was working hard to be seen as a 'good person' so they wouldn't bully me. There's one kid I still remember. Song Boyoung.

The youngest daughter of the Palhyun Police Captain. Song Boyoung bullied whoever, whenever she felt like it. Her most frequent target was Chunja-ne's granddaughter.

Chunja-ne was the village grandma who helped out with odd jobs. Her daughter was called Chunja. Though she, Lee Yeonja, of course had a name, people used her daughter's, calling her Chunja-ne. Everyone knew Chunja, the infamous nuisance of the village. I'd heard plenty of rumours about her. Started drinking at fourteen, slept with all the problem boys the village had already given up on, started fights with the local girls and got called to the police station, stole money from her family. Thinking about it now, I wonder whether all of that was true. Unsparing words to describe someone undeserving of this life. But one thing definitely was true. One day, Chunja came home pregnant; exactly four months before the baby was due. People said Chunja spent the rest of her term patiently at home. Her father, who'd been struck down with chronic illness, passed away. Chunja-ne borrowed money, and took whatever work she could to raise her grand-daughter. She helped out in kitchens and on farms, lent a hand in kimjang season and cleaned the village hall. And she didn't turn her nose up at working for small change, either. People in the village felt bad for Chunja-ne, but they still didn't treat her with generosity.

They knew. That if they didn't give Chunja-ne work, the family wouldn't survive.

Song Boyoung knew. That if she didn't play with Chunja's daughter, no one would be seen with her.

One day she was friendly. The next she was cold. The following day she'd be friendly again. Afterwards she'd be cold for a whole month. I often saw Chunja's daughter crying. The cruellest thing Song Boyoung did was give her a friend. Sometimes she'd let her get close to someone. Then she'd tear the two apart, telling them not to play with Chunja's daughter anymore.

I stayed out of it. After all, Song Boyoung wasn't the only one to walk all over that family. What could I have done? I could've been picked on at any time if I got on the wrong side of Song Boyoung.

Whenever she saw Chunja's daughter go by, my grandma used to tut, 'She'll go rotten just like her mother.'

My grandmother was a good person. Warm and kind. One day she lost her temper at Chunja-ne, saying she was too slow and that she wouldn't give her any more work. Later, my grandmother said Chunja-ne didn't understand a word she said.

'That Chunja girl must've been at the end of her tether with you. No wonder she left home.'

I don't know how the rumours got so out of hand from there. Word went round the village that Chunja had looked her mum in the eye and hissed that she couldn't hack living with a deaf old cow like her any longer, and walked out. There was also talk that Chunja had tossed her crying newborn on the bed, calling the child dumb just like her grandma, and told Chunja-ne to deal with it herself.

Then Song Boyoung said to Chunja's daughter's face, 'Heard your grandma's deaf as a post.'

I'd been standing behind Song Boyoung as she spoke. It wasn't as if she was the only kid at school; I could've hung out with some of the others instead. But it never went down well—Song Boyoung would put a stop to it. But regardless of that, in truth, I liked playing with her.

Kids the teachers took a shining to. Kids who made the others jealous. Kids popular with the parents. Being around them, it felt like I'd become one of them. I didn't want to become Chunja's daughter. Maybe Song Boyoung had worked out what I was really thinking. That was probably how she wrapped me round her little finger. Come to think of it, people know from a very young age how to use others' weak points as a weapon against them.

'You want to come, right?'

Another message from Tana. I'd been holding back tears, but I soon felt my eyes burn. I sent a reply.

'I'll think about it.'

'What is there to think about now? Stop thinking, won't you?'

I laughed. For the first time in a long while, I felt in a really good mood. Like somewhere deep within my body was being cleansed. If I'd never met Tana, I would've never known that I, too, had a lot to offer. That moment, it felt like my body was being dragged towards the floor. I'd trusted Lee Jinsub in the same way. And I'd trusted Kim Miyoung, too. I liked them.

Why? Why would Kim Miyoung do that to me?

Even when I first posted my story, there'd been critics. Some said I was doing it to get his attention, and others said I was exaggerating. But those comments never really got to me. No—they got to me, but I could handle it. They didn't know me. I could tell myself what they were saying about me wasn't true. That I was okay. That I wasn't that kind of girl. But Kim Miyoung's post I couldn't ignore.

That was why.

Why I spent all day scouring the internet for my name, scraping together the useless words spoken about me. Not to read what was said by the people I didn't know, but by the people I did.

*

And that was the real reason I walked away from my job. I spent day after day trawling Twitter, Facebook, and all the search engines for my name. I read articles and comments about me over and over. I wanted to know exactly how I'd come across, how I looked. Was I really a worthless human being? Was that why I'd been assaulted by someone I loved, why I'd heard the words 'I'll kill you', why I'd been stabbed in the back by a colleague I'd thought was a friend? What kind of person was I? How had I ended up like this?

After he beat me, he always wanted sex. It was once he'd sunk to his knees, sobbing and begging for my forgiveness, and I'd be losing my resolve. 'This person isn't me. I've never done this before, I swear.' At his anguish, my own only grew greater. I couldn't tell him. I couldn't say how I hated the way he pulled my hair during sex, or how he'd block my nose and mouth without warning so I couldn't breathe. I couldn't tell him it scared me, the way he ordered me to lie back, never looking at me once the whole time; how he forced it even when he could see I was in pain. I couldn't call it rape—I didn't have the confidence. And so I said nothing. Because I hadn't resisted. Never said I didn't want it. But I couldn't free myself from that sense of continual violation. Couldn't escape that feeling of misery. And so I forgave. Then I felt better. Was it because it relieved me of the heavy heart that came with hating someone? No. It was because it allowed me to feel somewhat in control of these dirty, humiliating circumstances. If I saw it as my choice to reinsert myself into this horrific situation, then I could also see it as my choice to remove myself whenever I wanted.

There'd been just one occasion where I took action. It was the day he'd beaten me a third time. The day he 'absolutely' hadn't raped me. I called the sexual assault support line. The operator asked me questions. Was it someone you didn't know? Did you express non-consent? Did you tell him to stop during? Did you show that you didn't want to?

No. No. No. No. No. No. No. No. No. No. No. No. No. No. No. No. No. No. No. No. No. No. No. No. No. No. No. No. No. No.

No!

I hung up the phone and took the time to forgive him again. Yet I couldn't stop the billowing doubts. Why? Why couldn't I sense a shred of affection when the person I loved touched me? Was there a problem with me? I wanted to know. I needed to know. I still do.

I searched for the reason in amongst those immense unknown voices—the ones who slagged me off, and the ones who took my side.

How had things ended up like this? Who was I? Why was I the only one who didn't know the reason?

The reason why I was the kind of bitch who deserved to get slapped around.

That's why I'm not going back to Anjin. I chucked my phone across the room and sat in front of the computer. My fingers moved first. Comments I'd been reading returned to my line of sight.

Stupid, calling me stupid.

This won't give me the answer. I'm sick of this.

I decided on Twitter this time. I typed my name and pressed enter. All sorts of posts lined up. There were more links to articles than there were real-time opinions. Twitter definitely wasn't as noisy as it had been a while back. Most of the conversation surrounded other women. Women like me who'd been knocked around by their partners. Women like me who hadn't been able to leave. I was now being remembered as just one of those women. It's weird. When I'd been flooded with every kind of hurtful word, it'd felt like nothing at all. But now the interest in me has faded, those careless comments really get to me. A layer of my heart peels lightly away.

I guess I was nothing special, after all. The same old story. A stupid one.

That moment, I halted my gaze.

A strange post caught my eye. I read it slowly. My hand began to tremble.

Kim Jina is a liar. Vacuum cleaner bitch. @qw1234

It feels as if my insides are about to explode again. Like I'll snap, *crack*, in two.

4

Vacuum cleaner

PRACTICE

VACUUM CLEANER? Oh, you mean Ha Yuri?

She's so easy. Say you like her and she'll do whatever you want. The girl's desperate. Won't bother to find out what kind of guy you are. She'll just fall straight in love with you. Like a vacuum cleaner—sucks anything.

First you need to act like you've never felt this way about anyone before. Say you're out of your mind you like her so much. As if the ball is in her court.

Won't be hard at all.

A few days and she'll have opened up completely, stars in her eyes, thinking that this time she's finally met a genuine guy who loves her. Girls with low self-esteem are perfect to practise on.

Then you get her on her back. This is the important part. Act cold towards her. Just the right amount. At the end of the day you're not planning on seriously dating her, right? But

44

if you're too heartless it'll be a headache for you. You don't know what she could go round saying. The other girls would never protect her, but information will be shared if nothing else. You can't let your life be ruined. So you've gotta be like this. Give her the impression that your mind is elsewhere, that she can't read you.

I'm telling you, it'll be easy. You've never had feelings for her anyway. Keep getting mad at her. Like it's her fault. You did wrong and now I feel bad. I'm hurt. You're not putting in the effort. Keep emphasizing it. Then drop this in. 'Were you really ready to date me?' Then she'll seriously start to fret. She'll think she's going to lose this fated love because of her own mistake, and go crazy. Never give her a choice. You're the one taking the reins. Tell her you're being loyal because you once truly loved her, but that you can leave whenever you want. Of course she might resent you. Or question you. How can someone change so much? Like that. Then tell her this. 'You were the one who never bothered to get to know me. Because you liked me, right?' The important thing is to keep telling her she's wrong. Don't acknowledge any of her opinions. Then she'll keep working to get your acceptance and always look to your response. Each time drop your guard a little. Make her think that depending on how she acts, true love could return. That's it.

As long as you're together you can do what you like with her. She'll do whatever you want.

So, what do you want to do to her first?

IMPRESSION

Ha Yuri? No? I don't know her. Just because we go to the same uni doesn't mean we all know each other. What? You call that pretty? Looks super desperate to me. Beauty's in the eye of the beholder, I guess. And then what? Her looks are just going to waste.

She's an orphan? No wonder. This is why upbringing matters.

INCIDENT

Oh, yeah. Didn't Yuri try to commit suicide that one time? Signed up to some kind of suicide website and went to a motel, then the police were called and shit went down. Right! It was in the newspaper, too. She put on one good show, at least. Think her attention-seeking turned her a bit crazy.

MEMORY

Yuri. Right, Yuri.

Not sure. I remember her always caring a lot what other people thought. It was as if she was so worried her presence was making people uncomfortable she couldn't even pour herself a glass of water.

Now you ask, I do remember. That's right. There was one time we went for drinks.

It must've been right after the new students' welcome party. I don't know how this conversation came up but we... haha, yeah. That's right. Us, who'd been grouped together under the weird name Eurasia Cultural Content or whatever. Because we'd all just turned nineteen, we started talking about *Jane Eyre*. Guess you weren't there so you won't remember.

Not all of us had read *Jane Eyre*—not everyone who's studied Korean literature has read Ki Hyongdo's poetry, either. And we weren't even from the English Lit department. But we'd heard we had to read the English source text for one of our compulsory classes.

About *Jane Eyre*... I knew it was about a lonely girl living in the Yorkshire wilderness on an island far away. That the main character was a woman, at the end of her hardship she's united with the man she loves, and that it's a really beautiful story. We were all saying our piece about the novel. Then the topic moved on to film.

Who was it that spoke? Anyway, someone asked, 'Who was the main actor again?'

It must've been when someone was talking about Franco Zeffirelli's 1996 film. Anna Paquin, who acted the part of Jane, standing next to Helen with a rebellious look in her eyes, bowing her head, saying, 'Cut my hair, too.' That film. Yeah, I really liked that film.

That resolute face of the Jane who stuck by frail Helen's side—it becomes thin and weak as she grows into an adult, and some said it didn't suit her character. But I liked it. For me, once she'd left Helen and spent so many lonely years, it was no surprise she'd change. I liked how before she spoke, she would stare at Rochester, face full of concern, and how she'd hunch her shoulders as she glanced around with a timid look in her eyes.

I remembered a fair bit about the film, but I didn't see any need to share this. Didn't want to draw attention to myself. Know what I mean? What use is it mouthing off about things you like? People will think you're a show-off. Or that you're obsessed with your hobbies. They'll judge you. I thought everyone knew that.

Then out of the blue someone next to me called out, 'Charlotte Gainsbourg!'

I was really taken aback. Her voice was so loud. It hurt my ears. Yuri. She shouted out how much she liked the film, how happy she was.

And then I noticed something weird.

Yuri was pretty, remember? Porcelain skin and eyes wide like a doll, long straight hair down to her waist. I could feel all the guys' attention drawn to Yuri the moment she entered the restaurant. But then as soon as she opened her mouth, the look in their eyes changed. It was understandable—loudmouth Yuri wasn't so attractive. Her face turned red and her nostrils flared. And she flapped her hands the whole time she spoke—I thought she was ADHD or something.

But I'll tell you what was hardest to watch. How she was like, I know that film! I know it! So speak to me, now! Listen to what I have to say!

Think I can explain what it was now. Yuri was so lonely— all it took was for someone to talk to her and it was like she'd fallen in love.

It was awkward.

Think it was Jina who replied to her.

That's right, it was Jina.

Jina told Yuri she liked the film and had seen it several times. From what I could tell, Yuri was being so loud that Jina had simply been trying to shut her up. But Yuri immediately latched onto Jina. Do you know what she said? It was so hilarious I still remember it now.

This is what Yuri said.

'I knew it! I knew I'd make friends when I came here!'

You should've seen Kim Jina's face. What do you mean why? It's so embarrassing. It was like she was reading a line from a film or something. Keeping on acting a part like that in front of people, isn't that hilarious? It's ridiculous, no? And Yuri didn't stop there. She moved in on Jina, told her she had the DVD, and suggested she come over the next day to watch it.

Jina's reaction was pretty unforgettable too—that's why I remember. You could tell she was disgusted by Yuri. I don't know, I guess you could be right. My feelings towards Jina could've got mixed up in it, and my memory might not be entirely objective. No offence, but I didn't like Jina. Thought she was a snob. It wasn't as if she'd been the only one who'd wanted to go to a better uni, but every day she came in looking depressed. It was like she was looking down on everyone. Seemed to me Jina thought she was too good for the place. Why did she have to make her feelings so known to everyone? Who did she think she was? To be honest, I reckon Jina reacted that way because she saw part of herself in Yuri. Made the effort to come to the welcome party and then ended up sat next to a girl like her. Jina must've hated it. And she must've been scared people would discover the real her. Don't take it the wrong way. That's just how I felt. Anyway, I still remember what Jina said. She gave Yuri an icy stare, as if to warn her, never speak to me again, and said, 'I have plans with my friend tomorrow.'

'My friend.' I found her response really cold. At the time I thought she was lying, but she must've been referring to you, Tana. I can't be expected to be right about everyone. I barely understand myself. Anyway, I'm pretty sure Yuri then became obsessed with Jina. Sat next to her every class, followed her every mealtime. I witnessed it on several occasions. Jina didn't hide her disgust. It seemed super harsh, but would I have done any differently? If I'd helped Yuri out, she would've come to me. I don't think I could've handled that.

Yuri was a burden, and there were all sorts of rumours about her.

Guys made bets about how long it would take to sleep with her. Right, I know. Obviously it was just a race over how quickly they could get on top of her. So disgusting.

But here's the thing. I thought those rumours only passed between the guys who were losers. That kind of cowardly story starts from cowardly people. People who find out others' weak points and do whatever they can to use it against them. Words only used by the type of creep that centres a relationship purely around sex, and ignores actual feelings like empathy and support. But I found out later that even the 'normal', decent guys saw Yuri as nothing more than a girl they could get straight into bed.

You remember Hyeongyu sunbae, right? I heard from one of the guys in our year that even that wonderful oppa thought Yuri was easy. Hyeongyu sunbae is a guy, too, I guess. That oppa just had better manners than the rest of them. He never actually went ahead and did anything like those pervs I was talking about, but in reality everyone saw Yuri like that.

They thought they could sleep with her whenever they wanted if they only set their mind to it—they just hadn't had the opportunity yet. A girl so lonely and vulnerable was always ready to take her clothes off.

Wonder what it is—I mean where you draw the line between a girl you love and a girl who's easy.

Vulnerability? Loneliness?

Why is it that vulnerability always becomes a target for attack and exploitation, let alone care?

The guys who judged Yuri and called her a slut said she'd go crazy for anyone as long as they had a dick. But that wasn't the case.

The way I see it, Yuri went crazy for literally anyone.

REALITY

Yuri died in a traffic accident aged twenty. It was winter.

5

Jina

'I T'S JUST AN ID someone randomly came up with. I'm telling you, they've seen people talk about you and probably just said the first thing that came into their head.'

Tana tried to reassure me. Unable to keep it together, I screamed down the phone.

'You really think it means nothing? Vacuum cleaner?!'

Tana let out a sigh.

'Listen to me, I asked another one of my friends, too. It's just a sick thing all the creeps used to say. You think Ha Yuri was the only one they called that? They must've talked about loads of girls that way.'

'Yeah, you never know. Might've called me that, too.'

As I spat out the words, I grew even more enraged. Calling me vacuum cleaner?! Me, the same as her?

Wait. I've got to settle down. Tana wasn't wrong; it was a childish, disrespectful nickname. But it's that memory of Yuri—the girl they called vacuum cleaner—driving the words into my chest. How they treated her, the way people talked—I remember it all clearly. Calling me a liar. And why drag the dead into it? My whole body turned hot. Whoever wrote this definitely knows me. For sure. Me, twelve years ago. Twenty-year-old Kim Jina. Someone who knew Yuri.

Pulling me into memories of that time; shaming me. Because back then, Yuri had been our department's vacuum cleaner, and I the liar.

'Jina-ya, you're not a liar.' Tana's voice was firm.

I was choking up. But Tana doesn't know. She hadn't been there for me then. That first term she was always at her part-time job, or off travelling, and never at uni. Then, during summer break she'd left Anjin completely. A round-the-world trip. For almost a year.

It'd been because of a guy. Aged sixteen, Tana had gotten pregnant. At first her boyfriend spoke affectionately—our love made this child, let's keep it—but really the issue had been money. Maybe fear had got the better of him, but whenever they met up he asked Tana if she was *sure* she was pregnant, whether it was definitely his. In the end, he said he didn't believe her. He didn't love her anymore, so what was the point of having the baby?

Piece of shit. Should've said he didn't want it from the start. Wanted to look good; didn't want to take responsibility. A guy and a girl make a baby, but it's only the girl whose stomach swells.

That bastard could escape the situation using whatever excuse he liked—I don't trust you, it was a mistake—Tana, however, couldn't. She couldn't talk to her parents. It's strange. They're the ones who bring us into the world, but we can never talk to them about what matters most.

Tana's parents were anti-abortion and devoted Catholics; civil servants with severe personalities. She'd have died before she told them. We were girls. Girls who'd learnt far more about the things we couldn't do than about the things we could. Girls who'd grown up hearing 'not okay' far more than 'okay'. Tana hid it from her parents right until the end.

Because of that, Tana understood when I suffered alone without breathing a word about Lee Jinsub to anyone. It's understandable. Of course you'd feel like that, she said.

This, understandable?

And these 'understandable' things keep on happening around you?

Once that lowlife was out of the picture, I withdrew from my bank account the money I'd been saving since middle school and met up with Tana. Through some acquaintance we found a hospital that did it. We held hands from the moment we entered the building right until we stepped out the door again. I thought that'd solved Tana's problem. That she'd been hurt, but, with time, would get over it.

That was until Tana left for her round-the-world trip; until I found out that every day she'd been writing letters to her 'dead baby'.

'To some people it's no big deal, but it doesn't work like that for me. Why do I have to be so sensitive? Why can't I let go of the past?'

Tana told me this the day before she left, when she confessed about the letters. Into the pages she poured out all her remorse, guilt and self-reproach, she said. That was why she was going away. She just couldn't take it anymore. It could've been my fault, too. I was the person who knew everything, who existed together with her in the core of that memory. And when Tana returned, she was completely changed. I knew that she'd truly loved. The kind of love that embraced her, that treated her with value, that gave everything. And as the colour fades in an old photograph, the experience of that love gradually dimmed.

I'd been a complete mess—I'd disappointed my parents once again when I hadn't got the grades for a scholarship, and after I fell out with Hyeongyu sunbae's girlfriend, rumours started to spread. Yang Sujin. That girl made my life so difficult. Every kind of terrible thing happened. My desperate search for someone to lean on ended up with me dating a guy from our year called Kim Donghee, but it was the most awkward relationship imaginable, and fizzled out after four months. And I was still showing up at drinks so I could see Ryu Hyeongyu sunbae. Moving universities was my solution. I'm sick and tired of Anjin; I'm leaving. It's this place that's the problem, not me.

That was the state I'd been in when Tana returned. She was my only friend, and I could talk to her about so many things. I was happy Tana was back. But I couldn't tell her everything.

I just about managed to pull back my voice. 'You don't know what you're talking about. This is about me. You don't know. You weren't in Anjin then. And why has the vacuum cleaner thing come up? How can they still treat Yuri like that? How can someone treat another human being like that?'

As soon as I said it, I could no longer control my anger. Yeah, how could someone treat another person like that? Why do they have to do this to me?

Who'd be willing to do such a thing? Someone who despises me, ridicules me, who'll never stop hating me.

Someone who delights in my suffering.

Someone who'll never forgive me.

A familiar face appeared before me. Tana spoke.

'Hmm. There was that guy you were seeing back then.'

'Kim Donghee?'

'Yeah. Think it could've been him?'

'No way.'

My response was immediate. Not Donghee. I was certain of it. So skinny that holding his hand was like being poked with a screwdriver. Donghee spent most of our dates slagging off his army sunbaes or complaining about university bureaucracy. Donghee hated Ryu Hyeongyu sunbae—he said there was something off about him. But I thought he was just jealous. Donghee wanted to take the lead in our department, to be seen as someone who meant something. I never once felt that he liked me, or that I liked him. Tana asked once how Donghee and I had ended up dating. I couldn't give an answer. It'd just happened, we'd just ended up together, I said. It was a strange reply, but it was the truth. I hadn't meant anything to Kim Donghee, either. And if it was Donghee behind it, he would've chosen to reveal and draw attention to himself, not to carry out this kind of childish prank.

Besides, a person capable of such a thing was already floating across my mind.

'No way,' I said again, resolutely.

'Nothing happened between Donghee and me to make him say something like that.'

'Really?' Tana said, seeming to find it strange. 'Didn't something happen with him early on?'

My hair stood on end as the puzzle pieced together. Tana was right. Something had definitely gone down between Donghee and me. But *she* was the one who'd started it. It was her fault.

Strong jawline and nervous mouth. Sharp eyes piercing into me. Someone who'll always hate and despise me. She was the reason I'd stopped trusting people.

Right, the thing that'd made everyone think I was a liar. Yang Sujin.

I asked Tana, 'Remember Yang Sujin?'

'Yang Sujin? Oh, Ryu Hyeongyu? Yeah, I remember.'

She halted her words for a moment, before slowly asking again, 'Are you telling me you think Yang Sujin wrote this?'

Tana didn't seem to believe what she was hearing. She had no idea. No idea how wickedly Yang Sujin treated me all throughout uni. I hadn't really told Tana everything.

I'd been planning to leave Anjin, anyway. When Tana returned from her trip, I only spoke about the future. Plans, dreams, mistakes never to be undone.

And so, even now, Tana thought that what happened between Sujin and me had just been a minor misunderstanding. That I'd been mildly humiliated by Yang Sujin and her friends when they found out I liked Ryu Hyeongyu sunbae.

Only mildly.

Tana cautiously asked me something else. 'You're not seriously still hung up on that, are you?'

I didn't reply. I wondered myself. Had it really, seriously been Yang Sujin? Did she hate me even now? Of course, Yang Sujin could easily still hate me. I still hate Yang Sujin, after all. And then the vacuum cleaner. I'd once witnessed Yang Sujin's face as she looked at Yuri. Eyes brimming with contempt. Sure, she wouldn't have understood her. Must've hated her.

But even so, did she have to bring up the dead just to slag me off?

I have to know, I thought. Who'd written it, why they'd said these words to me. If it really had been Yang Sujin, I had something to say to her, too. It'd been twelve years. I had things to say. And even if it wasn't Yang Sujin, if nothing else my chaotic rage would surely settle. Anyway, I had nothing to lose. I asked Tana to find out Yang Sujin's phone number.

I remember a rainy day in Anjin. The lake crowded with fog. There, within the mist that reeked with the stench of grass and fish. Times when I couldn't do a thing, and so did nothing.

Memory breaks off like decomposing flesh. A repulsive smell like crushed ripe persimmon spreads.

What should I have done back then? What could I have done?

Way back, whenever she saw Chunja's daughter, my grandmother used to say, 'She'll go rotten just like her mother.'

My grandmother would no longer be able to say such words. But she hadn't been wrong.

Yang Sujin was Chunja's daughter.

The next day, Tana sent me Yang Sujin's phone number.
She left a message urging me to think it over one last time
before I contacted her. She didn't want me to do something
I'd regret, she said.

But Tana-ya, I made enough mistakes back then.

Our department had been new, and so we had no sunbaes—but because the university actively encouraged double-
majoring and transfer between departments, lots of students
switched. Hyeongyu sunbae had been one of them. As soon
as he returned to uni after finishing his military service, he
changed major from English literature. It later turned out
that Hyeongyu sunbae had been one of those who'd come
to Anjin Uni knowing the Cultural Content department
would be set up. Apparently his grades had been significantly
above the requirement. He was the youngest son of the Anjin
Newspaper Company family, and so that had probably been
why. At the time there'd been all sorts of cultural projects
going on. His family's intentions had been to gain a strong
foothold in Anjin, so I heard.

I hardly ever saw Hyeongyu sunbae studying. He'd always
be at his part-time job at the university's think tank, at meals
with professors or uni executives, or working in the Chancellor's
office for his scholarship. After graduation, he went on to
the Anjin University Law School and became a solicitor. A
precisely calculated path, like the solution to a mathematical
formula. But those who knew him wouldn't have found it 'too
obvious'. He was both kind and principled—the perfect guy.

Saying the 'correct words' within the path of the law really suited him. Hyeongyu sunbae was like the male lead, and so it was only right that Yang Sujin was his female equivalent.

Yang Sujin sat at the back of the lecture theatre and led the judging panel for the other girls. Her head's too big, her legs are too short, her posture is bad. She's pretty when you first see her, but look a bit harder and she's nothing special. What is that? Her, pretty? Listen, that's trying and failing to be pretty. That face is half-finished. People should know their place before getting dressed in the morning. I, of course, had been one of the targets, and so had Yuri. Our lecturer, Lee Kanghyun, was also the object of ridicule. She was the woman who'd made us read *Jane Eyre* in English. I still remember because her name sounded like a man's. Maybe she had a bad stomach or something, but her breath always smelt—Sujin made fun of her for this. No one stopped her—Yang Sujin only went for the easy targets she could get away with bad-mouthing. Like Yuri.

Lee Kanghyun was old, and a horrifically bad lecturer. Yet she always used the source texts. She made us read British and American novels like *Jane Eyre*, *We Were the Mulvaneys*, and *The Heart is a Lonely Hunter*. She was a bad teacher, but rumour had it her supervisor had thought highly of her and so she kept being allocated compulsory lectures. It was impossible to tell what she was thinking, and she'd look down on us from time to time with a sardonic gaze.

Sujin must've spat those words back then believing she'd never become like Lee Kanghyun. An old, talentless woman, who cared only about getting ahead in the world. Lee Kanghyun is now the Eurasia Cultural Content department's associate professor.

The kind of stupid woman no one wanted to end up like. Yang Sujin, claiming she didn't want to smell Lee Kanghyun's breath, sat at the back and bitched about people. Once she even left in the middle of class. That day we'd been reading *We Were the Mulvaneys*. Everyone was stifling their laughter at Lee Kanghyun's terrible English pronunciation, but Yang Sujin, as if she couldn't stand it any longer, walked out the lecture theatre. Lee Kanghyun's pride looked hurt as she glared across at the empty seat. Yang Sujin didn't care.

Hyeongyu sunbae, however, would go around saying he'd never met a kinder girl than Yang Sujin—I suppose she never revealed her true colours to her boyfriend. According to rumour, Yang Sujin used every technique at her disposal to seduce him. Permanently wore short skirts, got drunk and threw herself at him, came up with excuses so he'd always escort her back to dorms. In sum, Yang Sujin mobilized any method possible to entice our innocent sunbae. I had no sympathy. Guess it wasn't just me that thought perfect Hyeongyu sunbae had no taste in women, but girls would confess their feelings to him on a daily basis. Yang Sujin saw them as easy targets, too. But Hyeongyu sunbae wasn't moved. He waited for Yang Sujin to graduate and married her. She now runs a café near the university in the best spot in town.

I remember the last time I saw him. Even the date—8th December, end of second year. No one knows I was there that day. There'd been a gathering at a BBQ place near uni, but I never went inside. I'd only gone nearby.

Hyeongyu sunbae was the only reason I went. I'd wanted to say goodbye. The restaurant was down a dim backstreet, but the light coming through its windows illuminated the whole alley. I remember standing in the only shadowy spot.

Coming out through the crooked path, I heard the clamour of voices and could see people inside the restaurant. Hyeongyu sunbae was standing. He'd been our department president that term, and from what I could tell he was saying some final words. Yang Sujin was sitting next to him. Lined up alongside her were her female friends, and across from her sat other sunbaes and hoobaes—all of them people close to Hyeongyu sunbae. If I had gone inside, I would've been forced to sit in a corner well away from him. It was nothing unusual. I always ended up in a position like that, stealing glances at Hyeongyu sunbae while he stood in the distance.

I hovered by a telephone pole near the restaurant and watched them. Wanting something I couldn't have; something that wasn't mine. To have it was impossible, and so I could do nothing but resent my own heart and hide in the shadows. Why have I come here? To tell you that I'm leaving? That I'm moving to a better uni? To Seoul? To ask you to finally see my true worth? But I knew—he wouldn't have had the slightest interest. To him it was like I didn't exist. He had no curiosity when it came to me. I'd been so stupid. There wasn't a single person in that place who would've been jealous, or missed me. They were there, happy, enjoying themselves. To them,

I'd be nothing more than someone who used to go to their uni before one day disappearing. I stared silently at Hyeongyu sunbae and the people surrounding him, then went home.

That was the end.

Sometimes I wonder—if it hadn't happened, would I have stayed? Would I be living a different life now?

Pretty Sujin. Kind Sujin. Honest Sujin.

You want to know what happened? What I did?

When I first found out Yang Sujin and I would be attending the same uni, I was in shock. In Palhyun, Yang Sujin's grades hadn't been half as good as mine. But in Anjin, no one referred to Yang Sujin as Chunja's daughter, and no one said she'd end up like her mum. It was unbelievable. Now-university student Yang Sujin was superior to me. How could she be at the same uni? And be better than me at everything? After I ranked in the bottom half of our year the first term, I avoided calling my parents, and didn't go to Palhyun either. Whenever I went, they talked about nothing but Yang Sujin. Can you believe she made it into a national university? Got a scholarship, too. Works part-time and sends her grandmother money as well. No one called her Chunja's girl anymore. Pretty Sujin. Kind Sujin. Honest Sujin. What a good granddaughter Sujin is. So good.

I'd go to the library alone and listen to music, and attend early-bird or late-night cinema screenings when no one else was there. If I did go to a department event, I sat in a faraway corner as if I couldn't care less, fiddling with my sleeves.

But I was watching Yang Sujin. Her smile, her ease, her friends. When I looked at her, I knew what I wanted. To fall in love, to be treated with warmth and acceptance, to feel happiness in the ordinary day-to-day.

That first autumn, a few students from our year had gone for drinks. It was there I heard Yang Sujin had started dating Hyeongyu sunbae, and kind of lost it.

Chunja's daughter?! Chunja's girl—are you kidding me?

That's right. It was me who did it.

Oh wow, is Sujin's boyfriend really that wealthy? Gosh, we in the village always knew things would turn out well for her.

It was then I told the others.

'Ryu Hyeongyu sunbae? What, no way! Thought she was dating Kim Donghee? I saw them together in a café near the bus station.'

It hadn't been a lie. I'd seen Yang Sujin and Kim Donghee together during the summer break, on the way back from my first visit to Palhyun that term. I still hadn't had much of a chance to talk to Kim Donghee, but I knew who he was. He stood at 1.89m—two centimetres taller than Hyeongyu sunbae. Though I hadn't had enough interaction with him to know what kind of person he was, I remembered his standout height. If you were looking for tall guys in our department, it'd be either Kim Donghee or Ryu Hyeongyu.

It was the middle of summer, and there'd been heatwave warnings. The sun beat down on my head as soon as I stepped off the bus. My vision blurred and I grew short of breath. As I walked, sweat dripped from my forehead and dampened my eyes. I wanted to get back to the dorm as soon as possible and feel the cool breeze of the air conditioner. As I waited at the crossing, I let out a sigh. It felt like my own breath might scald me.

If you crossed the bridge and walked about three metres, that was where the buses for uni stopped. But you wouldn't necessarily be able to get on one right away. The service was infrequent, and on a bad day you'd be waiting up to thirty minutes. I was irritated just thinking about it. My book-crammed bag was insufferably heavy, and the air smelt of stale dust. I tilted my head and waited for the lights to change. Then, without thinking I turned my gaze, and to my right I saw a familiar face. Kim Donghee. I could tell from his stature. He was stood in front of a café looking at his phone, apparently waiting for someone. *What's he standing outside for?*

Mid-thought, the lights changed. I crossed as fast as I could. Once on the other side, I glanced behind me again. No Kim Donghee. Instead, it was Yang Sujin standing in front of the café.

What's all this? I immediately wondered.

Are they here to see each other?

I stood in the street watching Yang Sujin for a few seconds. It was the height of summer, and she was wearing all black with her hair in a ponytail. But not only did she not look hot, she looked freezing cold. The level crossing was only a few steps wide, and so I could make out Yang Sujin's facial expression. She was frowning, like something was bothering her. That had been my guess; though it was also the kind of look you'd expect given the weather. But I wanted to imagine something bad had happened to Yang Sujin. Just then, through the café's enormous window I saw Kim Donghee with a drink in his hand. I then watched Yang Sujin go inside, before I turned away. I went over the bridge and waited for the bus.

Are those two an item? By the looks of it. Keeping it on the down-low? Could be.

I wiped the sweat from my neck with the back of my hand. Hope it rains, I thought.

I told no one. They'd met up well away from campus—I'd assumed—in case people talked. I kept my mouth shut, though it wasn't as if they'd asked me to. It felt good, keeping Yang Sujin's secret safe. I felt like the better person.

That was until I found out her secret hadn't been Donghee, but Hyeongyu sunbae.

No way was it true. No way Yang Sujin would dare date someone like him. I genuinely thought this way. No way Yang Sujin could have something I couldn't. That's not hers! I'm not lying, that's mine, I swear.

I said it: it was Kim Donghee, not Ryu Hyeongyu—I saw them.

Word spread. Just like how my grandmother's remark—that she couldn't understand a word Chunja-ne said—ended up as rumours that Chunja-ne was deaf as a post.

What had people said? How had word gotten out?

Yang Sujin is dating Kim Donghee, not Ryu Hyeongyu.

Yang Sujin is two-timing Ryu Hyeongyu and Kim Donghee.

Yang Sujin and Kim Donghee are friends with benefits.

Yang Sujin is using Hyeongyu sunbae.

The rumours came back around to me, and people started asking questions. They wanted to confirm it; to find out what the truth was, and how I knew. I was taken aback, and had no idea how to respond. Then Yang Sujin searched me out.

Whenever my grandmother disrespected her, Chunja-ne sat back and took it. But not Yang Sujin. Seething with rage, she tracked me down and commenced her interrogation. It was the first conversation we'd had in almost four years.

'Where was it you saw me then?'

When, where? Doing what? You really saw me? With Kim Donghee? What was I doing? Standing next to him? Sitting somewhere? Were we embracing? Eating? Holding hands? Did you hear us using first names with each other? Did I see or acknowledge you? How did I look? But you said you saw me? What did you see? What was it you saw? Tell me. Isn't starting rumours supposed to be your family's speciality? Spit it out. I said tell me when and where and what it was you saw me doing!

I couldn't give exact answers. A whole season had passed since then. 'I definitely saw you,' I'd said—at first. But as the questions went on, my already hazy confidence vanished completely. 'Look, I'm pretty sure I saw you,' I said. Later, it became, 'I'm sorry. I thought I'd seen you.' I hadn't said hello, and we hadn't crossed paths. I'd done nothing but think from afar, 'Oh, it's Kim Donghee. And Yang Sujin!'

Even so, I'd been holding onto the last remnants of my pathetic conviction, when one day I saw Hyeongyu sunbae walking up behind Yang Sujin. In that moment, I realized what I'd done. Only then did I understand. I hadn't just done wrong by Yang Sujin, I'd done something terrible to Hyeongyu sunbae, too.

I turned around as fast as I could and kept on walking. Yang Sujin called my name. I quickened my step. I wanted to get away. Just then, I felt my bag yanked from behind. I turned round to see Yang Sujin's icy face.

'What are you doing? Are you taking the piss?'

I made up an excuse that I'd suddenly remembered something urgent. Hyeongyu sunbae had almost caught up with Yang Sujin. I was losing my mind; I wanted the ground to swallow me up. This person I'd barely even spoken to—what had I gone and done to him? He must hate me now. Probably remembers me as the worst kind of person. This was all I could think. I flushed bright red and searched around for an escape. And then she met my gaze. Yang Sujin was looking at me. An expression that said: I know everything, now I get it.

'You,' Yang Sujin said. 'Did you say it on purpose?'

No.

It wasn't like that.

'Because of him?'

Yang Sujin pointed at Hyeongyu sunbae and asked again. Her voice was calm. She looked to be shaking a little, too. Because she hated me. She was angry. Couldn't hold it in any longer. I don't know. There's so much I'm not sure about now. I felt sad, tormented. Simply ashamed. I should have explained back then, I know. No, it wasn't like that. But what wasn't like what? What, exactly? I didn't want to make excuses to Chunja's girl. I turned from Yang Sujin and walked briskly away. She didn't follow.

That was how I became the liar.

*

And that was also how I became the number one target of Yang Sujin's back-row gossip. Rumour-starting liar. Bitch doesn't know her place. Hyeongyu sunbae's stalker. Again, and again. I... I was just another bitch. I could've become just anyone; and that was what I'd already become; later I'd be capable of whatever, however.

I'll wring the neck of anyone who doesn't find this horrific.

That was twelve years ago. But why now, again? A liar? I'm still a liar?

There was no point thinking any longer. I picked up my phone, typed in the number and held the speaker to my ear. Hearing the dial tone, the words I'd held in so long rose to the tip of my tongue.

I'm not a liar.

Yuri died. Properly remembered by no one; eternally the vacuum cleaner. This can't be right. It's not fair. No one deserves to be treated like that.

The dial tone stopped.

'Hello?'

Yang Sujin's voice. Spiky and full of confidence. I recognized it right away. Sujin-ah, how could I forget your voice? I swallowed. I wasn't afraid anymore. Back then, Yang Sujin had spoken to me in that same tone. You have to be really thick to start rumours. Had no idea you'd get found out, right? That's why you can go round saying stuff like that. Because you're stupid.

Now I wanted to give her a piece of my mind. I was ready.

'Hello? Who's this?'

That moment, I felt the conviction risen in my throat wane. What if it hadn't been her? If I was wrong yet again? Yang Sujin spoke once more.

'Hello? Who's there?'

I braced myself and replied.

'It's me.'

My resolve was gone. But I still believed I could bring myself to ask the question. Was it you that wrote it? Are you *still* angry at me? That's right, I *can* ask all of this. Should've done it sooner.

Even as Lee Jinsub hit me, I thought only of ways to avoid his fists. Ways to appease him, to lighten his mood and dodge his blows.

But it was my own voice that was really needed. Stop that.

Don't hit me.

'Excuse me? Who is this?' Yang Sujin asked again.

I replied. 'It's me, Kim Jina.'

With difficulty, I let out a long exhale. There was no answer from Yang Sujin. The responses I'd prepared gathered on the tip of my tongue. I can't delay any longer. I need to ask quickly, properly, precisely.

I was about to call out to her, when I heard an exasperated click of the tongue. A resolute voice followed.

'Stupid bitch.'

Then the line cut. Yang Sujin didn't pick up again.

6

Examination

I 'LL ASK ONE LAST TIME. These records definitely aren't
yours, right?

Fine. I'm concerned, that's all. I'd be dragging you to the
hospital this instant otherwise.

Okay, let me explain.

Basically, this patient's been to hospital over and over; their
condition isn't good—they've been through a *lot*.

Abnormal cells were detected during cervical cancer
screening, and later testing found two high-risk factors and one
low-risk factor for HPV. As you probably know, HPV develops
into cervical cancer. The patient had a biopsy, too. They'd
reached the dysplasia stage—essentially the pre-cancerous
stage.

So there's the dysplasia stage. There are three stages leading up to cancer, and this patient is between the second and
third. Are you with me? In rare cases we just keep an eye on
things, but in these circumstances the hospital director would
recommend surgery.

It's a procedure called conization—basically you're cutting
a cone-shaped portion out of the lesioned cervix. But the

patient's records end here, so I can't know whether she went through with the surgery or not.

You come across all sorts of patients working in a hospital. It affects me, too. As an obstetrics and gynaecology nurse, the thing I feel most is how life just isn't fair. Especially when I see patients like this one. You probably know this, but HPV has almost no effect on a man's body. But in a woman's it goes off like a firecracker.

I sometimes wonder whether whoever created this universe was in their right mind.

Not enough to make women the ones to bear children, but give them the disease, too? If it'd been up to me, I would've made it so both men and women could get pregnant. So when you have sex, you won't know which one of you it'll happen to. Then you'd never get men going on about how it 'just doesn't feel the same' when they wear a condom, or people claiming that men 'can't control their urges'. I've seen so many women cry at hospital. Especially those with STIs. It's not a big deal. Really, it's not. Anyone can get an STI, but some women get really scared. Think they're now dirty. What's up with that? What has contracting a disease got to do with being dirty?

Bacterial STIs get better with medicine and treatment. But viruses can become cancer. You could get ill and die. It all started from something both of you enjoyed, but the disease only manifests itself in the woman—how does that make any sense? We ought to sue the creator of this universe. For the women who end up like this, there's no one to tell and no one to hold to account.

Think about it. For other illnesses, you can place the blame somewhere. Like if you develop gastritis from eating too much spicy food, or don't exercise and put on weight and get a lifestyle disease. Then you have a woman who's caught HPV, but in most instances it can't be located in the man she just had sex with. Without sticking a swab right inside his urethra, it's difficult to detect. So men can go ahead and say: I don't have the virus, this is your problem. And because it's not widely understood that both men and women carry it, it's even worse. It's even called a *cervical* cancer screening. As if it's only the women who need to deal with and take responsibility for their bodies.

But more than anything else, men aren't the ones who get sick. When it comes to illness… Right. No matter how close you are to a person, no matter how caring and empathetic you are, if you're not the one with the disease, there's a limit to your understanding. Men and women's bodies are built differently, right? A woman's sexual organs are inside the body. So she can't examine them herself. Can't know when something is wrong. She just feels uneasy. When her period's late, stomach hurts, she senses something she can't see and continues to feel anxious. Thinking—am I all right? Is something wrong? You stay living like that. But what if something really is wrong? If you have caught something? It's my body in pain. The man beside me can comfort me, but in the end, it's not him it's happening to.

Shall I tell you a story?

There was a woman who developed cervical cancer after she got married. Her husband devoted himself to her care. It wasn't serious, and she recovered after a brief ordeal. Happy ending, right? But you know what the woman struggled with? Her husband. The loving and devoted husband.

All the husband thought about was tending to this fragile woman. He worked his whole schedule around his wife. And they couldn't have sex, of course. It was a given, but people wondered at how marvellous the husband was. Couldn't believe a man like that actually existed. Sure, it's impressive. Stopped by the organic supermarket after working late at the office to buy strawberries for his wife—how can you not be impressed? People said it was thanks to this devotion that his wife's condition slowly improved. They weren't wrong. It's not easy caring for someone sick. To him, it was worth it. Worth being the man devoting himself to the woman he loves. People's praise. All he had to do was wrap a scarf round his wife's neck and he'd be seen as a good husband. The more he cared for his wife, the more he felt like a good man, and it was a truly meaningful experience for him. But what about the wife?

She had to go through the surgery, chemotherapy, diet and exercise regimes, as well as battling with the depression that came alongside her illness. Then one day she was forced to hear how irresponsible it was just to eat some fried chicken. As if all her hard work until then had meant nothing; that this one thing made her a 'bad' patient. And then every time her husband did something for her, she had to make the effort. How had things ended up like this?—she had to stop herself thinking this way. What if his love fades? Is she keeping this man prisoner? Is he staying with her out of duty? What if he's only waiting for the day she gets better? If he's just enduring her? These were the kind of thoughts she had to suffer through.

She loved her husband. And so she had to put in even more effort. Had to battle with this devil of a disease in order to keep his love. Losing the will to fight would disappoint him—he'd feel as if everything he'd done for her had gone to waste. Fighting with all her might like this was the far preferable option. If she kept holding onto anger, there'd be no outlet for her resentment. She couldn't allow herself space to think this way: why me?

Pain is clear and simple as red dye splashed on a white sheet of paper. Every day the same pain presses through your body. You can't feel anything other than pain. Not taste, not sound, not texture. Not emotion.

Every time you feel the pain beneath your skin, you learn. Experiencing nothing but that sensation, you realize. That even emotion can disappear.

But she had to pretend like she was okay. Had to fight against the desire to break down and cry. She was scared of dying, afraid of losing her husband, and so hated her diseased self. Loathed it.

That's right, that was what I went through.

It was lonely. So lonely.

During treatment, I met another patient who thought the simple fact of becoming ill made her somehow less of a woman. She wouldn't make her pain known to anyone else. The man thought she was okay and so kept wanting sex, and each time she conceded, and ended up in an even more terrible state. It made her condition worse. Think that woman was an idiot? Yeah, she was an idiot. Naïve. But I don't know. When you're ill you lose resolve. If you can't see a future, your vision narrows. To that patient, the person beside her was her whole world. Is that wrong? Being ill is painful enough in itself without getting judged as pathetic for feeling lonely and clinging onto someone. It was sex that gave her the disease in the first place. If there'd just been proper recognition that responsibility lay with the two of them, things wouldn't have ended up like that. Yeah, there are lots of confident and unwavering women out there. Women that perform their duty in any given situation. But not everyone's born that way. We don't all grow up like that. And why is the bar raised yet again here? Why does the patient have to endure everything whilst also holding herself together mentally?

In fairness, the thing you end up clinging to most is the disease itself. Please, get better. Please, disappear.

You're already desperate and so you cling to anything and everything. It was like that for me, anyway. There are people who lose all will to fight, who give up on everything, but I was the opposite. I wanted to hold onto it all. I hated feeling like that. Desperate, impassioned, needing to do everything I could. Then, one day while I was sifting through the dregs of my emotions, I felt it. I want this over. I want all this pain to go away. I want a break, please.

I want to die.

Becoming ill is no different from leaving your happiness in the hands of others. It's uncertain, agonizing.

This patient would've been through so much.

More than words could say.

I didn't mean to get sentimental like this. Anyway, I'll continue.

Between 20th August and 1st December she came to hospital nearly twice a month. The main points based on information about her condition are:

29th August, blood came out from inside the vagina. Intense piercing pain. Result, vaginal injury.

14th September, hospital visit after pain in entrance to the vagina. This was when she got tested for STIs. And the doctor told her to stop having sex.

And then on 24th September she complains of continued pain in the vaginal entrance. Came following another injury. You can see the results of the STI tests here, but trichomonas and chlamydia bacteria were detected, and the doctor again recommended she stop having sex. After she was prescribed medication, I see she was retested. The bacteria had gone. This was 5th October.

She then came on 24th and 25th October, saying her symptoms were the same, and once more she was told to stop having sex. She was tested for STIs again. One week later, trichomonas and chlamydia were detected.

This means her partner wasn't treated, so she got reinfected. Some people don't show any symptoms. This means they pass it on without realizing, and you end up in a situation where you don't know who gave it to whom. But given the bacteria was detected again, it seems she never told her partner.

Wonder why she didn't tell him? I dread to think.

She didn't come for a while and then returned in November. This time it was really bad. There was even pus coming out from her vulva. So she had a cervical screening, then one week later the virus was in full force. She had a biopsy that day, too.

Results came out 8th December. Stage two dysplasia.

I don't want to make any more judgements. But look here. The doctor kept telling her to stop having sex. And then even when she was treated for trichomoniasis and chlamydia, the same bacteria were detected. It doesn't make sense. She kept on having sex even when she was ill. She must have been in so much pain—surely she couldn't have enjoyed sex during that? Though some people enjoy pain—could it have been that?

This patient definitely wanted treatment, that's for sure.

Who is this?

Do you know them?

Okay, all right. I won't ask again. But if it's someone you know, you have to take them to the hospital.

But when are these records from? Last year? Oh, it was then. But what's that?

Yeah, the notebook you're holding. Are those hospital records, too? No? Then what is it?

What is it you're hiding?

All right, fine. I won't ask any more. Anyway, I've said everything I wanted to say.

Someone needs to help this person.

PART 2

7

Donghee

'THIS IS FUCKING CRAZY,' Donghee muttered to himself, collapsing on the bed. 'What do I do about this bitch?'

No matter how hard he thought, he couldn't decipher the reason. Nothing had happened that day. Kim Donghee had eaten out with five of his undergraduates; they'd then gone for drinks before moving on to a noraebang. He remembered singing four or so songs, though he'd been tipsy so couldn't say for sure. While the students sang, he sat and watched. Of course, it was true he'd been sitting next to Kim Eyoung. Of all his students, she was the smartest—though only in her second year, her understanding and analysis of the texts was well beyond her sunbaes about to graduate. She had zero talent, however, when it came to letting loose at the noraebang. These days, even girls that studied hard partied hard too, but Kim Eyoung was your stereotypical intellectual. She sat quietly in a corner and watched her friends sing. Earlier in the night, though, Kim Eyoung hadn't been so quiet. She'd chatted excitedly all through the drinks after dinner. But at the noraebang, all she did was stare at the wall looking depressed. Donghee wondered if she was putting it on, or if she'd had an argument with one of the others. She was so quiet, he couldn't help but notice—it was uncomfortable. He'd felt like he should do something. Whatever the problem had been, he'd wanted to cheer Eyoung up, and so gave her a quick pat—*tuk*—on the back.

It really had just been a pat.

Your typical gesture from teacher to student. A pat on the back to encourage someone to keep going. Patting a scolded child on the back to reassure them everything'll be okay. Or a friend you haven't seen in a long time. You even do it when asking someone you don't know for directions. Literally, 'a quick pat'. No more, no less. He'd literally given her a brief pat—*tuk*—on the back. So, when a few days later, he found out Eyoung had reported him to the Student Support Centre for sexual assault, he was completely stunned.

A quick pat.

He couldn't recall a single thing aside from that. As far as Donghee remembered, that was the only physical contact he'd had with Eyoung.

And I'm supposed to have sexually assaulted her?!

This is what Eyoung reported to the Student Support Centre Gender Equality Service:

'While my friends were fully absorbed in singing, Kim Donghee seonsaengnim from the Eurasia Cultural Content department came and sat next to me. I'd drunk a lot and wasn't feeling well. My body felt slightly numb, so I was just sitting quietly. That was when Kim Donghee seonsaengnim stroked my back. He groped the part where my bra strap was.

I clearly remember the tips of his fingers arriving at my back. Shocked, I twisted my body away and he laughed. Then he got up and started singing.'

Donghee burst out laughing when he first got the Support Centre's call. He thought it was a joke.

'I did *what?*'

But the centre manager's voice—asking whether it was true Donghee had gone out drinking with Kim Eyoung—was cold and severe. That moment, he knew something was wrong. Donghee knew that if he didn't respond proactively, things could get a whole lot worse. He immediately rushed over to the Support Centre. The employees' gazes instantly flooded towards Donghee. Judging him.

The manager saw Donghee and greeted him stiffly. They were old acquaintances—Donghee thought if he explained face to face, the two of them could come to a mutual understanding. Yet, out of nowhere, the manager was keeping Donghee at a distance. They all believed this girl, barely twenty years of age. Twelve years Donghee had been at Anjin University. How is this possible? The centre manager had known Donghee since he was an undergraduate. He'd been part of the humanities administration staff, but was later promoted to administrative manager. Donghee had interacted with him when asking about scholarships, and had come across him countless times while working as a grad school TA. Back then, the manager had been working on his psychology doctorate. He was quite a bit older than Donghee, but they were both still students, and so often ran into one another at postgrad drinks. He was affable, manly, and liked Donghee. At one of the gatherings, he'd said to Donghee, now that male students were shying away from the humanities, it was a relief to still have a kid full of energy like him.

The manager had slapped Donghee on the shoulder. 'This is a proper man. A proper guy.'

Donghee watched him progress from ordinary staff member to administrative manager. Meanwhile, Donghee moved from his twenties into his thirties, and from student to teacher. The manager had been transferred to the Student Support Centre two years prior. Donghee had even sent him flowers. Fresh white hydrangeas in full bloom. Donghee had spent a full thirteen minutes debating options in the florist. But Kim Eyoung was a child, who'd barely been at the university a year and a half. A year and a half! Known Donghee for twelve years, yet the man gives more weight to the words of this budding liar?! Just because she's claiming to be the victim? That's all it takes?

The manager led Donghee into the inner meeting room. It was like entering a police interrogation. Right now, the manager was presumably thinking of his reputation. Sexual assault was a highly sensitive matter. The problem didn't end at victim-perpetrator. It was important how the report was filed, as well as how quickly and reasonably it was handled. A mistake during the investigation could operate as yet another act of violence against the victim. In this case, the institution would be accused of protecting the perpetrator. And this is why it goes beyond victim-perpetrator. Institution and assailant are tied together and branded as a set. And then what happens when the victim is a meticulous, clever girl like Kim Eyoung?

Donghee sat down and scowled. Kim Eyoung must've gone on about the rights of female students, the power held by the teacher, and so on. Said that if they didn't deal with the incident properly, she'd inform the press and make a scene. The manager had gotten scared. Donghee understood the situation perfectly. The very first time he'd seen Kim Eyoung, he'd known she wasn't one to mess with. How she thought and acted was different from the other students. A kid who was well aware she outshone the rest, determined to get herself to the position she deserved. In truth, this fascinated him about Eyoung. She reminded Donghee of himself as an undergraduate. Even though part-time lecturing had been just a way for him to earn a living, he'd had the makings of a teacher. This was triggered in him whenever he saw Eyoung: the uncut gemstone. She had a lot of questions.

Donghee understood Eyoung.

The university was flooded with elderly professors who made their students give presentations while they dozed off at the back of the lecture theatre; who killed time making students write on the blackboard like in high school; who gave out endless assignments and never taught a thing. Leniency with grades was the sole reason for their positive lecture feedback. On the other hand, as soon as registration for classes taught by well-known professors opened, there was a deluge. Close to a hundred students would huddle into the lecture hall, where they'd have to divide the spoils of knowledge like sharing a roasted sweet potato. Unsurprisingly, there were no questions, and debate was impossible. Hearing the academic's voice had to be enough to satisfy. Way back, this was something Donghee had gone through himself. He'd instantly recognized the dissatisfaction weighing down on Eyoung—it was just as he'd been twelve years before. But it wasn't as if Donghee had been paying special attention to the girl. The thought that all he'd worked for might be about to dissolve into nothing—it threw him off balance. How had he ended up in this situation? And then Lee Kanghyun. That witch with the foul stench coming from her mouth will click her tongue and tap at her mental calculator. She'll look at me with that icy expression on her face like I'm no longer of value.

The manager had been aiming for centre director the following year. He wouldn't want everything ruined because of a minor thing like this. Naturally his own twelve years of experience would mean a lot more than his twelve years with Donghee. Donghee tried to stay calm. But there was only rage, bubbling over. Would the manager have acted the same if Kim Eyoung had been one of the stupid girls? Donghee was suddenly reminded of someone from long ago, who'd also disappeared from the university without a word.

Vacuum cleaner. He wanted to laugh. One of the guys in his year had forced Ha Yuri to kiss him once. But Ha Yuri didn't put up a fight. Didn't cause a fuss. A docile girl. Right, it doesn't matter whether it's their wealth, power, or personality—the victim needs to have something that prevents them from being an easy target.

'This is a setup.'

Donghee just about managed to blurt out his words. The manager placed a paper cup filled with cold water in front of

Donghee. He explained, in detail, the situation as he remembered it. For the first round, they'd had meat and soju at the BBQ place, and for the second round they'd gone to a pub for some beers. The manager was careful with how he asked his next question.

'Apparently at the pub you were pressuring the students to drink?'

Donghee let out a sigh. Kim Eyoung's face flashed before him. How am I getting screwed over like this—after I took them for dinner, bought them coffee, taught them all I knew? Regret seeped in. But he coolly explained the situation once again. Three out of the five students had been male. There'd been another female student aside from Kim Eyoung. That girl could handle her drink even better than Donghee. And so he kept topping up her glass. Kim Eyoung looked to be a lightweight. The male students and the other girl could've easily drunk the night away all by themselves. So Donghee hadn't paid much attention to Kim Eyoung. To be honest, he hadn't recalled her drinking a great deal. It was true that, seeing her sip water while everyone else was drinking, he'd said on more than one occasion, 'Have another drink, come on.' But it wasn't as if he'd threatened not to let it go if she didn't, nor had he poured the alcohol down her throat.

All he'd done was told her to have another drink. Fucking hell.

He wasn't one of those domineering old-timers who guffaws as he forces alcohol down the necks of his hoobaes and the freshers. Donghee hated those men. He was constantly checking himself in case he ended up like one of them. Donghee prided himself on being a decent guy.

KANG HWAGIL

Donghee replied with confidence, 'There's absolutely no way. The other students will back me up on this. I'm certain of it.'

The manager's face was unchanged. Donghee continued, his tone now irritated. Then why hasn't the other girl made a report? If anything, it was her making people drink.

At Donghee's remarks, the manager replied in a familiar tone of voice, 'Then why did you go drinking with your students in the first place?'

Donghee felt like he might finally get through to him. He replied straight away. Donghee had noticed them because they'd taken his classes for three whole terms. He got the sense they were considering grad school, so he'd wanted to talk with them. Donghee made sure to stress that it'd been the students who'd originally suggested drinks. Kim Eyoung had said that! Kim Eyoung had asked him to take them out for a drink!

Ordinarily, Donghee would've just laughed off the suggestion, he said, but his afternoon appointments that day happened to have been cancelled, and as it was nearing the end of term, he thought—why not spend some time with his undergraduates?

But what Donghee didn't say is that it'd been decided last minute.

It was because of Lee Kanghyun. The day before the incident, Donghee had found out that the new research centre, which they'd been pushing for since the year before, would be going ahead. His academic supervisor told him it'd be run by the project team set up the previous term. Donghee had been involved since the initial plans were first written, so naturally he'd be joining the research team. For five years

88

now, Lee Kanghyun had been leading all the department's key projects. That day, Lee Kanghyun had phoned him directly. She explained what his duties would be, and complimented him on his hard work.

And then she went on to say, 'Oh, and think you could get a move on with that translation?'

Donghee hung up and cursed internally. Evil bitch. Ever since joining the graduate school, he'd been translating whatever documents Lee Kanghyun needed for her research. He even wrote whole sections for her. No one apart from Donghee and Lee Kanghyun knew. Donghee had no idea he'd end up tied to Lee Kanghyun—whose bad breath he'd trashed behind her back as an undergraduate—like this.

From Donghee's point of view, Lee Kanghyun should've left the university long ago. The woman had been teaching feminist research on nineteenth-century English literature for twelve years. But the problem wasn't that. Donghee didn't take issue with feminism classes. If anything, he'd been the one pushing for a greater number and variety of lectures on the subject. But parroting the same argument that all men oppress women, that women are the long-standing victims of discrimination, using the same text and teaching the same class for twelve years was, as he saw it, violence. What does it mean to be a researcher? Isn't their role to come up with new theories and lead progress? Of course, Donghee was well aware of his own limitations in this aspect. He wasn't part of the academic faction at the forefront of new discourse.

His goal was different. But Lee Kanghyun—she took things to a whole new level. She didn't have the slightest sense of responsibility. Lee Kanghyun wasn't a nineteenth-century women's English literature researcher. She was simply a woman who'd stuck her flag in the topic, holding on at the university like a fossil. Call that feminism? Donghee abhorred Lee Kanghyun with everything he had. Still single at forty, she'd married a Korean medicine doctor from Anjin after becoming associate professor two years prior. Her parents had introduced her to countless men. At department drinks, she used to openly say, 'A man needs to have a house, a good family, and a decent income before you marry him.'

Hypocritical bitch, Donghee thought to himself. Reading *Jane Eyre* and going on about women's financial independence to your students, yet you're saying the *man* needs to buy the house?

The woman was a con artist. From the English Literature department, but couldn't teach a single proper lesson on the source texts. Yet she got the highest scores when it came to lecture feedback. Because of the grades she doled out! She sprinkled grade As all over the place like handing candy to children. Lee Kanghyun could get away with it because she was only allocated compulsory classes where she had the final say on marks. It was all thanks to how she sweet-talked her supervisor and the other humanities lecturers.

But Donghee did also respect Lee Kanghyun. He truly hated her, but her political talent was remarkable. As soon as he entered grad school, he instinctively knew that Lee Kanghyun was the person to cosy up to. But Lee Kanghyun hated Donghee. She readily called him a pathetic macho shit. Donghee couldn't understand. He'd never acted like that in front of her.

In truth, Lee Kanghyun was the only one who referred to Donghee that way. His friends, especially the girls in his year, were confused. No girl thought of Donghee as 'macho'. Donghee decided Lee Kanghyun was a strange woman with a serious victim complex. It was typical. She'd reached that age having never once properly dated, having done nothing but study. She wasn't pretty, and her breath stank. What man would choose her? Probably used feminism to vent and explain away men's lack of interest in her. She wouldn't have been able to control her anger at guys like Donghee getting along so well with the opposite sex. Donghee usually avoided women like her. But at grad school, he couldn't avoid Lee Kanghyun. Donghee tried his best. At department events, he'd sit by Lee Kanghyun and pour her drinks, then at the noraebang he'd strain out high notes well beyond his range. At the end of the night, he stayed and saw her into a taxi, made sure to call on holidays, and didn't forget to send a gift.

Yet Lee Kanghyun was still cold. He couldn't understand why. Donghee grew agitated. Lee Kanghyun had recently become the most influential professor in the department. She had her eyes set on full professorship, and so needed visible results. She'd of course written swathes of papers, and was heavily involved in university projects. Many wondered out loud what the world was coming to when a person as talentless as her could become professor. But as Donghee saw it, these people didn't know how the world worked. Skill? It was important. What was really important, however, was clear research performance that shows itself in concrete numbers. When it came to stacking up research credentials, Lee Kanghyun was exceedingly capable. There were plenty of skilled researchers, and plenty of researchers with good academic backgrounds, but there was no one like Lee Kanghyun.

That was the talent Donghee had seen in her. Donghee was a pragmatic guy himself. He'd taken on classes as soon as he finished his doctorate, and published four papers on the trot. It hadn't been easy, but Donghee managed it. Donghee loved academia, but it wasn't a passion for academics that drove him. To be precise, he loved the status that came with being a scholar. Donghee hadn't gone to grad school because he liked studying. He was no different from those joining large companies or taking the civil service exam. This was a profession. The profession of scholar; the status of professor. The work of using another's annotations on your writing to expand on ideas and produce new theory. The honour of becoming someone's reference. Donghee openly coveted that position. But in this field full of all kinds of clever bastards, he had no intention of using ordinary tactics.

While some researchers, try as they might, could only just about manage a paper a year, others churned out work of a high quality every few months. Academic background posed a considerable barrier. In Seoul, countless researchers spoke foreign languages like their mother tongue. And then what about resources? The majority of discourse was produced and consumed around the capital. Donghee was a researcher at a local university. He had no illusions of competing over the same topic on an equal playing field with that lot.

Donghee's goal was crystal clear. It always had been. Twelve years ago, he'd applied to this middle-of-nowhere university with grades much higher than the requirement, because there were two things he could definitely get out of it. One was a scholarship, and the other was a job. At first his plan had been to acquire every library- and information-related certificate available whilst he studied, and then apply for jobs at public firms. But then he started to change his mind. Firstly, he liked studying. He was pretty good at English, and was learning Japanese as a second foreign language. As the name Eurasia Cultural Content department might suggest, there were numerous classes dealing with foreign-language texts, and Donghee stood out. He excelled amongst his peers. He thought more and more about graduate school, and began to put feelers out.

As he wrote about and debated texts, Donghee came to realize that talent was also required in the research field. An eye for choosing topics, writing skills that develop discourse, the ability to understand and synthesize huge volumes of text; all of this needed talent. Around six months after completing his military service, Donghee decided on graduate school. Was he confident? Yes. Because he was talented? No. Donghee never once thought he had talent. He understood very clearly, however, what he was and wasn't capable of.

Donghee wasn't the type to be at the forefront of new discourse, but if nothing else, he had an eye for choosing conversation-starting materials. He wrote quickly, and read his surroundings quickly. He was good at languages; many other researchers were too, but not in Anjin. The department was new. Aside from his sunbaes who'd switched majors or transferred departments, he was part of the very first cohort, and was planning to be the very first graduate student. It wasn't only the professors; all the instructors were brimming with enthusiasm—showing rapid results and securing the department's future would in turn cement their own positions. As an undergraduate, Donghee was one of the students the professors and instructors had most often called on. They recommended graduate school to him on multiple occasions. Full scholarship, research funding, think tank activities. There were endless ways to keep studying without having to worry about money, they said, and Donghee was convinced. Once he'd calculated the time and money it would take to apply for jobs in the public sector, and then how long before he'd be promoted, it seemed graduate school wouldn't leave him hugely out of pocket. He also had the advantage of being an alumnus. Half the professors had come down from Seoul, and half were from Anjin University. Educational background wasn't much different from the aristocratic Silla Dynasty bone-rank system, where proximity to the throne, and thus authority, was strictly hereditary. Donghee could've easily applied to grad schools in Seoul, but that would mean coming up against impenetrable, devoutly accumulated connections and vested rights, which he didn't have. Donghee knew himself well. Maybe if he'd been a true talent it would've been different, but he'd never be able to break out of his preassigned bone-rank. Though if nothing else, he'd remain part of the powerful Anjin clan. Donghee was a pragmatic person; for him, clear results were the only thing worth fighting for. Where you studied for undergraduate, postgraduate, if the department was newly established, foreign-language ability—after weighing up this and that, he came to the conclusion he'd advance in life faster in grad school than he would at a half-decent company. Even if it took a bit longer, with postgraduate experience, he'd be able to do all kinds of work with Anjin businesses. By the time he moved on to grad school, his goal was set firmly in stone. He would become Anjin University's number one.

Lee Kanghyun was much the same. Everything—from the projects she chose, to the subjects of her papers, to the connections she made at the university—was based on pragmatism. It was also the source of people's scorn. His colleagues and sunbaes, the so-called 'researchers who'd given their souls to academia', lamented that it was people like Lee Kanghyun that meant those with real skill were overlooked. How could she put politics over study, valuing projects that made a profit over the purity of academia? They raged that Lee Kanghyun was the reason Anjin University was stuck in a rut. Donghee didn't refute what they were saying. Making enemies by going against others' opinions wasn't his style. To their faces, he frowned appropriately, wearing the costume of the young scholar fallen to scepticism and suffering. But they were the ones Donghee really despised—those who'd pledged their souls to academia. Academia, passion, the university's true substance? I study for academia itself—he loathed remarks like this. Human language really was impressive. There was nothing better than language for hiding your true self and forming a guise. The endless linguistic embellishment used to express 'sincerity' was incredible. Saying academia has to pursue truth; how it's the world's last remaining fortress questioning human existence; how we must ruthlessly self-censor and continue searching for what 'academia' is; in this capitalistic society where profit is now the only good, academia must remain to throw out the uncomfortable questions.

But these individuals laying bare their hearts—what they really wanted was Lee Kanghyun's seat. That was the real reason they hated Lee Kanghyun. It was 'me' who really deserved to be recognized and given special treatment—they hated that it was her instead. And likely the fact she was a woman. The way Donghee saw it, compared to the scholarly crowd who couldn't distinguish between their need for acceptance and love of academia, Lee Kanghyun was the far more competent one. And it would have been perfect, if only Lee Kanghyun hadn't hated him.

Literally, why?

When during classes Lee Kanghyun would openly tease him as the 'pathetic macho type', or stare into him with that disinterested expression, Donghee could feel beads of sweat dripping down his spine. He paid close attention to how he spoke and acted in front of Lee Kanghyun. What exactly had he done to rub her up the wrong way? Donghee really did have a good reputation with women. All his ex-girlfriends so far liked him. Of course, he'd heard his share of abuse during breakups, but how many couples actually end on good terms? He wasn't controlling, and was never violent. Donghee understood almost perfectly what girls looked for in a guy. Obviously he hadn't been great in the beginning. He'd learnt, all that time ago. From Ryu Hyeongyu sunbae.

Watching Hyeongyu sunbae, Donghee had discovered that girls like kind and affectionate guys. The secret to scoring points was making her feel she was precious to him. And in that respect, Ryu Hyeongyu was impressive. Donghee hadn't liked observing him at first. He had so much that Donghee could only assume he'd been born with a silver spoon in his mouth. But Hyeongyu sunbae was a genuinely good guy. Guys like him are rare in this world; it was almost impossible to find a man like him. It was thanks to Hyeongyu sunbae that Donghee's girlfriends said he was 'different from other guys'. If Donghee acted based on what he learnt from him, everything was easy. Everything aside from Lee Kanghyun. It was almost like she was telling him: no matter how hard you try, you'll never be like Ryu Hyeongyu.

Bitch.

Donghee couldn't stand being openly belittled by this idiotic woman with bad breath. Planning to settle things once and for all, he had gone to see Lee Kanghyun.

Lee Kanghyun glanced briefly at Donghee with disinterest before returning to her book. Donghee went to stand before her. Lee Kanghyun sighed. Donghee held his breath. He felt the rank odour with every step closer.

For a moment, Donghee stood wordless in front of her.

As usual, Lee Kanghyun showed no interest in Donghee. Donghee swallowed. He glanced at the book she was reading. An English source text. A thought ran through his mind.

And he opened his mouth to speak.

'I've come because I think I can help.'

It was only then that Lee Kanghyun looked momentarily up at him. Her lips curled into a faint smile. A scornful expression.

'With what?'

'I thought I could lend an extra pair of hands.'

Lee Kanghyun continued to peer indifferently at Donghee. 'Is that right?'

That was the start. He went over Lee Kanghyun's English papers. He translated documents. He wrote draft sections for her. After that, Lee Kanghyun grew surprisingly kind towards Donghee. She brought him along to important events, and complimented him to other professors. Later, Donghee found he was basically writing all of her English papers himself. He didn't see it as lowering himself. He didn't see it as exploitation, either. It was a clear give-take relationship. If Donghee helped Lee Kanghyun, she gave him proper treatment in return. And because Lee Kanghyun wasn't Donghee's supervisor, no one was suspicious of their relationship. It was only then that Donghee realized. That Lee Kanghyun had hated how he'd wanted special treatment without doing anything in return. How hadn't he seen that! Hadn't Lee Kanghyun been a pragmatist just like Donghee?

However, the truth was Lee Kanghyun had the upper hand. After all, Lee Kanghyun was on the giving, and Donghee on the receiving end. And she'd often work Donghee to the bone like it was nothing, just like she had that day.

'BITCH!'

That day, after his conversation with Lee Kanghyun, Donghee sat in his car and screamed. Establishing a business relationship with her hadn't got rid of the unpleasant feeling. He didn't know what it was, but Donghee sensed Lee Kanghyun knew something. She always looked at him suspiciously. 'Everyone thinks you're so nice and intelligent, but you won't fool me.'

Arrogant witch. And she would've been dead and buried already if it wasn't for that political instinct she'd had since she was in her mother's womb. Lee Kanghyun was too high up for him to fight. At times Donghee had wanted to lay bare the truth, but he restrained himself. Donghee couldn't tear down all he'd achieved just like that. He wasn't idiotic enough to direct an all-out rebellion and face the ensuing damage.

It was then that he'd seen Kim Eyoung in front of the humanities building. Kim Eyoung was probably a hundred times smarter than Lee Kanghyun had been as an undergraduate, but she had exactly the same personality as that witch. If he could go back in time and meet Lee Kanghyun at that age, he'd never let her get away with it. He'd do what he wanted with her. Until she clung to him, and cried, begging for mercy. Donghee got out of his car. He strode forward and called out to her.

'Kim Eyoung!'

Eyoung turned round to look at him. She was smiling brightly. Instantly, his overwhelming rage subsided. This young student, far sweeter and more intelligent, with no bad breath; this girl, far prettier and more feminine than Lee Kanghyun even at her peak, respected Donghee. He walked with Eyoung to the lecture theatre. A fragrance wafted from her. An indistinct, gentle scent; that soft type only young women her age have. Something you could never smell on the likes of Lee Kanghyun. Kim Eyoung, who hung on every word Donghee said. Kim Eyoung, who looked at him as if he had the answer to all the world's mysteries, and asked every kind of question. She was at his side.

He spoke. 'Perfect weather for a drink, don't you think?'

Even until that point, it was obvious Kim Eyoung had respected Donghee. He could tell from the way she blushed, like she'd been waiting for him to say those words.

'It is, seonsaengnim! Will you buy us a drink sometime?'

'Are you free this evening? I'd like to have a drink with you and the others who've taken my classes the past three terms.'

'Sounds great! I'll ask the others, seonsaengnim. I'm sure they'll be fine!'

Donghee smiled again. Then he gave Eyoung a pat—*tuk*—on the back. The memory returned to him. It hadn't only been when they were drinking—right in front of the humanities building for all the students to see, he'd given Eyoung a pat—*tuk*—on the back. Why hadn't she said anything about that, then? It didn't make sense. Dammit. Women. Fucking women, all think *they're* the victim.

'Kim seonsaeng!' the manager called out to him. 'If your accounts don't line up, we'll have to open a fact-finding inquiry.'

'Go ahead and tell them to open one. I'm a victim, too, after all.'

Donghee's response was pointed. The manager let out a sigh—he was opposed to the idea. Donghee knew, too. If it went to a fact-finding inquiry, if he was investigated and things went wrong, next came the police investigation and then things would really get ugly. He understood what the manager was recommending. To admit that he didn't remember properly, that he'd been drunk and made a mistake, and move on.

Donghee raised his voice again. 'What am I supposed to admit when I've done nothing wrong?!'

The manager then told Donghee it wasn't looking good for him. If a fact-finding committee was set up, this would imply something very serious had taken place, and there'd be no way to reach a reasonable compromise. Hearing this, Donghee started to suspect Kim Eyoung had made demands. Otherwise there'd be no need to keep skirting round the issue like this. The manager was trying to make Donghee understand that he was in a disadvantageous position, that he had no choice but to accept Kim Eyoung's terms.

'What is it she says she wants?'

The manager avoided Donghee's gaze. Kim Eyoung wanted Donghee fired. Perhaps anticipating that Donghee would raise his voice once more, the manager immediately went on.

'You'll be able to lodge a complaint.'

He pushed the paper cup closer to Donghee and continued.

'But at the very least, we'll have to suspend your next term's lectures. As well as your campus activities.'

Donghee gave no reply and rose from his seat. He went straight home.

Donghee couldn't sleep. There was no way he'd be able to right now.

'What do I do about this bitch?' Donghee muttered to himself as he got up from the bed. All of his experience had been at the university. Donghee couldn't change careers, and it was too late for him to take the civil service or teacher certification exam. He flung his pillow against the wall. Why am I trying to hide? Why should all the experience I've acquired so carefully have to go to shit because of *this*? Word had probably already gone round the university. His supervisor had likely been contacted, too. But he hadn't received a single call. Not one person had asked him about the situation. About *his* truth. Maybe they think it's better to cut ties completely than be seen taking the side of a molester?

Donghee laughed. Should I get in touch with all my exes? Just ask them. Did I once do anything you didn't agree to? Ever do something wrong? Idle thoughts came flooding alongside a feeling of misery.

He sat in front of the computer. No chance of sleep now, anyway. His thoughts were making it difficult to breathe. I'll watch something, he thought. He needed to find a film, TV show, something to block out the pointless thoughts and give him room to inhale. He opened the browser and clicked on the download page saved in his favourites. But an article on the search engine caught his eye. Man taken to court by girlfriend for assault receives three million won fine.

'If you're going to date, at least try and be classy about it. Unbelievable.'

Donghee was mindlessly scrolling through the comments when he saw the woman's name.

'Hang on—Kim Jina?'

Doubting his own eyes, he checked her age—the same as him. 'Surely not?'

He continued reading the comments. Someone was telling people to stop digging up the woman's personal details. The important thing was what she went through, they said, and linked to the message board where she'd originally posted her story. Donghee followed the link and burst out laughing.

It *was* Kim Jina. The sentences reeked of victim complex and self-pity. He did feel bad that she'd been knocked around. But at the same time, Donghee understood the man. Kim Jina had been the worst girlfriend he'd ever had. Impossible to read, so consumed by her own issues that she had zero interest in the people around her. But he could tell she wanted a boyfriend by the way she always checked out the guys. Weirdly, that'd caught his attention and they'd ended up together, but how it finished had been a joke. He thought they'd had a decent four months, when one day, suddenly, she broke up with him in tears, saying all their time together had been fake and she hadn't once been happy.

He'd thought she was a fucking nutcase.

All that was fake? Going for meals, trips, hanging out, spending all night together studying for exams, going to the seaside in winter and scribbling on the mudflats—those happy times had all been lies? Donghee even felt kind of hurt. But he wasn't angry. They'd had a clean break. And then he'd seen the way Kim Jina looked at Ryu Hyeongyu sunbae.

Donghee chuckled again. To be honest, the whole time they'd been dating, Donghee had known he was out of Kim Jina's league. He never let it show, but it was true. Not only was Kim Jina plain, she was an odd person and so guys never gave her a second thought. He'd literally just ended up with her. They trudged along those four months, but Donghee had given it his all. But Ryu Hyeongyu sunbae? Donghee found it hilarious, and was left lost for words. Just who does Kim Jina think she is?

'I treated her so well. Bitch doesn't know her place.'

People never change. Kim Jina was no different. The man had abused and treated her like shit on a daily basis? Crushed her self-esteem? All right, guess it could be true. Beat her up, strangled and kicked her down an alleyway? Probably true. And so she was scared he might kill her? Yeah, that must be true as well. But what about the rest? Kim Jina had only described how the guy had hit her, but written nothing about what she'd done to him. That was Kim Jina all over. You're the victim? You weren't happy? Then we'd better hear from the perpetrator, too. Never wondered just how uninterested, how bored out of my mind I was those four months dating you, did you?

Donghee continued scrolling through the message board. There must be something here. The Kim Jina he knew made everything about her. Yeah, just like that bitch Kim Eyoung. How has this happened to me twice, with two of the exact same whores? Lee Kanghyun's face suddenly flashed through his mind. She always looked at Donghee that same way. I know what you did. As if he'd done something to Lee Kanghyun herself. Then what is it?! All of you think you've done nothing to me, don't you?

Here we go.

Donghee caught sight of a post written by one of Kim Jina's colleagues. There was even a screenshot of a company group chat discussing her. She'd demanded the perpetrator buy her designer goods, and hadn't paid a thing on their dates. No surprises there. *You haven't changed a bit, I see.*

A viciousness wrapped itself around him. Every day he'd worked hard. Donghee had done his best for his people and tried not to cause them harm. If he'd made a mistake, it was opening himself to liars like them. Those two weren't the victims, it was him. Donghee, who'd showered those liars with kindness just so they could turn the blame round on him and indulge in their own self-pity—it'd been his mistake.

He made up a random Twitter user ID. @qw1234

Kim Jina. She'll think it uncalled for. But this is what you really are. Her heart will sink. He typed a tweet.

Kim Jina is a liar.

Something was missing. He wanted to make her realize her true nature, for her to be tortured by a guilty conscience—this wouldn't be enough. Suddenly he felt the countless souls who'd given themselves to academia raise their heads. All this time he'd been ignoring them. Don't turn from the truth. Question what you think is real. Create a problem. Showing people the boundary for separating truth from lie is the scholar's duty. Since the incident, people had been railing about the man's violence, when they should've been focusing on what's beneath it—the problem existing between two people. The moment someone becomes a victim, no one gives the slightest consideration to the perpetrator's perspective. Is this the truth? Only the victim has the right to sympathy—no one questions it, but is it really true? The world's gone rotten. All that's taught is how to become a victim. Mass production of idiots who can't distinguish between real and fake. Thinking Kim Eyoung smart had been a miscalculation. That bitch is the most stupid, most pretentious brat out there. Probably think you've achieved something now. Your petty lie has torn down authority right before your eyes! But the truth always comes out. There are people in this world who live decent lives having nothing to do with that kind of lie. It was that moment. A face Donghee hadn't thought about for a long while popped into his head.

Ha Yuri.

Yuri, entangled in every kind of rumour, but still sitting there aloof and upright. At the time, Donghee'd had a sort of respect for Yuri. How could someone trust people so easily? And cope with all that hurt by herself? He pitied the girl. Donghee had never dated Ha Yuri. But he'd always been drawn to her. And who despised her the most? The girls. Those bitches claimed they were nothing like Ha Yuri, spouting nonsense like it was the truth. Must've prided themselves in being 'different' from her. You were the biggest devils. You lot were all the same. Donghee wrote some more.

Kim Jina is a liar. Vacuum cleaner bitch. @qw1234

Donghee switched off the computer and went back to bed. He felt at peace. It was as if the rage inside him had all come spilling out. Reason slowly returned as he began to grasp the situation. Still no word from his supervisor. He was a fair person. At least when it came to this kind of thing, he'd be level-headed. Donghee's allegiance to him thus far was irrelevant. There was of course a chance he'd protect Donghee, but there'd be so much to deal with as a result. The bad name would carry more weight. Donghee quickly redirected his thoughts. What if I give my supervisor no choice but to offer his help, despite the tarnish it'd bring on his reputation? There needed to be something in it for him. It needed to be worth him going through all that. Then the story would change. Just like it had for Lee Kanghyun.

Yeah, he needed to become like Lee Kanghyun. He needed to be someone of help to the university. For that he needed help himself. All answers, of course, lead back to Lee Kanghyun.

Lee Kanghyun pretended she knew nothing, that her hands were clean when it came to this matter, but she'd never be able to give up on Donghee. If this was the way he was going to go, then he was prepared to play his final hand and drop a bomb. That's right.

Lee Kanghyun. I'll go find her.

Just like the first time I went to her office and laid my cards on the table.

Yeah, Lee Kanghyun.

You and I are in the same boat. We can't go down like this.

Tomorrow, as soon as I walk in the research room I'll say it: I'm going to make public the list of all the translations I've done for you. Donghee laughed as he imagined the look of panic sweep across her face. Out flowed a sigh of relief. He felt, now, that he'd get some sleep. Donghee lay down and closed his eyes. And he forgot all about the hilarious truth he'd posted on Twitter. Just like all the other events he'd considered insignificant, it vanished completely from his mind.

8

Jina

'WELCOME!'

I opened the café door to see Yang Sujin sitting at the counter. Her relaxed face reserved for customers stiffened the instant she laid eyes on me. It'd been almost ten years. Yang Sujin stared at me; before I could speak, she pointed over her shoulder. I turned round and saw an empty seat. Her arrogance was infuriating, but I said nothing and went to sit down.

How is this place so empty? I know it's early, but still. Business bad or something? Judgmental thoughts slipped into my mind.

After yesterday's phone call, I'd gone straight to the bus station and bought an overnight ticket to Anjin. Tana had looked unsurprised to see me. I'd lain wide awake the whole night, and headed to the café first thing in the morning. Whether it was the sleep deprivation, or the instant coffee I'd gulped down as soon as I woke up, my heart was pounding the whole way there. I heard it thump through my chest.

A minute or so later, Yang Sujin came and sat down in front of me.

'You want a drink?' she asked.

I shook my head. Sujin was sitting opposite me. Staring vacantly, like butter wouldn't melt. I held her gaze. Where do I start? I'd been selecting my words, when Sujin confronted me, 'What are you doing here?'

'What?'

'I said, what are you doing in Anjin?'

I wrinkled my forehead. She always had been the expert when it came to humiliating people. Married and in her thirties, I thought she might've changed by now—but no. I suppose then she never would've posted that comment online to begin with. I looked Yang Sujin right in the eyes. Given how she was acting, there was no need for niceties.

'Why did you write that?'

'What?' Yang Sujin frowned as she asked.

I went through all the words I'd prepared. Twitter, @qw1234. I know it was you. I can report you. This is libel. You're used to getting away with this kind of thing, you probably think it's nothing, but I could report you for this.

Sujin kept staring, like she still had no idea what I was on about. She thought me pathetic, I could tell. Realizing Sujin wasn't taking me at all seriously, my anger rose and I grew impatient. I spoke faster. Then it all came pouring out—not just my story, but the stories of everyone Sujin had trashed at uni. As the tales went on, the rage piled up thick, and my face grew hot.

'You've never once thought about what you did to people, have you?'

Sujin didn't respond. Little by little, my voice began to tremble.

'You can't treat people like that. You insult and belittle others, but you're nothing special yourself.'

Then Yang Sujin cut me off.

'Why did you come here, seriously?'

She hadn't changed a bit. Once Yang Sujin had slagged someone off, she would always pretend she'd done nothing of the sort. As if she was so thoughtful, so considerate; meanwhile she was pushing people off the edge of the cliff. This time was no different. I was certain Sujin had written it.

I raised my voice. When I called that day, I'd wanted to have a conversation with you. You didn't even listen to what I had to say; you just cursed at me. The more I spoke, the more my courage welled up. That's right. I've done nothing wrong. I was confident. I could easily sue you. That's what I'm going to do. You have no right to insult me. Do you have any idea how much I've wanted to talk to you?

I went on, 'Do you know what I've realized? That no one has the right to walk all over me. Feels good to comment on other people's business, doesn't it? Makes you feel big. But in the end you're just picking scraps of their self-esteem up off the floor. And about Yuri.'

I held my breath for a moment.

'The dead… How can someone treat another human being like…'

I was struggling to speak. Surely you knew what it'd been like for her?—the words flew out. You get it. Isolation. Loneliness. My eyes reddened. I felt the tears would erupt any moment, but weirdly I wasn't embarrassed. It was strange. There'd been times when the most vulnerable parts of me, ones I couldn't show even Tana, had burst out in front of Sujin. Perhaps because we both recalled the smell of Palhyun; the moment the yellow fields flushed red at dusk. I said what I wanted to.

'You're a woman, too.'

But Sujin was still staring at me, irritated. Like I was making a big deal out of nothing, like I disgusted her. I'd full-on cried in front of Sujin—it made me cringe. Sujin let out a brief sigh, looked me straight in the eye, and spoke calmly.

'You really are a liar.'

I was ashamed. How could I let the likes of her see me cry? Getting sentimental over my home town in front of someone who couldn't care less about how I feel. I calmed myself down. I didn't want to steep myself in any more weird emotions in front of Sujin.

I spoke as coolly as possible. 'Let's see what the law has to say, then.'

Sujin laughed.

'Be my guest,' Sujin replied, with disinterest. 'You really haven't changed at all. You're creepy, seriously.'

There was no reason to stay any longer. That's right, just you wait and see. I picked up my bag.

Then Sujin spoke again.

'Let me ask *you* something.'

I raised my head.

'That winter, did you really see my husband?'

'What?'

'Don't act like you don't know. I know it was you who started the rumours.'

I frowned. I was ready with my comeback—What are you on about?—when suddenly a memory rushed back to me.

8th December, the winter I turned twenty. I'd stepped out of the backstreet where the BBQ place was.

I saw Yuri.

'Jina-ya!'

I was in front of the telephone pole, and turned around; Yuri appeared from the neighbouring alley, calling my name.

'Jina-ya, you came! I was wondering when you were getting here. I've been waiting over there for you!'

'Oh, hi.'

I was flustered. I'd planned to drop by without anyone knowing—I just *had* to run into *her*, didn't I? Yuri had always irritated me. Ever since we'd spoken that one time at the freshers' party, Yuri had gone round telling everyone we were friends. I'd never once thought of Yuri as a friend. Hoping I could say a brief hi and be done with it, I quickly moved my feet. But Yuri followed.

'Jina-ya, aren't you coming in?'

I pretended not to hear. But Yuri was persistent. I told her I had something to sort at home. Yuri looked disappointed. Then, though I should never have asked, the words came out.

'Why were you waiting for me?'

'I had something to talk to you about.' Her words sounded forced, as if she'd memorized the line from a theatre script.

She lowered her voice and whispered to me. 'Listen, can you help me with something?'

Yuri's damp, warm breath enveloped the rim of my ear. I rubbed at it irritably. I was annoyed. Annoyed someone had already discovered me here, and even more so that it'd been Yuri. Why did I have to be standing here with *her*? Not Hyeongyu sunbae, not anyone else? Yuri was about to open her mouth to speak, when I asked, belligerent, 'What is it you want help with?'

Yuri looked at me with a severe expression. I hated it. I could tell from her face she was acting. I let out a sigh. This is agony. Why am I still talking with her? I'd decided to go home regardless of her response; it was then.

'Yuri-ya!'

Someone called out from the end of the alley. A man. Yuri flinched and turned to look behind her. I strained to hear the familiar voice. But there was silence. Yuri glanced back awkwardly. The man's shadow hung dimly under the street lamp's glow. He looked tall. Yuri shifted her gaze back and forth indecisively; him to me. She wanted to go to him, it seemed. That attitude—that I was no longer necessary—sent my rage soaring. Now there's a guy here, just one of your endless string of men, I'm nothing to you? Guess in the end the last person I'll see is you, then. I felt like venting at Yuri. But I bit my lip, turned around, and walked on ahead.

'Jina-ya?'

Yuri called out, but I didn't turn back. I'm never coming back here again. The voice calling my name echoed on through the alley.

On my way home, the student representative from our year called me. Naturally her tone gave no hint of wanting to see me. It suggested: everyone else is here so we should probably at least try phoning her. I felt the voice she'd tried hard to conceal ring in my ears. We're not excluding you. You've misunderstood. Look, we told you about the gathering today, and we're even calling you right now, okay?

She asked whether I was coming. When I said I wasn't, a mildly sarcastic response came back at me.

'Really? Yuri said she just saw you, though?'

I silently furrowed my brow. Then I realized. Of course it wasn't because they wanted me there—they'd called to confirm that I'd come and gone. Wanted to bitch that I was stalking them. I lied, saying I'd run into Yuri a while earlier, and quickly pivoted the conversation. To that topic everyone pretended to be disgusted by, but in truth fascinated them. Seems Yuri has a new guy, I said.

'There's a surprise.'

As predicted, she acted uninterested, but then wanted to carry on talking about Yuri's man.

'Who is it this time? Someone from our department again?'

'Dunno. But the guy was super tall.'

I'd guessed people might mistakenly think it was Hyeongyu sunbae. I didn't want to cause him yet more trouble. Even so, I didn't take back what I'd said. It was no longer any of my business. It'd had nothing to do with me to begin with. Just like this place, and these people. I'm leaving, and never coming back. I remembered Yang Sujin and laughed. Would she come to Seoul just to interrogate me? Yeah, so be it.

All I'd said was that he was tall.

A few days later, Yuri was dead.

*

'Thanks to you, people started saying my husband was fucking Ha Yuri. You know that, right?'

'No, I...'

I had nothing to say. I wasn't unaware. I'd been worried people would say exactly that, and so had confirmed it myself. People were ridiculous. Hyeongyu sunbae and Donghee weren't the only tall ones by then. A new cohort had come in, and there were tall guys amongst our sunbaes discharged from the military. If you searched the humanities department you'd find at least ten. It made no sense that rumours had centred on Hyeongyu sunbae. But it soon went from my mind. I no longer had any connection to Anjin University. And honestly, I only really cared about whether Yang Sujin and Ryu Hyeongyu had broken up because of it. They hadn't. I lost interest. I couldn't say I'd completely forgotten, but I never remembered. It was like stealing a package from outside someone's front door, opening it up and destroying it. Later, I put the object back inside the box, resealed it, and returned it to its original place. As if nothing had happened, as if I knew nothing. Is Sujin still angry because of it? Is that why she wrote I was a liar?

Sujin spoke coldly. 'You're good at that, aren't you? Saying you saw something you never did. Acting like you know when you don't.'

I felt pathetic and ashamed, but I needed to make things clear: that'd never been my intention. I needed to say it properly this time. Then Sujin spoke.

'That Twitter post, it wasn't me.'

She got up from her seat. As if she had nothing more to say. I was the one who'd come looking for her, but Sujin was the only one who'd said her piece. Sujin left me alone and strode back towards the counter. I clenched my jaw and stood up. I went over to Sujin.

'I could report you to the police.'

Sujin replied frostily, 'Go ahead. I didn't write it.'

I stood completely still. It felt strange. I'd come to get answers, but now I was the one in the wrong. I didn't want to back down.

'So it was because of the rumours. That's why you called me a stupid bitch?'

Sujin didn't respond. I didn't understand, and I wasn't convinced.

I asked again. 'Well you've asked now, haven't you? Why didn't you grill me back then?'

Childish. If it'd all been because of that, it really was childish. How could she act like this when she'd seen everything I'd been through, and knew how I'd felt? Sujin looked at me and smiled. She was cold, like she thought my question utterly trivial.

It's hard to believe how little people change.

'All right, then.' Sujin spoke as if she'd made her decision. 'I didn't write that tweet and the rumour you started was false. Happy? That settles it. Also.'

Sujin paused for a moment. She was torturing me. *You're not the only one who finds me disgusting. I do, too.* Sujin spoke.

'I'm not a woman. So will you get the fuck out of my sight?'

I left Sujin's café and walked a while. I found a random place for lunch, but humiliation flooded over me like nausea. Stepping outside, I stifled my breath and kept on walking. By the time I'd pulled myself together, I was at the Anjin University campus.

A familiar path.

Coming through the main gate, cherry trees lined up like an avenue. Cherry blossom was the Anjin University emblem. In spring when the flowers were in full bloom, Anjin locals would come for walks in the university grounds. But the real spectacle came at night. When the street lamps in between the cherry trees lit up their white petals, the reflection would float up softly beneath the night sky. When the wind blew, petals scattered from overhead and settled white on the ground. Though very different from spring, winter carried its own atmosphere.

My body trembled as I walked. I didn't know if it was the cold, or the bitter taste in my mouth. I continued straight ahead without diversion. The main gate soon stretched into the distance. If you followed the first curve five paces ahead, there was a slender path leading to the humanities department. I counted my steps as I walked.

One, two, three, four, five.

The trees vanished, and in their place appeared the path, as if it'd been waiting for me. When I first started uni here, it felt like a tunnel from a fairy tale. A narrow, deep portal to a whole other universe. Until I turned nineteen, Anjin University had been where the cherry blossoms bloomed radiantly at night. Once I became a student here, I realized there was another world beyond the blossoms. Where I needed to go, where I needed to be. Like crawling into the depths of a cave, I crept beneath the blossoms and entered that world.

I halted my step; the humanities department was in front of me. Students were wandering around outside. A sour smell like alcohol wafted from inside the building. It was like walking through my own memories. I continued on as if possessed. Cherry trees packed the rear side of the building, too. It was also where the humanities mini sports field was, which connected to the back gate. Across from there was the studio apartment village. The studios were closer to the humanities department than the dormitories. There were always students who'd arrive for class with hair still dripping wet. Living in the dorms myself, I was jealous. Kim Donghee lived in the studio apartment village. Ha Yuri, too. At the end of first year, Yang Sujin also moved out of the dorms into a studio. They all lived there.

Trapped inside events of the past, unsure what was memory and what wasn't, suddenly my phone's message alert sounded. I opened the chat window and immediately closed it again. Lee Jinsub.

It's all happening today, isn't it? I was so frustrated. I thought of just going back, but there was nowhere to go. It'd still be a while before Tana finished work. She'd given me the entry code to her place, but I didn't feel like going back to an empty flat. I looked around. Lee Jinsub wouldn't have followed me all the way here, would he? I surveyed my surroundings and walked towards the entrance to the humanities building. My plan was to walk one lap of the sports field to calm myself, then leave. It was then. A handwritten poster stuck in front of the building caught my eye.

My jaw dropped.

'I am reporting English Literature department lecturer Kim Donghee. On 16th December, we went for drinks, where I was sexually assaulted by him. He groped my back where my bra was. Four of my friends had been there, but because it happened on the sly while they were absorbed in singing, no one noticed. I twisted my body away, but lecturer Kim Donghee shamelessly stretched out his hand, and continued to rub my back.

'I reported this to the university's Gender Equality Student Support Centre. They told me I could either choose to follow official or unofficial procedure, and could also request disciplinary action against the perpetrator. Unofficial procedure would involve negotiation with the accused via the Support Centre's intervention, and official procedure would mean opening a fact-finding committee to investigate the incident. The first thing I asked for was lecturer Kim Donghee's dismissal. I wanted to follow official procedure, but also didn't want rumours about my personal business spreading round the university. Given the situation, the Support Centre recommended the unofficial route. Lecturer Kim Donghee wanted to come to an agreement, they said. In the end, I agreed to follow unofficial procedure. Our testimonies were misaligned, there were no witnesses, and as there was no proof, even if a fact-finding committee were to be opened, a dismissal was off the table. As a result, disciplinary action of one term's lecture cancellation was ordered. Although rubbing someone's back can be regarded as sexual assault, the intensity, as well as the bodily region in question, was not "definitive" enough to warrant dismissal, in addition to the fact that there was no

evidence or eyewitness. It was doubtful whether the humiliation I felt can be deemed "definitive" on objective terms. But
I decided to accept lecturer Kim Donghee's class cancellation
as constituting a certain degree of punishment. However, I
then found out he would be giving lectures for the humanities exchange class in the Engineering department, as well as
teaching at the University of Natural Sciences. It was also
made known that he would take on key projects at the graduate school and continue his involvement in external activities.
When I protested to the Support Centre, they responded that
as lecturer Kim Donghee's humanities department classes had
been cancelled, I, the victim, would not come into contact
with him, and thus reasonable measures had been taken. I
would like to make this matter known to all my university
friends and colleagues. An incident that has been reported
and settled cannot be re-reported. Lecturer Kim Donghee was
someone I respected. An individual I believed would protect
and guide me has instead scarred me for life. The Support
Centre is there in name only; in reality it does not consider
the demands or position of the victim. And so I would like to
ask for your support. Please help me get a fact-finding committee opened, and last term's incident properly investigated.

'Kim Eyoung, Eurasia Cultural Content Department.'

Donghee's face flashed in and out of my consciousness. It'd
been a long time since I'd thought about him. Our whole
four months together had been unpleasant. It wasn't proper
dating—though I was clueless and new to such things, I
knew that much at least. What happened between me and

Donghee wasn't a relationship. Lee Jinsub's face shot into my mind. Thinking about it now, I know why Lee Jinsub had felt familiar the first time we met.

All that time I'd thought it'd been because of Hyeongyu sunbae, but actually, it'd been Donghee. The idea made my hair stand on end.

Two men walked out from inside the building. In one fell swoop they ripped the poster in half. I stepped back in shock. Sensing my reaction, one of them spoke to me.

'We're from the administration office. This has been put up without permission. We have no choice.'

The other man sent him a reprimanding look for his useless comment. They scrunched up the torn poster like a piece of rubbish and went back inside. Kim Eyoung's words vanished without trace.

It felt like I was dreaming. I went inside the humanities building; the smell of old dust burrowed through my nostrils. Kim Donghee. Things didn't turn out so well for you, either, I see. I glanced around just in case.

I absolutely did not want to see him.

That man was nothing to me.

I hastened my step. When I came outside, the sports field was before me. Some male students were playing football. Cherry trees encircled the field, with a collection of benches dotted beneath them. Funnily enough, coming outside brought back crystal-clear memories of Kim Donghee. This was the bench we often sat on during our 'dates'. Of course, I often sat by myself, too.

I observed a lot of people from the bench during that time. Friends, sunbaes. Humanities students idling away the time between classes, couples on dates like Donghee and me, university societies day drinking. And Yuri was there. I closed my eyes tight and opened them again. Ha Yuri's image appeared in perfect photographic detail.

Yuri always sat over there, alone.

I shut my eyes and opened them once more. In the distance, I saw a female student putting up posters. Baseball cap pulled right down, zip-up hoodie with a well-worn windbreaker on top. Is that Kim Eyoung? She looked tired. Plenty of people walked past, but no one looked in her direction.

A car accident. Yuri had evidently been on her way to uni—she'd been hit just across from the main gate. She'd most likely been going to submit her 'Content Creation' class paper. The 15th December deadline had long since passed. She may have been planning to hand it in directly and plead with the professor. The last person in our year to have messaged Yuri called her annoying. Yuri had been texting all morning saying she'd missed the deadline, and asking what to do; they'd replied telling her to go hand it in herself, and didn't look at their phone again after that. That was what I heard along the grapevine. Yuri was making a big deal out of nothing. We'd been given the assignment to write freely what we thought about ourselves at the beginning of second term. The whole term, Yuri texted other people in our year whining. She messaged me, too. I have no idea what to write. It's too difficult. I can't do it. I find this kind of thing so tough. It's way too hard. Is it no big deal for you? What kind of person do you think you are? What about me? How do I seem? What do I want to become? What kind of person do I want to be? Wait, maybe I'm already becoming someone? The kind of person you'd never want to end up like. People pretended to comfort Yuri, telling her not to worry, that she'd be fine, before gathering in a separate chat to bad-mouth her. Stupid bitch. Attention-seeking, yet again. She's way too much, I can't deal. So fucking annoying. Oi, then answer back properly. But if you were to reply, then the messages would come—Let's have lunch together!—from her day after day. You couldn't not realize: that was the first thing people always said about her. I received Yuri's messages, too. I never once replied.

Yuri's accident had been a hit-and-run. It was my first confrontation with death. Though I'd been to my grandparents' funerals, in Yuri's case it'd been unexpected. With my grandparents, it was like quietly drawing life to a close. For Yuri it was different. Twenty years old was too young to comprehend death. It was for me, at least. Given Yuri's suicide attempt a few months prior, her death surprised me even more—I'd thought she'd just been attention-seeking. To me she was childish, over the top. I think that's why I'd been so cold to Yuri that evening in front of the BBQ place. After hearing of her death, I thought more seriously about what she might've been going through. I remembered that voice calling me through the alley. Maybe something really had been going on?

Though people sneered at her attention-seeking suicide threat, in reality it'd been a very serious incident. The newspaper even ran a story on it. She'd joined a suicide group and they'd met in a motel.

Six including Yuri gathered that day. As it said in the article, there'd been no deaths. I heard from Tana that the group's organizer was now pianist for the Anjin Cathedral choir. Recalling that time, he said he'd been all façade, and had lost touch with who he was. An act of bravado during a period when he'd worshipped death, spat on life, and believed he had the right to do whatever he liked with his body. Yuri had been in that group. It happened four months before her death. Then maybe the car accident was a suicide?—the thought crosses my mind. She'd wanted to die, anyway. Like that. In the end, she'd gone like that.

I heard they kept the funeral small. No family to speak of, there was no one to take charge, and so it'd been a simple affair. One of her distant relatives did attend, but went home immediately after the cremation. And so no one knows where Yuri was buried. I heard from Tana that Hyeongyu sunbae helped with the funeral right until the end. He was also the one to clear out her empty room. After hearing the landlady was going to sell all Yuri's things second-hand, Hyeongyu sunbae took some of his male hoobaes and went over there. Cleaning, sorting out any keepsakes—he did all of it.

I wonder what Yuri wrote for that assignment.

I walked a while as I thought back on those events, and soon I was in front of the studio apartment village. I often passed by here when I was seeing Donghee. His place was easy to find. First you looked for the convenience store, followed the road and turned left at the water leak inspection sign. Two blocks from there you'd see some flats; the semi-basement studio was Donghee's. Diagonally across was a new-build, where Yuri lived on the fifth floor. I'd seen her a few times taking the rubbish out or on her way to the market.

I stood for a short while in front of Yuri's building. It'd grown run-down over the past eleven years, but the entrance gate and its surroundings were exactly as they had been. I had the indistinct feeling of being twenty years old again, when a doubt abruptly slid open the bolt to my heart and flew out.

Why exactly had Hyeongyu sunbae been the one to clear out Yuri's room?

To be honest, it'd always bothered me. Of course, it was exactly the kind of thing he'd do. Someone so caring and considerate of others. But why clear out the room of a girl you'd had nothing to do with? Hyeongyu sunbae would've, though. Given his personality, maybe he felt a compassion for this hoobae he'd been unable to protect. At the time I didn't give it a second thought—after all, I hadn't heard the rumours about him and Yuri. Now I find it difficult to understand. Why go and clear out the room of the girl people said you'd been fucking?

I pictured Sujin. It may well have been my fault those nasty rumours spread. But a long time had passed since then. Does that really warrant her *still* treating me like a stupid bitch?

Could something else be bothering her?

I swallowed. Maybe something she'd tried to bury deep, something she'd hoped no one would ever discover had come swelling out without warning—could that be why she was angry? Still?

In that case.

Maybe he really had been sleeping with Yuri?

The idea gathered speed and sprinted through my mind. A person who'd never do something like that. Someone you'd never think would. Whom you never would've suspected.

I no longer trust people who always have their praises sung like that. Lee Jinsub held everyone's confidence. People complimented him until their mouths turned dry. Just as for a whole year no one had known what I'd been going through—some people are able to completely pull the wool over others' eyes like that. It was Lee Jinsub who was the liar. To look good in front of others, to become the subject of their envy, he fabricated himself. Child of a rich family, beloved son, doting older brother, caring partner. I fooled people, too.

Pretending my boyfriend loved me, pretending I understood it all.

I remember the day he first hit me.

We'd been drinking that afternoon. It was probably the alcohol, but he'd started opening up, sharing all sorts of things about himself. Where he grew up was as far in the sticks as Palhyun. He wasn't proud of being from the countryside. It was because of his family. He hated the term 'eldest son'. Having to take responsibility for the household angered him. That day, I learnt for the first time that he'd worked his way up from nothing. I was shocked—that wasn't what he'd told people at work. He'd often talked of growing up in a loving home, his good relationship with his younger sisters; but what I heard that day was a completely different story. According to him, since university he'd gotten by without any help from his parents. Yet his family believed they'd sacrificed so much for him.

'Of course I received a bit of help. But I don't know.'

Given one more piece of meat at dinner than his sisters? The only sibling to attend hagwon during high school? And the only one who went to a private university in Seoul? He couldn't deny what he'd had. But he'd received scholarships all throughout uni, and worked part-time to support his living costs. The hagwon had only been a small one in their neighbourhood that offered supplementary classes, and when his sisters got married, he took out loans for their dowries. He'd also been sending money to his family every month ever since he'd started working. But his younger sisters continued to complain how he'd always received special treatment, and so he needed to take good care of their parents, they said.

'Whenever they say that I want to beat the shit out of them, just like when we were kids.'

Taking a beer from the fridge, he continued, 'I liked when we were young. I could slap around those idiots and no one said a thing.'

He already seemed tipsy. I thought I'd better not let him talk any more about himself. I started to talk about my own family.

Once both sets of grandparents had passed away, my family shrunk. Our relatives consisted of one uncle on my father's side and two aunts on my mother's. The uncle emigrated to America, and we didn't see my aunts often as they lived in a different part of the country. They couldn't come to Palhyun on holidays, either, as they'd be at their in-laws'. My parents began to keep holidays simple. They'd worked on the farm since a young age, and weren't fond of ostentatious family gatherings. We didn't make a big fuss of special occasions.

People are always surprised when I tell them this, but for me, coming from the countryside doesn't necessarily mean you uphold tradition. Every family is different. My parents spent their whole lives harried by work and debt. On extended public holidays when their shop didn't get many customers, they would've wanted to rest. Maybe that's why we didn't spend much time on the food. And Umma didn't like me in the kitchen, so I never helped with the cooking. She always refused, telling me to enjoy it while it lasted—once I was married, she said, I'd spend the rest of my life preparing food on the holidays. One day, unable to stand the sight of it anymore, I suggested going to the market to get some jeon, and Umma replied, 'All right, let's just buy the jeon this year.'

The jesa food was the same. 'And so I never once helped,' I told him.

'Really?' His expression abruptly contorted. 'I knew it.'

His tone panicked me. It felt like an attack. I stared at him, stunned, not knowing what to say, when like a shot he slapped me twice round the face—*tuk tuk*—with the back of his hand. It wasn't a caress; there was power in it. I felt my cheeks sting.

What? Is this a joke?

I was confused. My mind was all over the place. I didn't get why he'd said it. My family was laid-back—this was why I didn't cook on holidays. I of course helped with the washing up, laundry and cleaning. All I was saying was how my mum had a thing against me cooking, but he was talking as if I was a layabout who did nothing around the house. But I didn't contradict him. After all, it wasn't something to be proud of. Maybe I'm in the wrong? Should I have helped, regardless of what Umma said? Had I completely missed something? I could still feel the stinging in my cheeks. And what was that? Did he just hit me? Or had he done it by accident, not realizing his own strength?

Then, I thought to myself:

Oh, he's drunk.

Of course, these things do happen after one too many.

Seeing my expression stiffen, he smiled. Then slapped me round the face again.

Tuk.

Tuk.

Tuk.

I grabbed his hand.

'Stop it.'

He laughed loudly. 'Hey, it's a joke. A joke. Can you not take a joke?'

I let go of his hand. He stroked my hair. I felt ashamed for getting angry at him. He began talking about his family once again. On holidays, he always handled all the chores himself, he said. From the jesa preparation to looking after his relatives; not to mention preparing the food as well as taking care of the grave. Other families had a daughter-in-law to help out, but he was single and so had no one. He couldn't leave it to his elderly mother, either, so he'd no choice but to do it himself. His father had never helped with a thing his whole life, he said. But then he'd click his tongue at his son, asking what a young man was doing in the kitchen. His sisters used the excuse of having 'come back home' and didn't lift a finger.

Then he said, 'I want to beat the shit out of them.'

Without thinking, I asked, 'You mean your father?'

He furrowed his brow again. 'What the fuck? Do I look like that kind of dickhead? I'm talking about my sisters.'

'Oh.'

Not knowing what to say, I just smiled awkwardly. He looked at me and spoke again.

'Wouldn't you want to slap them up?'

I hesitated before whispering, 'Well… Even men cook, I guess.'

That instant, I felt the air around me sink. I raised my head. He stared into me, his face boiling with rage. I hurriedly went on, trying to cover for myself.

'I mean, even the men in your family help out, is what I'm saying.'

Just then, a sound came down like a crash and rang through my ears. I held my hand to my face.

'Even men?!'

His voice was incensed.

'You proud of playing about at home? Think your parents are understanding, right? Don't delude yourself. They're not being understanding. They're just not saying anything.'

Then he shoved my shoulders. I slipped from the chair and onto the floor, still clasping my face. I couldn't look at him.

'Even men? Aren't you ashamed?'

I was ashamed.

My cheeks burned, and I'd been so startled it felt like my heart would burst out of my chest; but more than that, I was ashamed of having said those words. 'Even men.' I remembered how in primary school, I'd worn a skirt to impress a boy who'd said girls look ugly in trousers. And yet I go and say something like that? When I was at Anjin Uni, I went to a drinks reception for a famous translator who'd come to give a lecture. A man. The female students there well outnumbered the guys. The translator told a story about a girl he'd dated as a student.

All the guys used to fall under her charm, and he'd been hurt by her himself, but once he became famous she got back in touch. 'I was so disappointed when I saw her. She'd aged horribly.'

Then he scanned over the girls and said, 'Don't let yourselves go.'

I laughed. I laughed! I didn't want to be a buzzkill. I wanted to come across as a 'cool' girl who lets those kinds of jokes slide!

During my last term at uni in Seoul, an elderly professor said to the female students, 'You're all sitting there, meanwhile the population is declining as we speak! Hurry up, get married and have kids!'

A few of the girls, angered, collected signatures planning to report the professor to the university. I didn't sign. It was my graduation term. I didn't want 'a thing like that' to come back at me. Women only call it discrimination when there's something in it for them. A female colleague at work reported her boss on charges of sexual assault. I didn't help her. It wasn't my business. I didn't want to come across as the kind of woman who makes a big deal and spoils the company atmosphere over such a minor incident—there were much more important things to worry about.

Despite all this. Me, of all people.

I was ashamed.

Even men? Why had I said that? In this day and age. I loathed people saying 'women should this' or 'women are that', yet out of my own mouth came the words 'even men'. Wait, I've never actively talked about something like this before. How did I let the words 'even men' slip out? I created this situation; no wonder he hit me. I was in the wrong. How could I have said that knowing his situation? I have no right.

But the fact was, he'd hit me. When he went to the toilet, I gathered my things and left. For three days, I ignored his calls. Every day he left messages and voicemails saying he was sorry. Saying he'd lost control of his emotions and acted without thinking. That it would never happen again.

'I'm sorry. I shouldn't have taken it out on you.'

His parents' business had gone bust and he was paying off their debts, he said.

'Can you consider me a little more before you speak, though? It was my fault as well, for not explaining my situation better. But it's all on my shoulders. Just because I'm the eldest son. The simple fact my parents are still alive puts a burden on me. Any idea how guilty I feel just for thinking that? But *even men* help out? When you said that, it was like something snapped inside my head. I'm sorry. Really, I am. It took me by surprise, too. I couldn't believe what I'd done, either. This isn't me. You know that, right? I'm an affectionate person. Can't you bring out that side of me?'

On the fourth day, he came to my place and fell to his knees. He stood at almost 1.9m, but knelt down like that, he looked so small. Seeing him beg for my forgiveness, my heart softened. This commanding, confident man, the object of everyone's envy; my forgiveness was now the only thing he hoped for.

I realize that him hitting me was not something to be 'understood'. But I tried nonetheless. I needed to convince myself that I understood what had happened. I didn't want to accept that I was the kind of woman who gets beaten by men. So I accepted everything as the 'truth'. That he'd been hurt by me. That his life was hard. That he was really sorry. That, despite everything, he really loved me.

I love you.

I really love you.

And so in the end, the person who fooled me the most was me. Anyone is capable of deception. It happens. Was Hyeongyu sunbae any different? Was he really the person I remembered?

Just then, the door to the studio block opened. A middle-aged woman walked out talking on the phone.

'Okay, I'll head over to the estate agents now,' she said.

I recognized her right away. The landlady. I'd seen her before. The studio apartment village was relatively small, and students moved about a lot. And so the faces of a few decent landlords were known among the students. I'd been itching to move out of dorms, and so I remembered this place even more clearly. She'd aged a lot, as well. I wasn't certain it was actually her; it was only an inkling. Sensing my gaze, she glanced over at me. I rushed over. I might as well ask.

'Excuse me!'

She turned around when I called. I immediately spoke.

'Excuse me, you remember Ha Yuri, don't you? She lived on the top floor a long time ago.'

Looking at me doubtfully, she slowly stretched out her words.

'Oh... The young girl that died? Why now, all of a sudden?'

It *was* her. And she remembered Yuri, too. I hurriedly continued.

'I was in the same year as Yuri at uni.'

She sighed, and it was clear she was annoyed. 'You must be the thousandth one.'

'Sorry?' I spoke back.

'What's this about? Are you writing a novel, too?'

I had no response, and no idea what she was referring to.

The landlady continued. 'Always come saying they're writing a novel, article, whatever. What are you writing? A novel? Article?'

I shook my head. She waved me off. She had little to say about Yuri, she said.

Quickly, I asked, 'Just one thing. Back then, a guy came to clear out her room, right? Really tall. Do you remember him?'

I rushed to explain. 'Before you put the room up for rent again, did a guy come to clear out her room?'

'Yes. What about it?'

'Do you happen to remember who came with him? Should've been three or so of them. I was wondering if you remembered exactly what they got rid of.'

The landlady stared at me in bewilderment. 'What are you on about now? Why are you asking that?'

'The thing is…' I swallowed.

'Go. You shouldn't be digging around the dead like this. If it's a novel you're writing, use your imagination and write it on your own.'

I turned and grabbed her. 'I want to clear up a misunderstanding people have of me. Please, help me out. Could I at least know who it was that came?'

She looked at me in confusion.

'People are saying I'm lying,' I said.

'Lying about what?'

'People suspect it was me who went with him to clear out Yuri's room. It wasn't. I can't get in touch with him, and they keep saying I stole something…'

My words trailed off and I looked at the landlady. My face burned red; probably because I really had lied now. The landlady frowned. She still seemed dubious. Given I'd already lied once, I thought, why not tell another? Yeah, if I'm able to fool myself, I should have no problem deceiving others.

'The rumours keep getting more serious, and if things don't get cleared up, I'm thinking of going to the police.'

At this, the landlady's expression darkened. She tutted, asking what I wanted to go to the police for.

'Seems like everyone's been misunderstood. You, and the other girl.'

I listened. The landlady continued on.

'Two people came that day, not three. The boy and one of Yuri's friends.'

'Yuri's friend?'

'Yeah, she used to come to Yuri's place a lot. She'd asked her boyfriend to help her sort Yuri's belongings. The two were so close, I thought it'd be all right to leave her to it. Yuri had no family, after all. But what are they saying was stolen? Her friend took everything important. Said she'd send it all on to Yuri's relative.'

The landlady's explanation was long and drawn-out, perhaps concerned she'd be misunderstood herself. I'd brought up the police—that was probably why. She continued to speak resolutely, clearly not wanting to get caught up in a headache.

'I remember well—it was Yuri's friend. Yuri had introduced her to me as her really close friend a while before, telling me not to worry if I saw her coming and going when she wasn't there. I can't deal with this! Anyway, that Yuri was a strange girl. When she signed the contract on the place she went on about how she was an orphan, telling me every last detail about her life. Then one day she suddenly told me her friend would be staying with her for a while. I went through a lot because of that girl. People like you asking me these questions causes me so much stress, you realize? Anyway, that girl was certainly Yuri's friend. She used to stay here days at a time. I'm sure. Whenever Yuri saw me, she begged me not to talk to her friend when I saw her. That's why I remembered the girl and let her in the room. I wouldn't let just anyone in someone's room, dead or not.'

The landlady's voice grew higher and higher as if to prove her innocence. I could tell she was sick of me. I kept on listening. Not because I was convinced, but because I couldn't understand a thing.

Sujin and Yuri had never been friends.

The landlady said she was busy and carried on her way. I stood where I was, perfectly still. Alleyways spread out ahead.

The small, pretty face staring into me. That morning, Sujin had said to me, 'I'm not a woman.'

Why?

At first I'd thought it was a sarcastic remark—that she wasn't a woman like me. Or maybe she'd been ridiculing me, telling me not to look for sympathy by making a comment like that. I'd simply thought she was acting like a stubborn child because she wanted to contradict whatever I said. Then I suddenly realized another potential meaning to her words. Another, hidden meaning.

Sujin and Yuri. Yuri and Hyeongyu sunbae. Then me.

The deeper my thoughts went, the less I understood; soon the sun was setting and darkness began to unfold. I stayed where I was, groping around for old memories. I hadn't a clue where I was supposed to go.

9

Sujin

S UJIN WENT PAST the apartment nursery on her way to work again today. A little boy was sobbing, refusing to let go of his mother. Without making it too obvious, she carefully examined the child's expression. Sorrow was stained across his screwed-up face. As the tears forming round his eyes began to drip down, Sujin felt her own heart sink; it must be breaking his mum's heart. The woman managed to pry her child away and turned around. She looked utterly exhausted.

Sujin turned her head. She pretended not to have seen.

Eleven p.m. Sujin had closed up the café and was on her way home when her husband called. He said he was working late and not to wait up. Fine, Sujin said. A brief silence hung between them.

Sujin stopped a while outside the nursery on the way back, too. What a cliché, she thought.

Obvious, ridiculous.

If you live nine years with someone—having known one another three years before that, too—you pick up their feelings and habits. Silence wasn't a habit of his. Neither was working overtime. She'd always been able to read his thoughts, so clearly it was like she could reach across and grab them; but lately they'd been beyond her grasp.

Hyeongyu was a good husband. He'd been a good boyfriend, and was an even better husband. But recently there'd been an awkwardness between them. He'd been acting strange ever since they'd gone to that concert about a year ago. Nothing unusual had happened, but they had run into two girls from their year at uni. One was now a civil servant in the Education department, and the other a librarian, but given they'd never been close, Sujin wouldn't have known it was them if they hadn't recognized her husband first.

Had something gone on between them and her husband? It was possible. Her husband had been the most popular guy in the department, and Sujin certainly hadn't been his first girlfriend. But even if she were to find out he'd, say, slept with his professor, she could've lived with it.

Since *it* happened, she'd always tried to live in the present.

Yet there was no reason to suspect those girls had history with her husband. They were the kind who'd done nothing but study at uni. Some people don't need anyone else in their future plans. They'd been like that. It wasn't that they'd had no interest in dating or wanted to be alone forever. But they didn't feel a particular need to be with someone, and enjoyed their single life a lot—they had their books, studies, friends, all sorts of interests. Sujin had been in a similar category, too.

If she'd had a little more time, she might've ended up friends with them. Sujin had wanted to become a librarian.

Classifying books, putting them in order, storing and preserving older texts—that was the kind of work she'd wanted to do. Running into those two, it felt like discovering something long lost, and for a moment Sujin disappeared into her memories. If things hadn't happened as they did, she would've turned out like them, too. If she hadn't met Hyeongyu, that is. And if she hadn't thought running a book café was a better idea than becoming a librarian. And if *it* hadn't happened.

Really? Sujin was confused. Had it really been because of that?

But Sujin couldn't fall deep into such thoughts—her husband had started acting weirdly. No matter how many times she went over it in her mind, she was still sure nothing had happened—yet ever since running into those two at the concert, her husband had been off. From the very next day.

In the middle of breakfast, he'd said, 'Those two have really changed a lot.'

At first, Sujin laughed. She assumed he hadn't been able to recognize those two, who'd practically lived in the library at uni, they were so pretty now. Her husband didn't smile.

He stared at Sujin hard before saying, weakly, 'It looks like nothing's changed for us at all.'

Sujin asked what he'd meant. Her husband smiled drearily. He looked a little depressed; exhausted somehow. Sujin didn't ask any more. She guessed he must've been having a hard time at work. Sujin's in-laws always asked why she wasn't having a baby. It wasn't about not having a baby; they couldn't conceive in the first place. Hospital tests revealed her husband's sperm wasn't particularly healthy. They'd tried IVF three times without Hyeongyu's parents knowing, each time without success. Sujin suffered more serious side effects than most. Hyeongyu said he couldn't stand seeing Sujin go through that, and so they stopped trying. He bought some time by insisting to his parents they weren't planning to have a child until he was at least thirty-four. Sujin always wondered whether this was what had got Hyeongyu so down. Her husband had never failed at anything in his life. But potentially not being able to have a baby? That must've been a shock to him.

'I'd be happy just the two of us. What do you think?' Sujin encouraged him.

She'd really felt that way. Of course, Sujin did want a child. Hyeongyu and Sujin's baby. But part of her also didn't want one. She thought life wouldn't be so bad if it carried on just as it was. Life really was good. And so Sujin started secretly watching the nursery children on her way to work. To try and find out whether she wanted a baby or not. Children looked beautiful from afar. Those tiny beings who believe Umma and Appa are their whole universe. Looking at them, Sujin realized she liked children. But if asked whether she truly wanted to raise one herself, she wouldn't have a response. Perhaps, she thought, it was enough to watch them like this. Not everyone has to live how society expects them to.

'I really would,' Sujin said to her husband.

He said nothing. After that, they never brought up the baby issue again. They carried on as if the problem didn't exist. Most of the time they enjoyed life, and were happy. But as he moved closer to thirty-four, his parents began bullying them. Sujin wasn't getting any younger—how much longer were they going to put it off? they asked. She wanted to admit the truth and be done with it. But lately her husband had been so miserable she was afraid to bring up these serious conversations. He'd been like this before. But if she left him to it, after a while he'd pick himself up and return to normal. So Sujin decided to wait.

But this time the wait was really long.

Sujin still didn't ask him anything. It was better, for his sake, to let him be, she thought. But really, the person avoiding the issue was Sujin.

Sujin knows what she needs to ask. Living with someone is working to stay together. Aware there's a chance you could part at any time. Because that person is not you. Effort is the will to keep on living with you, dear. But will on its own is not always enough. Sujin knows how easily her will can break. Will only exists to the extent that there is something worth protecting. Will exists only as far as you can endure. There were times Sujin wanted to tell her husband her secret. But she didn't. Would he be able to cope? Based on the person he'd shown her until now, and the trust she had in him, the answer would be, 'Yes. He'll be able to cope.'

He'd understand her. But would he really? Was it really possible for two people to perfectly understand and accept one another? Would he retain the will to keep living with her? Sometimes she thought about it the other way round. If he had a secret, would she be able to put up with it?

She would.

It would always be a nod of the head. She could. I can put up with anything. Sujin loved him with all her heart. While they were dating, he used to complain that she wasn't opening herself fully to him. But it was because she loved him! She thought that if she opened up completely to him, her hot heart might suffocate him to death. She wanted to love him with every part of her being. But would she really be able to put up with anything?

She would.

No matter what it was? She'd deal with it?

She would.

Even if Hyeongyu had been sleeping with his professor. Even if he'd had a secret child. Even if he'd been fucking Ha Yuri?

She would.

Wait!

Nothing had ever happened between Ha Yuri and her husband. Sujin had heard the rumour before he did. And it'd been Kim Jina that started it. Sujin ignored it. A few weeks later, Ha Yuri died. Supposedly it'd only been then that Hyeongyu had heard the stories. Sujin was totally fine, but Hyeongyu had asked to meet for a coffee, saying he had something serious to talk to her about.

'You will have heard a weird rumour. It's not true, and it's completely groundless. There's no point going into it, but I wanted to say it straight up to you, in case you were worried. Nothing went on between Ha Yuri and me.'

Sujin smiled and took Hyeongyu's hand.

'Obviously. You think I'd believe something like that?'

And she didn't believe it. Sujin really didn't believe it. Hyeongyu had never once lied. The honest face of an innocent man. He clearly hadn't done anything. She knew more than anyone else that nothing had gone on between him and Ha Yuri. He'd done nothing wrong. He'd never cheated on Sujin, and had never once taken advantage of lonely girls desperate to have someone at their side. She knew that face well—the one that spoke only truth. That face of integrity, that believed it had never hurt a soul. Thanks to *it*.

Spring, when she was nineteen. The face of the guy who'd raped her had been the same.

'I thought there was something between us, no?'

That expression, speaking as if bewildered. A resentful, chagrined voice. He spoke carefully to Sujin, who was hiccupping from emotional shock.

'Listen. Don't take this the wrong way, but you have a victim complex.'

Sujin smiled at Hyeongyu. She pushed the guy's voice to the back of her mind with all she had. Hyeongyu looked at her in relief.

'I think I should help out with the funeral,' he said.
'You?'

'Yeah, no one else is coming forward. I called her relative, too. They said they wouldn't be able to stay long. I was planning to get some of the guys to help me clean up her place.'
'Really?'

'You don't mind, do you? I feel sorry for her.'

Sujin was reluctant. 'But the rumours... Do you really have to?'

'It's all lies. None of that matters. I think I should do it, precisely because of those rumours.' Hyeongyu took Sujin's hand. 'She died. I feel bad for her.'

Sujin examined his expression. He seemed to feel truly sorry for Yuri. Sujin said she'd go with him. Hyeongyu looked at her, surprised.

'It's cleaning and heavy lifting. It'll be tiring. I think it's better you don't come.'

'No, let me help too.' Sujin looked right at Hyeongyu. At that innocent face. 'I feel bad for her.'

Hyeongyu nodded his head. He looked a little unhappy with the situation. Like something had gone wrong, like he was disappointed. But it was probably just her imagination. She didn't ask anything more. Didn't ask if she'd misunderstood, didn't ask if there was something she should know. Sujin loved Hyeongyu. She didn't want to break up with him. She wanted to stay together. She didn't want to discover a secret she couldn't handle. All Sujin had to do was not ask. After all, she had no intention of confessing her own secret.

Her husband stayed out the whole night. When she woke in the morning, he was standing in the kitchen eating a salad. Hyeongyu looked clean and fresh—he seemed to have showered and changed. Sujin inhaled the sour smell of balsamic vinegar. She went to take the bread out of the cupboard, but he shook his head.

'I'm not hungry. I'm all right with this,' he said.

She chucked the bread down on the dining table and crossed her arms. Frustration rose up inside her.

'You should've called to say what time you'd be home. Then I could've made something for you,' she said.

'I said, I'm not hungry.'

He placed the salad bowl in the sink and turned on the tap. Icy water flowed out onto the dish. Sujin stood motionless as she looked at his back, before opening the bag of bread. She bit into a slice, and he spoke.

'Don't eat that, have a proper breakfast.'

Without thinking, Sujin replied bad-temperedly, 'Forget it, I'll just have this.'

He didn't say anything. He wiped his mouth with a tissue, and walked out the front door saying he was going to work.

'Will you be late again today?' she asked.

'I don't know.'

Her rage soared. At least tell me what it is you've been doing, whether you'll be back early, late. She held in her anger, and just about managed to push out her voice.

'Has something happened at work?'

He turned to look at her. His expression was cold and unkind. She'd never seen him like this before. That same depressed, dreary smile he'd had that day one year before flashed across his face. Nothing's changed for us, he'd said. What about it? What's the problem with not changing? Isn't not changing what we're supposed to do? she wanted to ask him. Every day you begged me never to change, are you finally bored of me now?

'You're actually interested in how I'm doing, then?'

Sujin stared blankly at him. What's that supposed to mean? Before she could ask, he'd gone. The front door closed with a click. She was lost for words. Thought I was meant to be the one who was angry here?

She spent the whole morning raging. His words spun non-stop through her ears. She got the sense things were heading somewhere beyond her control. Was this rectifiable? Could they go back to before? Where had things gone wrong? Sujin felt like she'd known this day was coming. I knew this would happen in the end. While they'd been dating, at times he said he'd no idea what Sujin was thinking. He said it made him insecure. She burst out laughing. What are you talking about? I've never wanted to make you feel insecure and never will.

It was the truth. She had no intention of leaving. She was well aware she'd never be able to meet another guy like him. Was it because she was runaway Chunja's daughter? Because he was the loved-by-all son of the heart of Anjin's community? Because after dating, then marrying him, the position of Sujin, Chunja's girl, had just about shifted? All these things were true. But none of them were the reason.

Naturally, the rape broke Sujin. What was the most horrific thing? She got pregnant. It was almost impossible to believe. It had just been that once, but that one occasion had ripped her life to pieces. Could you get more obvious? Got raped then pregnant. Pregnancy wasn't anything mysterious. How could it be this easy and straightforward? To Sujin, her story was nothing but a cliché.

Was it difficult, coming back from hospital after getting rid of the baby, and weeping beneath the cold water of the shower? Or how you'd wanted to carry on life as if nothing had happened, but it was so hard you couldn't eat, had stopped seeing your friends, and lost more than ten kilos? Lying motionless on the floor three days straight? No, those things weren't difficult.

This was what was really difficult. 'Maybe I'm not as worthy of love as I thought', 'Guess I'm the kind of girl who gets raped'—it was being consumed by thoughts like these. That was the hardest thing. So when she started seeing Hyeongyu, Sujin was afraid. This was a man she could never let go of. Seriously, it was like every single girl at uni had wanted Ryu Hyeongyu. But that guy had told Sujin he liked her.

Why?
    Are you going to walk all over me too?

Sujin had never read a fairy tale about a princess who didn't trust her prince. She wasn't a princess anyway. Grandma had called Sujin her little princess—that was just you though, Grandma. Even as Hyeongyu held her hands tight, Sujin waited for him to do a 180. But Hyeongyu truly was a good person.
    He contacted Sujin every day. He messaged whenever he had a moment, and called before bed to ask about her day; well done for getting through the day, he always said. But Sujin still didn't let her guard down. Maybe it was all an act. He'll start treating me like shit soon enough. She thought again, and again: I need to prepare myself, that's the only way I won't suffer again. But she liked him. She loved the warmth in his voice, how he smiled shyly when he looked at her. He wondered about the insignificant things. The glass of water

she'd had in the morning, the number of minutes she'd spent choosing what to wear, the words that had come to mind as she composed her message to him—all of this interested him. And so Sujin sent insignificant replies. She'd had a late lunch and was feeling full; she'd worn thicker tights that felt uncomfortable; her mouth had felt dry for some reason so she'd made green tea, which she never usually drank. And as she slowly asked what he was doing, how he was feeling, it felt like Sujin was sharing her life with someone. That was what scared her. The more she liked him, the more afraid she was—that this happiness could disappear in an instant. But when she saw him, all Sujin's concerns vanished. It was like being compensated for all she'd been through. That's right, I deserve to be loved. I'm worth something. When she was with him, Sujin could feel first-hand for herself, not only his warmth, but that she had her own body heat, too. That her clenched heart existed, physically; that it was real—this was precious to her.

Ha Yuri. Until she heard that story. And until she read Yuri's diary.

Sujin knew where Yuri had hidden her diary. Despite living alone, Yuri used to stash it behind her bed. Yuri had told Sujin that when she was living with her relatives, she'd found out her cousin had read her diary once. Since then, she'd always hid it at the end of her bed, she said. She couldn't sleep otherwise.

People thought Yuri would do anything for attention. But Yuri never said what was really in her heart.

*

Hyeongyu said he was going to get some of his hoobaes to help, but in the end he came alone. They'd all told him something had come up, he told Sujin.

'It's Yuri, after all… Guess they felt uncomfortable.'

Hyeongyu seemed to be making excuses. He told Sujin to go home too; he didn't want her involved in this kind of thing, he said. Sujin stubbornly shook her head. She told him she wanted to clear out Yuri's room. To a certain extent, it was true. Hyeongyu didn't seem able to connect Sujin and Yuri. If he'd paid the slightest bit of attention, he would've noticed something was off. Hyeongyu seemed occupied by other thoughts. It was the first time Sujin had seen him like that. He looked uncomfortable; on edge. At the time, Sujin had assumed it was only her imagination. Sujin felt anxious herself, in case something linked to her turned up in Yuri's place. And so she needed to get into her room at all costs. But Hyeongyu kept trying to send Sujin back. He didn't want to put her through such exhausting work, he said. Won't it be uncomfortable for you? he asked.

That made Sujin start to doubt Hyeongyu. Why's he acting so out of character? Has he always known my secret? Was he hoping to go by himself and find some evidence? Yet she knew there was no way. Yuri hadn't told a soul. Sujin was certain. Her story couldn't have got out. Then why is he being like this? Sujin was obstinate. She'd clear out Yuri's room, no matter what. Eventually, Hyeongyu relented. There were no signs he'd worked out what Sujin was thinking.

He had no clue that the reason the landlady had let them in was not because she'd been moved by Hyeongyu's 'pure heart', but because she'd recognized Sujin as the girl who'd been so close to Yuri they'd practically been living together.

And the landlady didn't know either.

That the spring she turned twenty, Sujin had told Yuri she wanted nothing to do with her anymore, and said not to act like they were friends. That Sujin didn't see Yuri again after that.

Hyeongyu had no idea. He was a good, kind person; respected by everyone. That was his flaw—not realizing there could be another reason for something. He believed he could achieve anything if he set his mind to it. Here he was; the one and only Ryu Hyeongyu had come to help poor Yuri—of course the door had to be opened for him.

The room was a total mess. Starting with the kitchen, they did the washing up and put the plates in boxes they'd brought with them. Sujin went over and stripped the bed. While she was sorting out the sheets, Hyeongyu went over to Yuri's shelves and began putting away books. But something was weird. Hyeongyu was rummaging through the pages. Almost like he was searching for something. Sujin couldn't restrain herself.

'Are you looking for something?' Sujin asked.

'What? Oh. No, nothing.' Hyeongyu fumbled an answer. 'She tried to kill herself that time... I was wondering if she'd left a will or something.'

Sujin didn't respond. On the surface, there was nothing weird in what he'd said. Something wasn't right, though. Yet Sujin had other priorities: she needed to find Yuri's diary. While Hyeongyu emptied the bookcase, Sujin stretched her arm over the top of the bed. She slid her hand between the frame and the mattress. A thick notebook was in her grip, bulging with bundles of paper stuffed between its pages. Sujin glanced behind her. Hyeongyu was still absorbed in the books. She carefully removed the notebook and hurriedly stowed it in her bag.

Yuri had been the one to take the pregnant Sujin to hospital. Sujin had thought her secret might be written in Yuri's diary. Of course, Yuri had never revealed it to anyone. Even when Sujin told Yuri she didn't want to see her anymore, Yuri quietly nodded and said, 'I won't tell anyone what happened to you.'

You won't tell? Can't tell, more like. No one would take what you say seriously. Sujin wasn't afraid of Yuri.

There were times when Yuri had been necessary to her. When Sujin was lying on the floor, overwhelmed by self-hatred, Yuri had held her tight. But Sujin was heading towards a new life. She'd met Hyeongyu, and had new friends. Yuri. Sujin's secret. Memories she longed to forget. Sujin's stomach turned whenever she saw Yuri. Yuri would watch Sujin from afar, as if pining after an old lover. Sujin ignored her.

Yet Hyeongyu and Ha Yuri were supposed to have been fucking?

Don't make me laugh. There's literally no way. Sujin pushed her bag aside and went over to Hyeongyu. She reached over to help sort the books, but Hyeongyu grabbed her by the wrist.

'Don't.' Hyeongyu smiled warmly at Sujin. 'They're dirty. I don't want you touching them.'

Beside him was a box stuffed with stacks of papers. She glimpsed a few exercise books in between the piles. Could they be Yuri's diaries, too? Sujin moved surreptitiously towards the box. But once again, Hyeongyu stopped her in her tracks. He told her not to touch it. All her assignments, notes, presentations since first year; they were all dirty, he said. Covered in dust. Sujin said she'd throw them out, but Hyeongyu waved his hand fiercely, saying it was heavy.

Sujin wasn't able to lay a finger on anything else in that room. All she did was stare vacantly as he threw out boxes.

That night, Sujin read Yuri's diary.

But it wasn't a diary. It was a kind of strange record; from August to December. The calendar was covered in **o** and **x** marks. There were 26 **o**s, and 17 **x**s. Sujin had no idea what these symbols meant. Then she opened out the papers slotted between the pages. They were gynaecology treatment records.

29th August, 'internal vaginal injury', 'if symptoms persist, consider STI screening'. The records went on. 14th September, 'hospital visit after pain in vaginal entrance', 'avoidance of sexual relations advised'. 24th October, 'hospital visit following injury to vaginal wall', 'medicine prescribed, advised to avoid sexual relations'. The records went up to December. The huge number of technical terms made it difficult for Sujin to understand. After some debate, Sujin quietly asked for help from someone she knew who was a nurse.

Her friend said Yuri's case was serious. Really serious. Hearing her explanation, Sujin looked at the diary again and felt terrible. Maybe **o** meant she had sex, and **x** meant she refused? Her friend said the hospital kept recommending she stop having sex, and the patient continued to be examined and given treatment, but weirdly she kept returning complaining of the same symptoms.

Really, is that right? She'd tried to refuse but kept having sex? This many times?

Maybe she'd refused every time but sometimes she gave in and ●ed? Then do all those marks mean rape in the end? No, surely not. Sujin shook her head. It can't be that.

However, these things do happen. That's where clichés come from. No, no way. Sujin shook her head again. Maybe I have a tendency to look at everything like this. That's right, I always see things this way. Just because it happened to me, doesn't mean the world works like that for everyone else, too. This must mean contraception. When she used it and when she didn't. There was a prescription for oral contraceptives in the treatment records, too. And if it'd been rape, then she should have refused every time. Isn't that right? Yes! She had to have refused.

Yet Sujin didn't have any memory of refusing herself. It'd happened when she wasn't in a position to do so. No, no way. It must mean contraception. 25th September ●, then her period starts. Even during her period? She'd used contraception during her period?

Sujin slammed the diary shut. She buried it right at the bottom of her drawer. Her heart was pounding. What happened? What does this mean? Is it a record for just one person? Or for different guys? Come on, this is Yuri we're talking about. It's a promiscuous record for all sorts of men. For sure. Then who were they? Who's this diary about?

At times, every rumour comes close to the truth. Sujin and Yuri. Sujin and Hyeongyu. Then Hyeongyu and Yuri. Sujin stopped thinking here. She didn't want to delve any deeper. She vowed to forget. Yuri was dead; it was nothing to do with her. Sujin had been the one to cut ties with Yuri. It was Sujin who'd coldly said, let's live our own lives. There was no reason now to take any interest in that life. Sujin really did forget. She'd worked hard to do so. Yet sometimes, when she argued with Hyeongyu, the diary's **O**s and **x**s returned to her. Just like that, **OX** would appear out of nowhere. Any time, any place. The day before her wedding, Sujin thought of **OX**. When her mother-in-law went on at her, **OX**. When her grandmother passed away, up came **OX**. After their first unsuccessful IVF attempt, there was **OX**. She tried to forget, but **OX** kept popping into her life without warning. And recently, Sujin had thought of **OX** every day. When Hyeongyu turned his back on Sujin and stormed out, when he messaged saying he wasn't coming home, when the silence over the phone grew longer, Sujin thought of Yuri. She couldn't forget.

Sujin didn't ask Hyeongyu about **OX**. She could never bring the question to her lips. What if she couldn't handle the answer? Or if Hyeongyu was disappointed Sujin could think in such a way? No, those were all excuses. She worried the story would end there: this was the real reason. Sujin feared she'd end up telling Hyeongyu her secret. Why she'd been close to Yuri, what had happened between them. Maybe it would all be over. He'd of course understand. He wouldn't be fazed. The person she couldn't trust was herself. Can I really have faith that he hasn't changed? She wasn't confident. That body heat she'd just about embraced in her hand. The truth. There was no way she could lose a precious heart like that. It would've been better not to have known. How did this happen? How did she end up hearing those rumours?

Kim Jina.

Stupid bitch. Why can't you just leave me alone?

At eleven p.m., Sujin closed up the café and sat alone at an empty table. She didn't want to go home. Should I message him? But saying what?

Sujin opened her laptop and reread Kim Jina's post, which she'd found a few days before. Rumours about the Kim Jina thing had gone all round Anjin. At first, Sujin had thought nothing of it. Huh, so that's what's been going on with Kim Jina—that was as far as her thoughts had gone. But now she felt like joining the side trashing her, and wanted to post her own random comments online.

Sujin sniggered.

It was like that whenever she thought of Kim Jina.

What had taken place when they were young felt like a dream. How until they graduated middle school, the two had been known as inseparable to everyone in Palhyun. How whenever she went over to Jina's, her parents would look disapprovingly at Sujin, at which Jina would cry and yell, telling them not to hate Sujin, not to treat her like that. How because of this, Sujin liked Jina so much, and swore to herself she'd sacrifice anything to protect their friendship.

Just like a dream.

It really is all a dream. May as well never have happened.

Just then, Sujin's phone rang. Unknown number. She picked up.

'Hello?'

She couldn't hear the voice at the other end. Maybe it's a prank call?

Sujin spoke again. 'Hello? Who's this?'

Then, a reply.

'It's me.'

A woman's voice. Someone Sujin didn't recognize. But the person was speaking as if Sujin should know who she was. Sujin was tired. The whole day her head had been full to bursting, and now someone calls her at eleven o'clock at night? Sujin closed her eyes. Yuri's face suddenly flashed through her mind. And then, of course, the floating **OX**s. Her husband probably won't come home tonight. When Sujin had found out it would be difficult to get pregnant, she remembered **OX**. Sujin felt a vague sense of relief.

'Excuse me? Who is this?' Sujin asked.

She spoke. 'It's me, Kim Jina.'

Sujin slowly opened her eyes. Right, of course it's you. How could I forget your voice like that? You'll never leave me alone, will you? Eleven years earlier, Sujin had told Yuri she didn't want to hang around with her anymore. Sujin had actually been told the same thing herself long ago. I don't want to hang around with you, ever again.

We're different people.

Long ago, Jina had said that to Sujin.

The past that suffocated her. The memories and emotions she longed to forget, but never could. Sujin wished it would all just disappear. Forever. But right now she was so exhausted, and an uncontrollable anger rose up from inside her. She couldn't hold it in. Sujin spoke in an icy voice.

'Stupid bitch.'

Then she hung up. Her phone rang again. She didn't answer.

10

Jina

I RANG THE BELL. Tana opened the door.

'What took you so long? You said you'd be here an hour ago.'

Inside, cooking smells wafted through the air. I washed my hands and went over to the kitchen. Cheonggukjang with tofu was set out on the dining table. Tana had recently moved into a small civil servant's apartment. She'd taken a loan to cover half of it, but even so she was full of pride. I'd been saying for three months now that I'd come down to Anjin and see her new place; I'd never imagined it would be under these circumstances. We sat at the dining table. I carried a spoonful of stew to my mouth. The smell of beans reached my lips. I told Tana I'd stopped by the PC Bang on my way over. I'd originally planned to report the Twitter account to the cyber police bureau. But at the police station I was met with exasperated scolding. We can't do anything with this, they'd said. No obvious defamation had taken place, and even if it did go to investigation, they wouldn't be able to look into it until they'd dealt with the long backlog of other reports.

And so I'd gone straight to the PC Bang. @qw1234. I tried

a Google search. Nothing. The account had been created the day of the post, and there'd been no other activity on it.

I spent a while flicking through internet pages searching for similar IDs. There was nothing to speak of. Was there something else I could try? I wanted proof. So I'm a stupid bitch? A liar? Yang Sujin was definitely hiding something. I'll uncover the truth. But conviction wasn't enough. This time, I needed clear proof. But I couldn't find any evidence Yang Sujin had written it.

As soon as I'd finished speaking, Tana asked, 'What are you going to do if it's not Yang Sujin?'

'It was definitely her,' I replied, resolutely.

I considered telling her about my visit to Yuri's place, before changing my mind. There was still no proof for that part of the story, either. Tana seemed to think the Lee Jinsub thing had made me overly sensitive. I was frustrated. Was there nothing that could make Yang Sujin confess straight up?

'Anyway, good thing it's Saturday tomorrow. I'm busy all of Sunday, so I wouldn't have been able to take care of you,' Tana said.

'It's okay. I can look after myself.'

Tana went to church regularly on Sunday mornings. She attended Anjin's oldest Catholic church, built in 1914. A red brick Gothic-style building. Inside was a soaring domed ceiling, and a beautiful spread of multicoloured stained glass windows. I'd gone with Tana once when we were in high school. It was Christmas Eve. Everyone was praying, earnest and serene. As I went to sit down, they all shifted along to make room. It made me feel important. Then the choir at the front began to sing. They hit each note perfectly; it was the first time I'd discovered that voices could come together to make such a wonderful sound.

The choir.

I set down my spoon. Yuri's suicide attempt came back to me. The choir's pianist had been one of those with her that day, right? Apparently, since the incident he'd devoted himself to work at the church and was an active member of a suicide prevention organization in Anjin. He was using his experience to help others in danger, it was said. Anyway, I thought he might know something else about Yuri. People want to die for a reason. The more I thought, the more I realized that Yuri hadn't been attention-seeking. She'd had a reason. She'd wanted to die alongside these people—surely she would've revealed some of what she'd been going through to the last people she believed she'd ever see?

'Can I go with you to church on Sunday?' I asked Tana.

'What?' Tana raised her head. 'Why, all of a sudden?'

'I'm not interested in going to mass.' I hesitated briefly before continuing, 'That pianist is still there, right?'

Tana let out a knowing sigh. In a slightly irritated voice, she said, 'This is getting way too complicated. Yang Sujin says it wasn't her, can you not just let it go?'

I didn't reply; Tana continued on.

'You weren't even close with Yuri. Is it really necessary to drag up the dead just so you can get closure?'

'It wasn't me who brought her into it,' I replied.

*

I thought of the final time I'd seen Yuri. Yuri, rushing out from the alley, calling my name. It was winter, and it was cold. Yuri asked me to help her. I'd thought only of my own feelings. I wasn't kind to her. There'd been no need for me to act like that. Time passes on, and moments grow blurred. We hadn't been close, but I could have at least given her a warm goodbye. After all, Yuri may have been the only one sad to see me go. She'd always kept an open heart, no matter how others treated her.

I raised my head and spoke sharply, 'I'm not letting this go. I'm going to find out who the real liar is.'

Tana shook her head resignedly.

I did the washing up while Tana peeled some apples. We lay down in the living room and watched TV. A romantic drama was on. Lines in shows like that had once made my heart pound, but now I felt only coldness. Everything sounded like a lie. Tana was chuckling next to me. The sound of her laughter burrowed into my ears.

I rested my head on Tana's shoulder. 'Lee Jinsub messaged me this afternoon.'

Tana stopped laughing.

'Saying what?'

'He wanted to meet up and talk. Said he had some final things to say.'

'Talk about what? What is it he wants to say?'

'Don't know. He said I could bring someone with me if I like.'

'Look, just tell him to piss off. He'll never get down off

his high horse. Why does he always speak like he's granting permission?'

I didn't say anything. I'm not sure. The tone of Lee Jinsub's message hadn't been one of giving permission. He'd seemed concerned I'd be uncomfortable, or worried something unpleasant would happen, and so was seeking my understanding by telling me I didn't need to come alone. But I didn't back him up to Tana. Nor did I tell her that, when I saw his message, for a moment I'd softened. I was embarrassed. Tana picked up some apple. *Crunch*—the sound felt good. Tana turned her head to me.

'Did you reply? You told him no, right?'

'No, I just ignored it.'

'Forget that. Tell him you're not interested. You were the one who said nothing gets through to him otherwise.'

'Hmm…' I said, 'I just hate even the idea of talking to him.'

'Don't be like that. Give him a piece of your mind.'

I said nothing. Tana spoke seriously, 'Remember that guy I was seeing for a while when I was nineteen? Minwoo. I completely lost it when he dumped me, remember? Must've called him two hundred times. I was out of my mind. He never once picked up. I didn't realize how obsessive I was being. *If I call, he'll pick up. Then we'll be able to talk. If we talk, there'll be hope.* I was young, I guess. But the fact was, Minwoo couldn't bring himself to say yet again how fucking sick of me he was, and that's why he kept avoiding my calls. But I didn't realize and that's why I completely lost it like that. Then later his friend contacted me. Remember?'

'Yeah, you were…' I laughed. Thinking back on it now, it was funny. 'Extreme. He told you to stop acting like a stalker.'

Tana paused for a moment before continuing.

'I was in the wrong. I never realized I could do something so unbearable to someone else. But if I had to make an excuse, if he'd just told me outright to stop calling, that he didn't want to see me anymore, I probably would've realized a bit earlier.'

I was on the verge of crying. I lifted my head from Tana's shoulder and tilted my neck back; I thought then the brimming teardrops would slip back inside.

Meanwhile, Tana stared at me in silence.

'Are you still going to counselling?' she asked.

'No.'

'Why not?'

It didn't really seem to be helping, so I thought it was a waste of money, I said. Tana switched off the TV. I was afraid. What if I burst out crying now? I won't be able to stop. I needed to change topic.

'Wonder how Yuri handled it,' I said. She must have seen every kind of disgusting thing in her time. I've no idea how she coped with all that, I said. She had no friends, no proper boyfriend.

'I don't think that's fair,' Tana said.

'Really?'

'Yeah,' Tana replied. 'We barely knew her. I don't know what kind of person she was, but I reckon she would've dealt with it and got on with her life. What right do we have to feel sorry for her or whatever? Yuri would've had her own way.'

I was just about holding back my tears. I raised my head. 'Way of what?'

Tana looked into the distance and replied, indifferently, 'Just… a way of coping.'

I shifted closer to Tana. Our shoulders touched. Tana's skin was soft, yet sturdy. I carefully reached for her hand. Tana doesn't date anymore. Said she was sick of meeting someone new and getting close to them, only to eventually grow apart. Tana said she didn't get the point when the bad times far outweighed the good. Just the thought of trying to hold a relationship together was exhausting, she said. You don't date someone wanting to become unhappy, but it's inevitable. And as she approached her thirties, Tana had come to the conclusion that she wasn't cut out for relationships. She'd vowed never to date again. I hadn't thought it would last long, but she stayed true to her word. Tana seems so much calmer and stronger alone than she ever was in relationships. I'd once asked her whether it was lonely. My relationships were lonelier than this, she'd said.

I suddenly wondered. 'Do you still write letters?'

'Sometimes.' Then Tana grinned and added, 'I think you should find something, too.'

The letters were—to use Tana's own words—her 'way'. A method of overcoming those memories that, out of nowhere, came looking. Emotions held in memory. Tana had really liked that guy. It had taken her a long time to recover her abandoned truth. That's probably why Tana still writes those letters. Proof she's overcome the past; a record that, from now on, she'll be able to stand whatever comes her way. Tana was right. You need a method. A method of scraping out the things stagnating in your heart and dragging them into reality.

I smiled. This time Tana's head rested on my shoulder.

'Talking helps me, I think. That's why I keep speaking to you,' Tana said.

'Do you really tell me everything?'

'Just about.'

Tana laughed. My body shook alongside.

'"Just about" isn't enough. Until you spell it all out there'll be things left undealt with.'

We held each other's hands tight. Sixteen. When Tana stepped out of the hospital, we held hands, too, all the way home. If I'd ever made one right choice in my life, it was walking hand in hand with Tana that day.

The notes of the piano were cold and robust. But as voices were laid on top, the sound bent into a soft curve. Was it the high ceiling? Or the atmosphere of the light falling through the stained glass? The whole building filled with singing. I wasn't Catholic, but when I went to church with Tana, it felt strangely like my heart had been perfectly emptied out.

The priest's sermon was steadily drawing to a close. The congregation's complete absorption in his words intrigued me. There looked to be around fifty people. Where does this power to hold the attention of so many come from? How must the priest feel to have fifty pairs of eyes focused solely on him?

Giving presentations was always the thing I loathed most at work. I hated standing up in front of people. It was uncomfortable. Just the idea of all those people listening and looking only at me made me nauseous. I was scared I'd be judged if I made a mistake or said something wrong. I wasn't confident I could satisfy them. Maybe this pressure was why I kept relying on Lee Jinsub. But I never felt like I could do a good job, even after checking and double-checking what I was meant to do. And so it was fascinating hearing a voice like the priest's, so full of conviction. How could he have so much certainty? And how could these people hone in on the words of just one man without suspicion? I was staring towards the front, lost in thought, when everyone made the sign of the cross and began praying.

Through my fault. Through my fault. Through my most grievous fault.

I heard the words. They startled me. It felt like the tears I'd just about held in the night before would burst out once more. Through my fault? Seriously. Is it my fault? I felt guilt. My thirty-first year. The guilt of how every moment, every choice I make, is wrong; how my life will be a permanent disaster. The guilt of having destroyed my own life. I looked at Tana next to me. She was praying in earnest.

I hadn't once heard Tana talk about her religion. I'd never heard her say she couldn't forgive herself because of her beliefs or anything like that. The Catholic Church is anti-abortion. Even after it happened, she'd attended mass faithfully, and would search out services even when away on holiday. Through my fault—coming every week and repeating those words; is she really okay with that? But I didn't want to make presumptions about my friend. Tana's strong. And it's her religion. She must have an answer that ties everything together within her own world.

I don't know. I don't see what hearing the voice of the Almighty changes. But whenever I accompanied Tana to church, I liked hearing the words 'you're loved'. God loves us unconditionally. It's nice. They're nice words. If I could believe there existed someone who loved me without condition, I felt it might bring me peace. But would that really be enough? A love you can't feel, can't see? I wanted warmth. The instant warmth of holding the hand beside you; that real, tangible thing. It's only this warmth that lets you feel love indiscriminately.

Had it been the same for Yuri? Why is it some places talk about the greatness of love, then in others you're a fool for not being able to let it go? I couldn't let it go. One day he'll treat me how I deserve. I believed we'd become precious to one another.

I buried my head in my hands.

Fucking hell. Why can't I forget him, just for one day?

I had no idea what I was doing. Everything felt out of reach.

Mass was over.

Tana whispered for me to wait, then headed towards the pianist. He was overrun with greeting all the choir singers. Tana said hello, and the pianist looked happy to see her. She pointed over at me. It seemed she'd mentioned Ha Yuri. His face stiffened.

We went with the pianist to a nearby café. I was reminded of Yang Sujin again, and my stomach turned.

'What makes you curious about Ha Yuri?' the pianist asked calmly.

Tana apparently hadn't shared any details of why I'd wanted to speak with him. I selected my words. I'd been planning to tell him how I was looking for information on the culprit who'd bad-mouthed Ha Yuri and me on Twitter, but it felt pathetic somehow. I blurted out a random response instead.

'I'm… writing a novel.'

'A novel?' the pianist asked. I could sense Tana's surprise.

'Yes, Yuri's suicide attempt was the inspiration for my book, and so I want to hear from those who knew her.'

'What is it you want to know?'

His tone was highly distrustful. I tried to reply as naturally as possible.

'What Yuri was like back then, anything.'

The pianist smiled faintly. 'I'm not really sure I have anything to say.'

He'd said everything in interviews at the Support Centre and in his writings, he explained, and didn't think he had anything to add. I didn't mind if there was overlap, I said, and asked him to tell me what'd happened that day. Anything he remembered about Yuri. I really did feel sincere as I spoke. I asked him to help.

'Aren't there other people helping you?'

He let out a brief sigh, but soon began talking. Yuri had been the first to arrive at the hotel that day, he began. Him and his girlfriend had just broken up and he'd been full of rage.

In a fit of anger, he'd thought about dying. Then she'll have to carry that guilt her whole life. People began to arrive. There were five in total. It was awkward. It was to be expected—they were coming to die alongside people they'd never even met. They sat round in a circle and each told some of their story. Why they wanted to die, why they hated this world. He lied. Wanting to die because he'd been dumped by his girlfriend didn't exactly look great. So he said it was because the world was unjust.

This was what Yuri said: 'I'm unwell. I'm exhausted. I want it all to be over.'

'What's wrong?' another guy asked.

Yuri had looked over at him. Though probably a misunderstanding, at the time it had looked like Yuri was hitting on him, the pianist said.

'To be honest, Ha Yuri was strange. How can I put it? Like she couldn't read the room? I was just a cocky bastard, but the other two girls there were in a really bad way. They had a kind of darkness that was like, if you gave them a knife they'd slash their necks right there and then. But Yuri kept laughing and clapping at things that weren't even funny. It was so awkward being there, so I can understand why she might have overcompensated, but even still she was way too much. It was uncomfortable. I thought the girl was out of her mind.'

I understood what he meant. It was as if Yuri were there right in front of me.

'She wasn't listening to other people; it was like she only wanted to talk about herself. And then she suddenly burst into tears.'

The atmosphere turned strange, he said. Not depressing or despairing, but uncomfortable. That was when it happened.

Yuri started screaming. Let's hurry up and die. Let's do it now. Yuri got the weed killer out of her bag. She handed it out and shouted to hurry up and drink it. But no one did. Then Yuri handed the weed killer to the pianist. He took a step back. The others moved away from Yuri, too. Then there was a *bang bang bang* on the door. The police. They were all questioned before returning home.

It was the same story I'd heard. I then carefully brought up what I'd wanted to ask from the beginning.

'Did you happen to see someone come pick Yuri up? A tall man, or a woman?'

The pianist shook his head. 'No. Why? Is it someone you know?'

'No.' I swallowed. 'I just wondered if she'd been alone the whole time.'

'It was just her.'

I nodded. Then I thought of something.

'About the guy. The one Yuri seemed interested in. Was he tall, by any chance?'

He shook his head. 'No, he was shorter than me. Probably about 1.65m. Why do you ask? Was there a tall guy Yuri was close with?'

I hesitated, unable to reply, when Tana jumped in.

'What happened to the other guy?'

The pianist laughed. 'He's alive and well. You might recognize him...'

'Who is he?' Tana asked again.

'Oh... he's called Kang Seungyoung,' he said, before looking to gauge our reactions. We'd never heard of him before. The pianist shrugged his shoulders, like it couldn't be helped.

'Do you think he saw Yuri again after that?' I asked, as if to myself.

'I wonder. I don't know,' the pianist replied, and closed his mouth. There was a brief silence. He appeared to be debating whether or not to say something. I waited. Tana stayed quiet, too.

He peered over at me before asking, 'What's your novel about?'

'Sorry?'

'The book you're writing.'

I looked at him. He held my gaze.

'Guilt,' I said.

The pianist went quiet for a moment, lost in thought. Then he spoke again.

'Now I think about it, there's something I've always wondered.'

He began talking once more. It was the first time he'd considered how terrifying death was. Cutting all ties with the world; scary to think I once saw death as something so easy and straightforward, he said.

'I was twenty-six years old, but unbelievably immature,' he said.

He wasn't sure whether Kang Seungyoung ever saw Yuri again—but he himself had, the pianist said.

'She was strange, but she was pretty.'

He paused once again. I felt suddenly weird. It was like I was the priest and he was confessing; slowly, painfully laying bare the tales long held up in his heart. Through my fault. Through my fault. Through my most grievous fault. Is he trying to ease his guilt? But I soon sensed something else—he was sounding me out as he spoke. That was it. He wanted to keep my interest. Thinking about it, he was the one who'd considered killing himself just for attention. Does that desire remain even now, pressed down like a still-moist lump of clay in the depths of his heart? Maybe rather than helping others, he still needed help himself. For someone to see his heart, to see the ugly concealed truth? Then what about me? I, too, needed his attention; his help. I met his gaze and listened earnestly. It was only then that he—who, though speaking honestly, had hesitated and skirted around as he spoke—grew more relaxed.

He finally admitted that at the time, he'd sensed Yuri was your stereotypical 'easy' girl, that you could hook her in one fell swoop. That was why he'd contacted her again after. It really was easy to get Yuri to agree to meet.

'But that wasn't the only reason. I'd just started going to church. I thought she needed it even more than I did.'

They got something to eat before heading to a café for a cup of tea. Seeing Yuri, he faced a constant internal battle. He didn't express it in so many words, but it was obvious what he'd been thinking. Should I suggest going to a motel? Should I wait? No, I should take her to church. The two chatted. He was naturally unable to focus on what they were talking about. Yuri didn't exactly make for an enriching conversational partner. She kept laughing for no reason, and always wanted to speak about herself. Then, out of nowhere, Yuri announced she didn't want to die anymore.

'I thought you were exhausted?' he asked.

Yuri tittered with laughter. He had no idea what was so funny.

She almost shouted as she spoke, 'Yes! I'm even more exhausted.'

But Yuri said she didn't want to die. 'Why not?'

Yuri's response made no sense. 'To win.'

He abruptly cooled off. Am I really desperate enough to date a girl this strange? He grew disinterested. He wanted to get out of there as soon as possible. He asked if she wanted to come to church sometime. Yuri declined.

'I won't win like that.'

He found her response—like she'd lifted it from a book or film—embarrassing more than anything else. He wanted to die of shame thinking the people beside them might've overheard. She didn't intrigue him anymore, and he'd no motivation to stay any longer. He planned to quickly finish up his coffee and head home. Then, Yuri did something odd. She shot him a quick smile and pulled out a thick notebook from her bag. Yuri placed it on the table and stood up.

'I'm just going to the toilet.'

He sat there, speechless. It felt as if he were watching a play. The notebook lay there innocently in Yuri's empty spot, as if begging him to read it. It looked like a diary.

'Did you read it?'

'Yes, I did. To be honest, she'd essentially put it there for me to look at, so I didn't think twice.'

The diary laid out, asking to be read. It was the kind of thing Yuri would do. She went about screaming with her whole body for someone, anyone to see her hurt. What had been inside? Men? Lonely thoughts? Maybe Yuri had actually written a novel. What was in her diary? The tall guy. She probably wrote about him. Seriously, what had she written? What was it you so badly wanted people to know?

'There wasn't anything much,' he said. 'It made me laugh. Three or four pages had been written in, I think? And it was just a bunch of numbers. There was a calendar, too. With Os and Xs. Women keep those kinds of records, right?'

'Periods?'

He blushed slightly. 'Yeah, there was that. And there were also a few sheets of some kind of medical record slotted inside, but I didn't look in detail. I thought that'd be taking it a bit far. I assumed she'd got them for her medical insurance. And I wasn't interested in those things. The notebook wasn't what I expected, so before long I put it back. Oh, but I do remember one thing. There were numbers written on the front page.'

'Numbers?'

'Yes, I still remember them. 7-38. It was July. I thought it referred to the date, but obviously there's no 38th July. It was weird, that's why I remember. Later, when I heard Yuri had died, I thought of those numbers. I tried to find out what they were, but there was no way of knowing.'

7-38.

Unknown numbers. July had been five months before Yuri died. The Yuri the pianist had described wasn't much different from the girl I'd known. I felt weird hearing about Yuri like this. It seemed they'd all known Yuri so well, but in reality no one had. Even the Yuri in their stories didn't know herself.

The girl didn't appear to have known who she was. I asked if he wouldn't mind giving me Kang Seungyoung's contact details. He didn't know his number, he said.

And then he added, 'If you search online, he should come up.'

He was apparently involved in some kind of suicide prevention work. Whoever he was, I'd meet him. Maybe the pianist hadn't been the only one Yuri had tried to show her diary to. I can't be sure of anything right now. But I had a hunch. The diary must've been Yuri's method. Writing down her memories and feelings in symbols only she could decipher. Yang Sujin probably took it when she cleared out Yuri's place. What had Sujin done with it? Had she binned it? Or did she still have it?

I looked beside me at Tana. If I were to lose Tana. That won't happen, I'm sure. But if it did, and I were to read those countless letters she'd written, I would never throw them away. If Yang Sujin and Ha Yuri really had been friends, then Sujin probably wouldn't have gotten rid of the notebook. Even if there was something written inside it Sujin really hadn't wanted to admit, she wouldn't have thrown it out. The Sujin I know, at least, wouldn't have.

Just then, I thought of the numbers again.

7-38.

Yuri's method.

Yuri's words. 'To win.'

Something flashed into my mind. A distinct voice rising up, tearing razor-like through my memory.

'Number 4-98.'

April last year. The day Lee Jinsub beat me. The day he came to my house in the middle of the night, and out of fear I'd had sex against my will. I called the sexual assault support line.

They asked me, did you express non-consent? No.

Did you tell him to stop during? No.

Did you show that you didn't want to, and did he carry on regardless? No.

Question. No.

Question. No.

Question. No.

No. No. No. No. No. No. No. No. No. No.

The operator spoke again. 'You need to say no. Expression of non-consent is very important. You might consider it unfair, but expression of non-consent is the standard. There needs to be proof it happened against your will.'

'Proof? What kind of proof?' I asked.

'Anything. Write a diary. Record all the details of when, where and how. Threatening texts and emails can be used, too. It's good to obtain evidence of having been abused, whether emotionally or physically, after expressing non-consent. Only then can you win.'

You can win.

At the end of the call, the operator gave me a number. She told me to quote it if I wanted to get in contact again.

4-98.

That was my number.

April, ninety-eighth consultation.

*

The last time I saw Yuri, she said to me, 'Jina-ya, can you help me with something?'

The tall man's shadow, standing across the alley. I had my back to the BBQ restaurant. Anyone could've come outside. Hyeongyu sunbae cleaned out Yuri's place. Had that been what Yuri needed help with?

'What's wrong?' Tana asked from the seat next to me. I shook my head. I wondered if I should ask at the support centre, but I knew they wouldn't release details of someone else's case. But a hunch alone wouldn't get me far. I needed to check the diary. I needed to check everything it was possible to check. That came first. Then what if my suspicion turned out to be true?

I was afraid. How had Yuri gone all that time without telling anyone? Maybe she'd wanted to tell the pianist what was happening to her.

Just like when Yuri ran out from the alley towards me.

'Can you help me?'

I'd avoided her. She'd been asking for my help, but it hadn't registered, and I'd coldly overlooked it.

Suddenly a throbbing started inside my abdomen. Where Lee Jinsub had hit me. Pain pushed out from somewhere deep inside and my stomach churned. But it was still just speculation. I took a deep breath. Maybe I'm just blowing things out of proportion.

We said goodbye and rose from our seats. Tana turned towards the pianist.

'Sorry… There was just one thing.'

Tana said she'd been wondering about something. She asked why, when Yuri handed out the weed killer, no one drank it.

Yuri may well have ruined the serious atmosphere. But was atmosphere really so important when you'd come together to die, she questioned.

Carefully, Tana asked the pianist, 'Why was it you didn't drink the weed killer?'

The pianist turned towards the church. Hesitation rose on his face. We waited for his response.

'I guess I just didn't want to die with that girl.'

I looked at him quietly before lowering my head.

I understood him.

And I felt guilty for it.

11

Sujin

READING HAD BEEN SUJIN'S METHOD. Reading was easiest. It hadn't always been novels. At first it had been articles online. Search just a few words, and she could see all sorts of things. Rape, pregnancy, abortion. So many women in this country had been raped. She'd opened dozens of browser windows, but the incidents kept appearing. Women raped. Pregnant teenagers. Women filmed without them knowing. Women stabbed. Abandoned newborns.

The reason she kept searching was simple. She wondered what it had been like for others. Sujin hated the idea of attending counselling or survivors' meetings. Anjin was small—word might get around. Everything was kept confidential, they said; but Sujin wasn't convinced. She was afraid of people's malice. To be exact, more than malice, Sujin couldn't trust formless voices. Malice she could actually trust in—if nothing else, malice carried a clear outline and intention. Voices travelling all the way from Palhyun. Indifferent words pointing at Sujin: Chunja's girl, rebellious child, that poor thing. The people from the village were kind. They really were good people. But it apparently hadn't once occurred to them that their words could be hurtful. They said it, and they said it again. Careful not to trip on the stones! Sujin'll end up stupid like her mum. Look, there's an aeroplane. Chunja's probably run off somewhere and had yet another baby. Winter's here! It's snowing! Goodness, *Sujin* is going to university? They were like that. People didn't realize what they were saying.

Now, twelve years later, the guy still probably doesn't believe he raped Sujin.

That's why Sujin read the articles. Other women who'd been through what she had—where were they and how were they coping? After hundreds of articles, Sujin worked it out. The rape mentioned could generally be organized like so:

The victim had never reported it and died.

The victim had reported it and died.

The victim had reported it and lost at court.

The victim had reported it and carried on living.

Sujin felt nothing from these brief statements. That wasn't what she cared about—this was: so then what? How did you feel? Are you miserable just like me? Do you have nightmares? Do you see yourselves as scum like I do?

She wondered most about guilt.

Why does it feel like I've done something wrong when I haven't? Because I got rid of the baby? But can you really call that a child? That cluster of cells that came out of a situation I never wanted, a method I never wanted—do I have to call that a person? What about me? What about my life? And my body? What about you lot?

There wasn't a single answer in the articles.

Then, in class one day they'd read an extract from Joyce

Carol Oates's *We Were the Mulvaneys*. Lee Kanghyun was teaching. So typical. No doubt she was going to get her undergraduates to do a rough translation. Sujin had been irritated; but then she saw the word 'rape', and stared motionless at the text. Hyeongyu did the translation that day. The scene where Marianne comes home in distress after being raped at her graduation party. Mulvaneys, Marianne, woman, girl. The family falls to pieces, and for a long time Marianne drifts from place to place like an exile.

One part said this: 'I was drinking. I was to blame. If I could relive that night but I can't. How can I bear false witness against him?'

The moment class was over, Sujin ran out of the lecture theatre. She went to the toilets and cried. Sujin read that part over and over. She kept altering the sentences to fit her own situation.

I was drinking. I was to blame. If I could relive that night but I can't.

I was drinking. I let my guard down. If I could pretend that night never happened but I can't.

If I could pretend it never happened but I won't be able to. I'll never be able to.

Because it already happened to me.

It happened to me.

Sujin couldn't relate to Marianne in every respect, however. Marianne had remembered everything. She only said she hadn't to prevent charges being pressed against her father for assault. Sujin thought if she, like Marianne, had remembered what happened, things might've been different. But later

Sujin realized: she wouldn't have done anything about it. Of course—she was Chunja's daughter after all. Gosh, the kimchi has turned out really well. I told you Chunja's girl would end up like that. Chunja's umma, would you like some kimchi?

Sujin couldn't put her grandmother through that. Grandma had cried when Sujin told her she'd got into university. You'll be all right now, you can start a new life. Her grandmother had always said how proud she was of Sujin, how she'd do anything for her. Sujin couldn't do that to her. It was then that Sujin understood Marianne perfectly. So Sujin cried. It's enough I went through it. I can't do it to Grandma, too. I'll ignore it. If I pretend it never happened.

If I act like nothing happened, everything'll be okay.

She'd been nineteen. It was spring. Sujin had a lot to drink that day—her first ever taste of alcohol. It had all been because of her mum. Since her early teens, Umma had gone round getting drunk and sleeping with the village's lost causes. To that day Sujin still didn't know who her father was. She'd probably been a drunken mistake—Sujin believed that this rumour, if nothing else, was true.

Sujin detested that love of alcohol which potentially lay dormant in her genes. She had sensed she'd take a liking to drink; that she'd be the kind who drank just to get drunk. Sujin thought alcohol would bring her nothing but misery. Sujin had been in an unusually good mood that day, however, and so she drank.

It had been Lee Kanghyun's lecture. Sujin was complimented on an opinion she shared about *Jane Eyre*. The class was taught around source text comprehension, and Lee Kanghyun used to allocate five minutes or so for spontaneous presentations, for which she gave additional marks. It went like a relay: if someone presented first on 'female emancipation in *Jane Eyre*', someone else would give their opinion about that opinion, yet another person would give their opinion based on that, and so on. Sujin had resolved to devote herself fiercely to her studies at university, and so had no intention of missing out on extra points.

Sujin's presentation went something like this: 'Previously, you criticized how Jane Eyre ends up returning to the arms of a man. I want to concentrate on the fact that Jane Eyre saw her love for Rochester as just as important as financial independence. Jane Eyre is a character who carefully considers which decision will bring her the most happiness. If she'd defined herself only in terms of her relationship with Rochester, she never would've left him in the first place. She would've stayed by his side as his lover. But Jane Eyre didn't believe the courtship and marriage would make her happy, and so she left. She came back when she thought she could cope with him. When it came to her own life, she was straightforward and proactive. I think this woman's love, which she chose without hesitation or fear of the unknown, is worth supporting.'

After her presentation, Lee Kanghyun had told Sujin she had a unique way of looking at the world. Her words had no doubt been formulaic, but it had still put Sujin in a good mood. And because of this exact compliment, this prescriptive compliment from a teacher she didn't even like, Sujin drank that day. When other students in the class said they were going for drinks, she—much like Jane Eyre—freely pushed her way in, and when she sat down in the bar, the first thing she did was twist open a soju bottle.

It had been fun. Hyeongyu had been there, too. He was there, so of course the place had been packed. At first it had been just ten of them, but two hours in, more than twenty had gathered. Students from other departments crashed, too. Some came from the English Literature department (Hyeongyu's original major), as well as a few from Korean Lit. In the end there were so many it was impossible to know who'd come from where. Sujin slowly began to feel drunk. By the time they'd moved to the covered street food stall at the rear of campus, she was fully out of it. Sujin still can't remember how many people had been there at that point. She felt good, really good. Sujin had been feeling so good that she'd even wanted to go up to Jina—it had been almost two months now since the academic year had started, and she hadn't once properly spoken to her—and suggest they put the past behind them.

Jina-ya, honestly, I've really missed you. I know we can't even look each other in the eye, but when I found out we'd be in the same department, I was secretly happy. I missed you.

Jina-ya.

I missed you.

Sujin was wasted. Then, when she opened her eyes, she was naked. Completely naked beneath the musty sheets of a cheap motel bed. The guy was snoring beside her, also naked. Panicked, Sujin couldn't even scream. She removed herself from the bed. Sujin was shaking. Her mind had been wiped completely blank and she couldn't utter a word.

The guy awoke from his sleep.

'You're up?'

He smiled and reached a hand towards Sujin; he caressed her face warmly. Sujin shivered.

'What is this?'

'Huh?'

The guy looked at Sujin, apparently confused by her question. Sujin was ready to burst into floods of tears. She remembered nothing. Nothing! She had no clue what was going on. Sujin had never even held a guy's hand before. She'd felt sexual desire, but it wasn't something she fully understood; everything she'd known was from hearsay. Apparently it really hurts the first time, Apparently you need to push your hips out, Apparently you should close your eyes. Sujin was still a girl. But there was one thing she definitely knew. What had just happened, what had almost certainly happened—sex, it had to be her choice. Sex had to be when she wanted it, with the person she wanted. But had I wanted this guy? She couldn't remember. She sat dazed, her mind in chaos. He carefully opened his mouth to speak.

'Are you thirsty? Want some water?'

Would things have turned out differently if Sujin had broken out crying instead? Maybe he would've realized he'd done something Sujin hadn't wanted. But she was in a state of confusion, too shaken to shed a single tear. Yeah, she was confused. She needed to get out of there right away. Sujin hurriedly pulled on her clothes. Then he approached her. He put his arms around Sujin. She slapped his hand away.

Sujin, her voice trembling, just about managed to ask, 'What happened?'

'What do you mean, what happened? We came here together.'

Only then did his face contort. He stepped back from Sujin as if stunned, and stared at her for a moment before clicking his tongue in disbelief. Picking up his clothes from the floor, he said, 'I thought there was something between us.'

'What?' Sujin replied, her face flustered.

'You were the one who came on to me?'

'What did you just say?'

Sujin's voice cracked. She wanted to scratch his eyes out. She couldn't handle it. Sujin had been drunk the night before. So drunk she had no memory. That meant she'd blacked out. Whatever she'd done, she hadn't been in her right mind to choose. *I never wanted you.*

She was about to scream at him when he spoke. 'Look, don't take this the wrong way.'

'What?'

He looked her straight in the eyes and said, 'You have a victim complex.'

It felt like something had snapped—*tuk*—in her heart. There was nothing more she wanted to say. Sujin walked towards the door. Before opening it, she said, 'Let's pretend this never happened.'

Sat down on the bed, pulling on his socks, he replied, 'Right, it was just a drunken mistake. Let's forget it. Alcohol's to blame.'

Sujin ran outside and gasped for air. Nothing happened. *Nothing happened to me. I'm not a victim. No one needs to know. It was a mistake. Right, I made a mistake. When you do something you didn't mean to, you call it a mistake, right? Yeah, a mistake. This was definitely a mistake. But I wasn't the one who made it. Nothing was my choice. All I chose was to drink. Just like Umma—just like Chunja. I did exactly the same as Umma. It was literally just one night. People go through so much in this world, but you're making a big deal out of this? Naïve. So naïve. Shut up. I said shut up. Grandma! Grandma, what do I do? I'm scared, Grandma.* Sujin ran. *I'll go back to the dorms. I'll go back to the me who gave the presentation yesterday.*

Sujin slipped on the pavement. Blood poured from her skinned knees.

I didn't want it. But what if I had?

If I became like Chunja and wanted something, if I really did want something? Then would it be okay? A one-night stand can be a mistake. If I think like that, will I be okay? But what about the fact I didn't want it? How can this truth be reconciled?

Sujin staggered as she got up from her seat. The tears came. *What if he tells people?*

She was afraid. Tears flooded. She wanted her grandma. *Her grandmother hadn't gone through all that for this. It's my fault. If I'd just been more careful. It's my fault. My mistake.* Sujin curled up on the ground. She couldn't bear it. She wanted to die. That moment, a hand ran itself through her hair. Startled, Sujin raised her head. It was Yuri.

'Sujin-ah, what's wrong? Did something happen?' Yuri asked.

At that warm voice, Sujin collapsed completely. Her shoulders began to heave with sobs. Yuri wrapped her arms around Sujin. She gently patted her back.

*

After *We Were the Mulvaneys*, Sujin locked herself in the library. She wanted to read more novels. She searched for more Mariannes. Books with victims. That was Sujin's method. Just like drug addicts sharing their experiences at meetings in hope of recovery, Sujin read novels featuring rape victims. There was no need to tell anyone her story, or to cry as she listened to the stories of others. Unlike the articles, novels had a heart. She could feel that heart distinctly.

Sujin tried hard to remember that day. It would've been better if she'd had some mark on her body to prove she'd resisted. She had a vague recollection of stumbling and hanging onto his arm. But she had no idea what it had meant. Had she been coming on to him? Or had she just not been able to stand up straight? She couldn't remember what she'd said to him, either. We must've chatted. Yeah, must've just had a nice conversation. But she had no clue whether that'd been her flirting with him, or whether she'd just been caught up in the moment.

What was clear, though, was that she'd never wanted him. She'd never been interested in him in that way. No way she'd have suddenly wanted him just because she'd had a few drinks. Alcohol's to blame? Really? Is that really true? He said he'd thought there'd been something between them. What'd made him think that? If only she could remember *something*!

Then she could refute it. If she could remember something, she'd be able to say, 'There wasn't anything between us, I was just leaning on you because I was drunk.' She could say, 'How can you not tell the difference? Idiot.'

It was obvious she hadn't wanted it, yet she had no proof;

the fact was agonizing. It agonized her that if she couldn't prove it, no one would back her up. From her research she'd learnt that in the majority of situations, rape was only 'proven' when the woman had aggressively refused. And so only violent cases were accepted as rape. Sujin had found this fact incredibly disturbing. If the woman had to be beaten, threatened, made to scream out, and have her life put in danger for it to be called rape, then what'd happened to Sujin definitely wasn't. Sujin hadn't been beaten, threatened, hadn't screamed out, and hadn't felt her life to be in danger. But she hadn't wanted it. Sujin couldn't understand why the fact of whether she'd wanted it or not was judged based on how violent the perpetrator had been. For Sujin, rape was simple. Completely straightforward. Sex the victim hadn't wanted.

Just like it had been for Sujin. Something that happens when you're blacked out from drink and unable to do a thing. According to Korean criminal law, Sujin's case would come under 'quasi-rape'. Quasi. How can you put 'quasi' in front of a word like rape?

Sujin's case would be difficult to prove. If she did report him, she'd be torn to pieces. She had to think of Grandma. Of her own future. She didn't want to be called a rape victim. She didn't want to live life as someone who'd cried rape. She didn't want to carry on, having been unable to prove a thing, surrounded only by suspicion.

And so she read. Novels had lots of female characters. There were women who'd been in their right mind when they'd had things done to them against their will, and some who'd been unconscious. There were women like Sujin who'd wanted to pretend it had never happened. There were also women who would've done anything to get over it. Sujin couldn't have handled writing or giving interviews. She feared reading the voice of experience. It was easy to escape into made-up stories. No one realized what she was reading. During class they talked about connecting novels with wider discourse and ideas, but Sujin had no interest in that. To her, voices were important. One person's voice; their own story. The rage within that space was her encouragement; the hate, her joy. When she read the Mariannes, she felt calm. The Mariannes were characters she could understand; they eased her loneliness. That is, until she read the gruesome scenes where they were trampled to pieces.

One day, Sujin discovered the brackets.

Brackets.

(violence)(intimidation)(stripped)(suppression)(arousal)(erection)(penetration)( )( )( )( )( )( )( )( )( )( )( )( )
( )( )( )( )( )( )( )( )( )( )( )( )( )( )( )( )( )
( )( ).................................( )( )( ).............
( )( )( )( )( )( )( )( )( )( )( ).

The novels brought the brackets graphically to life. There were so many of them. Books that explained it all in horrifying detail—how they'd dragged in the women, how they'd frightened them, what position they'd laid them on the bed, how they'd overpowered them, what (   ) they'd performed in a state of arousal. The novels weren't, of course, justifying the perpetrator's actions. They expressed what disgustingly bad people they were. To show just how terrible they were, the (   ) of rape was colourfully depicted like a firework bursting open across the night sky. How can there be such bad people in the world! He must be really bad to have done something so cruel! Emotions that make the sadistic nature of bad men look even worse. That make you hate the bad guys even more. Those brackets; vivid and horrible enough to stir up desire for revenge. Showing quite how bad the bad guys were, later revealing clearly quite how awful the victim's pain had been; and so the graphic, detailed (   ) formed into scenes both aesthetic and necessary. It's all right—we've proven he was a bad guy. It's all right—this scene doesn't take it too far. It's all right—we've shown why the bad guy turned out that way. It's all right—he's been reported. There was a novel in which the woman who'd been raped took even more horrific revenge on the man. The (   ) the woman had been subjected to was nauseating. The lifelike, detailed brackets! The woman, full of hate, got her revenge; the payback was so satisfying that (   ) was forgotten. But can we really forget? Can the victim really forget the contents of those vile brackets? Just because she's had her revenge, just because the payback was satisfying, can we really call (   ) nothing? Even Sujin, who hadn't been through (   ), couldn't forget. Really? Is it possible?

Sujin was doubtful. Was she being overly sensitive? The brackets were nothing, really—was she assigning them way too much meaning? Was it her victim complex, like he'd said? One day, she read a man's voice in a novel that said, 'I want to rape that woman.' She stopped reading.

*

Actually, it reminded her of something she'd heard before.

'Feels like I've been raped.'

It had been at their department welcome drinks. Sujin saw Jina on the other side of the table. Sitting next to Ha Yuri. She'd only looked over because Ha Yuri was talking so loudly. Yuri seemed weird. But Sujin concentrated on the people around her. She was full of anticipation. Sujin had doubted she'd even get in to university. I'm finally at uni. I'd better study hard. Get a job ASAP and bring Grandma to Anjin. Live happily with Grandma. It'd be nice to have a boyfriend, too. An affectionate, good-looking boyfriend. Someone who'll treat me well, who I'll treat well; a relationship in which we'll love and care for one another.

Probably because it was a new department, there had been a budget set aside, and the professors bought lots of drinks and anju. People came from other departments to advertise student societies, and sunbaes planning to transfer majors joined as well. Sujin had never attended such a large gathering before. She was nervous, but in a good mood. She didn't drink. At some point, it grew raucous around her. Five or so guys were sitting beside her, and three of her male sunbaes had started playing a drinking game. Sujin, not wanting to drink, sat out. She just watched.

The guys, as well as two girls, began the game. When you open a soju bottle, a small ring separates from the metal cap without detaching completely; the cap is passed around and players take it in turns to flick the ring as lightly as possible—the first person to knock it off has to do a shot. It was amusing to watch; the same person kept losing. It was one of their male sunbaes who was moving over from the Philosophy department. No matter how gently he flicked it, the metal ring fell—*tuk*—off the cap.

Once he'd lost three times in a row, people began to gather round. He lost a fourth time. Everyone clapped their hands and laughed. Sujin laughed, too. So when the fifth soju cap came around, probably wanting to make everyone laugh, he deliberately made his hand shake. The atmosphere was cheery. Everyone roared when he flicked the cap. The ring fell off yet again.

The sunbae buried his face in his hands and shouted, 'Fuck. Feels like my dick's been cut off.' Everyone laughed. He went on. 'I've been fucking raped.'

Everyone laughed again. Sujin had laughed, too. She wasn't offended. Everyone was out to enjoy themselves, and it wasn't the time or place to take what he said seriously. He hadn't said it to piss anyone off, it was just a joke that'd slipped—*tuk*—out. The other girls laughed, too. Everyone knew it wasn't really rape; he'd blurted it out without thinking anything of it. Ah, a direct analogy. Metaphors have no limits; the bolder, the more beautiful. Sujin clapped, too.

When Sujin read the man's voice in the book—'I want to rape that woman'—she was reminded of her sunbae's voice that day. Sujin could no longer accept those kinds of jokes. Jokes like that. How could he think that was a joke? 'I've been raped.' How can rape be a joke? But wasn't that how the novels portrayed it? Weren't all types of (   ) used to depict it in a horrific, tangible way? You've been raped? You want to rape someone? Think this is the same as rape? So you think (   ) happened to you? You think you want to do (   )? A ring flying off a soju cap does not mean you've experienced (   ). That's not what rape is. It's (   ). How is it that some people make a joke of rape so easily, and others express it so luridly through (   )? Is it just an easy metaphor? To find the answer, Sujin kept reading novels. Then, at some point she realized.

These people don't know what it is to be raped.

The brackets the novels portrayed weren't the victim's pain. It was the level of abuse. The realness of abuse that made the depiction so vivid. Horrific, vile scenes. They didn't know what the victim's pain was like. They weren't completely clueless; they knew it was bad. That was why they drew the bad guys as even worse. Bombarding us with (   ) to pour out criticism on the bad guys.

But do they really know? Do they really know the physical sensation of part of the body being forced open, torn open, crushed? Do they truly know the pain that comes when the body's most delicate, sensitive part is injured? The only expression that appeared following (   ) was 'it hurt'. This isn't something that ends with stinging when you pee for a few days after. From the very next day, Sujin was tortured by pain. Her privates were sore, and it hurt both when she sat down and when she walked. Because the guy had performed (   ) on her to his heart's content. Sujin never thought of going to see a doctor. She'd never gone anywhere near the Gynaecology department. She'd never thought about pregnancy. She hadn't realized she could get pregnant, either.

Every day came the same recurrent throbbing pain in her vagina, like being split in two. But she didn't go to the hospital. She'd assumed it would soon improve, like a scratch on your hand. After three weeks of continuous pain, Sujin went to see a doctor. The inside of her vagina was seriously inflamed, they said. They did an ultrasound just in case. It was then they discovered she was pregnant. Even after the procedure, Sujin kept returning. She was still in pain. The doctor couldn't see anything wrong and sent her home. They just prescribed her painkillers. But the pain continued. Her lower regions throbbed and she felt a pain inside her womb like its flesh would fall out in pieces. A feeling of being in tatters, like her privates had disappeared completely. Her body felt like a shredded sheet of paper.

If (   ) had really happened, there was no way it would end with 'it hurt'. A pain even more horrific and gruesome than (   ) would follow. That's what rape is. But there was one more thing Sujin realized.

That the victims, of course, are depicted as trampled upon; oppressed. Those subjected to (   )-like oppression. A commentary on one of the books read something like this: the aesthetics of violence. Tragic characters locked in the chains of unending violence. They called it three-dimensional. The subjects of (   ), like snowmen with bulging backs and fronts. Understanding them was an act of beauty, they said. No, nothing was beautiful to Sujin. Nobody felt tragic to her. If feelings around rape operate for some people in that way, if that's the sole method of portraying violence, then what are those in the clutches of (   ) supposed to do? Is Sujin supposed to rape someone?

Sujin grew to loathe novels. That vivid tragedy and heart. She loathed the outburst of mangled hearts. She loathed the voices that could speak in no other way. Yet Sujin couldn't stop reading. At some point, she herself was tainted by that violence. Reading (   ), she imagined it from the perpetrator's perspective. Every day she pictured pressing that guy to the floor and carrying out all the different (   ) she'd read. She was out of her mind wanting to rape him.

Sujin left the library at closing time. She didn't go back to the dorms. Sujin went to Yuri's place. As Sujin sobbed, unable to sleep, Yuri stroked her back over and over.

That was all long ago now.

Once Kim Jina had gone, she went by herself to the alley behind the café and drew a deep breath. She kept remembering what had happened back then. Her grandmother had passed away two years prior. When they got married, Sujin told Hyeongyu she wanted to bring her grandmother to live with them. Hyeongyu accepted with enthusiasm. He said his parents would grant permission. Permission. That word bothered her. Why did she need permission to live with her own grandmother? It wasn't as if Hyeongyu was the eldest son, either. Yet why did they need permission? But she didn't let her feelings show. She'd expected Hyeongyu's parents not to be keen on the idea, anyway. Sujin thought it natural for parents to feel that way when it came to their son. Sujin found it odd that she instinctively saw it like that, though she'd never been married herself. The knowledge that she needed her in-laws' permission was inscribed in her genes. But in the end, she didn't have to say anything to them. Her grandmother refused.

It was bad enough they hadn't been able to send this wealthy family a proper dowry—she didn't want Sujin to have to bring this old woman in tow too, she said.

Her grandma was obstinate. She thought she'd be inconveniencing Sujin. Daughter of a family that had nothing. It was obvious Sujin would be treading on eggshells as it was—adding yet something else would make things really hard for Sujin, she said. Weeping and wailing made no difference. Hyeongyu even went to see her himself, but Grandma still shook her head.

A teary Sujin told her, 'They're not like that. They're not that kind of people. They don't have the same outdated way of thinking as you.'

'Sujin-ah,' she replied, 'trust no one. Not even your husband. Right now, I'm sure he treats you well and would do anything for you. But people never forget what they've done for you. They never forget their own kindness. It isn't important how the other person feels. Look at the village. You and I are the only ones who see me as working. Everyone thinks they're doing me a favour. No matter how we see it, we owe them. Do you want to live your whole life feeling like you owe him something? The more he thinks he's given you, the more he'll think "it's all right for me to ask for this much". But no one knows what "this much" will be. I know Hyeongyu's a good man. Maybe he won't turn out like that. But life is a whole series of what-ifs. Marriage is like a set of scales. Right now there's no unnecessary weight on your side. You're already starting on an uneven keel—there's no need to add more to it. The world's changed. Women have changed. I know. But that's only for the women who have the strength and background to manage in that changed world. Your grandma isn't one of them. I don't want help from anyone. You take it. You're starting without owing a thing.'

Even so, Sujin thought she'd see Grandma all the time. But whenever Sujin had planned to visit, something else came up. At some point, she had to admit it; Grandma wasn't her main priority. Whenever there were gatherings at her in-laws', double dates, cultural events, she'd put off visiting her grandma. 'I can see her anytime' was no different from 'I don't need to see her right away'. Sujin got even busier once the book café had opened. She'd wanted it to be somewhere researchers and students from the university could talk and freely spend their time. She stacked the shelves with everything from mainstream novels to academic works. The building was in her husband's name and so she didn't have the worry of rent. But Sujin didn't just want to break even. She wanted her café to become famous in the university district, and to increase business by making it known for its coffee. Sujin wanted people to say they preferred it to the library. To a certain extent, she'd felt lacking. When she got married, she missed multiple opportunities to prepare for a career as a librarian. By the time she'd gotten her act together, so much time had already passed. She couldn't concentrate on studying. She hated people saying she was living off her husband. Sujin wanted to show people her own ability. It wasn't as easy as she'd expected. It wasn't that she'd thought it'd be a cinch; it just took far more effort than she'd anticipated. She worked day and night. Even though it was the university area's prime location, business was still slow. It took almost five years to become stable. Sujin hardly ever went to see her grandma during that time. Holidays, New Year, end of year. Grandma didn't say anything. The most time Sujin spent with her grandmother ended up being in the hospital. She suffered a stroke and was admitted for a year. The longest Sujin had spent with her grandmother was whilst unconscious.

As she gazed over her grandma's wrinkled face, she'd always remembered the words.

'Live the life you want. Don't owe anyone anything. Be free.'

Sujin had cried when she heard those words. She wasn't angry with her grandma; it was because she'd told Sujin what she'd longed to hear. A weight on lopsided scales. Sujin knew herself—Hyeongyu's parents hadn't been keen on her. The marriage would never have been possible if Hyeongyu hadn't pushed for it. He'd persuaded his parents. 'Sujin is nothing like the people where she's from.'

Sujin knew, of course, her position. Fatherless child. Mother who'd left home. Registered under her maternal grandfather's name; granddaughter raised as a daughter. Sujin acknowledged it herself. She had nothing. She couldn't say what kind of person her mum was, what her personality was like. She didn't know her father. Sujin never had anything to say. What does your dad do? What about your mum? She'd never once given an answer. Sujin always told them her parents were dead. My mum died. May as well be true. Sujin's grandmother raised her. My sweetheart. My darling baby. Little princess Sujin. My dear Grandma. Sujin's grandmother had loved her. Loved her completely. Grandma's love had been enough for her. But people always brought up Sujin's dead parents, and made an issue of where she was from. My grandmother loved me. Why does no one ask about that? They say girls always end up like their mothers.

Who did you say her mum was?

That must've been Hyeongyu's best method of persuasion. Standing up for Yang Sujin; claiming the values of those surrounding her didn't concern him. Sujin is completely different from them. She's nothing like her mum. She's not like her grandmother, either. Because she met someone like me.

Passing the hurdle of marriage made Sujin's background feel very real. And forced her to accept it. Sujin's grandmother had loved her dearly, and Sujin had loved her back. Yet she was also a heavy weight on Sujin's shoulders. As long as her grandmother was around, Sujin could probably never become 'another person'. The person she longed and worked so hard to be. A person not to take advantage of or look down upon. A person who'd never be raped. Sujin didn't once vocalize resentment towards her grandmother. But in truth, she'd always resented the reason for the way people saw her. She resented the reason she'd never be treated differently. Maybe it'd been because of that. No, it'd definitely been because of that. People could do whatever they liked to Sujin. You can mess around with her when you're drunk. Let's be honest, she's Chunja's daughter after all. The girl will never be able to pay back all those who helped her. Sujin had secretly resented her grandmother. That's why Sujin had cried when Grandma told her to live the life she wanted. And then again when she passed. Sujin was released of her burden.

Grandma, I've always thought this way. I'd rather become a rapist than be raped again. That was how I thought.

Sujin saw the guy everywhere at uni. Whenever she'd catch sight of other girls chatting with him, she wanted to run over and warn them. She wanted to tell them—he might get you drunk and drag you to bed. You'll wake up naked and resent yourself for ever trusting anyone. But Sujin said nothing, and every day went to the library. Because he never said anything, either. He really did seem to think it'd been a 'mistake', and had since forgotten Sujin. She got pregnant.

How is that possible?

It was possible.

Because Sujin was a woman. A singular possibility had pierced through her body. It didn't feel like she was carrying a life inside her. What she was carrying was a memory. A memory she wanted to forget; wanted to pretend never happened; wanted to erase completely.

Before the procedure, Yuri had asked Sujin if she was going to tell him she was pregnant. She wasn't. That guy had no right. It'd taken place with no regard for her intent. She didn't get why she needed his approval. It was Sujin's body, and her choice. Sujin wasn't sad. She really wasn't.

Child? Life? Love? Fuck that.

But it was hard. She didn't regret the abortion. Given another opportunity she'd have done exactly the same. She wanted to pretend it'd never happened; but the past didn't disappear. Her body was in pain. She had constant nightmares, threw up all the time, and grew thin.

She couldn't understand. I've done nothing wrong, but why do I feel only guilt? Whenever she felt panicked, she burst into tears.

Each time, Yuri had held her hand.

Sometimes Yuri read Sujin poems she'd written. The lines were transparent and warm. The rumours that Yuri had slept with a different guy every night weren't true. It was true she'd had a lot of experience, but she'd spent the majority of her time alone, writing. She wrote diaries. Poems. The dead appeared in her verses. Lost kittens. Yuri wrote things like this: I'm a lost pair of gloves, I'm an old lost T-shirt crumpled up in a wardrobe, I'm a chocolate wrapper thrown on the street, I drink warm milk, On and on I hold a note off-tune. Yuri enjoyed writing assignments. She wanted to do a good job. Yuri knew people gossiped about her, saying she was way too much. But Yuri really did want to write something decent. That was all. Yuri knew she made people uncomfortable, and that in trying to convey her sincerity she'd caused far more misunderstanding than anything else. That was why Yuri wrote. Words were where she stored her heart. But at the same time, Yuri was embarrassed. And so she wrote on torn-up pieces of coloured paper, corners of receipts, the back of her bookcase, scrap paper. And then threw the pages away. Sujin secretly looked through them. Yuri told Sujin not to, but then quietly left her to it. If only someone would read her heart; if she could only get through to someone; if only someone would understand what she had to say. Sujin could feel her longing. Maybe that was why Yuri worked so hard at the assignments. Whether a book report, or a short personal essay, Yuri put great effort into her writing. I'll reach them this time, I'll definitely reach them next time. Yuri always worked that hard, despite not knowing where her writing would end up. Then she just left it. Just like the guys who'd dropped her as they pleased.

One day, Sujin asked her, 'Don't you find it unfair?'

They looked at each other beneath the covers.

'Yeah,' Yuri replied.

'Then why don't you tell people?'

Yuri stroked Sujin's face. 'People only believe people they like.'

Sujin then asked, 'Do you ever tell guys you don't want to?'

'Yeah.'

'What do they say back?'

Yuri laughed again. 'They don't believe me.'

'Tell them again, then. Get mad.'

'I do.' Yuri gently squeezed Sujin's fingers. 'They don't think that's me being angry. They think I'm just pretending.'

Sujin thought for a moment, then carefully continued, 'Has anything horrible ever happened to you? Against your will?'

'No, never.'

'It might if you don't make it clear you don't want it.'

Yuri looked at Sujin with a sad expression. 'It's okay,' she said, 'none of the guys have been that bad. And guys are nice to you until they get what they want. I like it when they're like that.'

Sujin felt frustrated. 'But then once they've got what they want, they treat you like crap.'

'Yeah.' Yuri frowned slightly. 'So I find another guy.'

Yuri was smiling, but Sujin couldn't. Yuri hesitated briefly, and then said to Sujin, 'It's all right. I don't like when things get complicated.'

'Yeah.'

'But I wonder.'

'Yeah?'

'Why in the end, none of them ever love me.'

Sujin said nothing. It's probably because you look so lonely. Because they can tell your heart is always open and find it easy to approach you, but when they discover the extent of your loneliness, it's too much for them to handle. She didn't say any of this.

'I'm sorry,' Yuri said.

'What?'

'I must sound pathetic. You're disappointed in me, right?'

'Stop.'

'Okay.'

'No,' Sujin held Yuri's little finger as she spoke, 'I mean, don't apologize.'

Yuri said nothing. Sujin closed her eyes. For some reason, she couldn't look Yuri in the face. She'd comforted Sujin, caressed Sujin with warm hands; but Yuri's hands were already covered in scars. She was thankful to Yuri. Truly. But that was all it was. Yuri shifted closer to Sujin. They slept, foreheads touching. As Sujin drifted off, for the first time in a long while, she thought of Jina. She thought she might know the reason Jina had drifted away from her.

Sujin had been in the library that day, too. First term exams were over, so time was ample. She read a repulsive novel. The story of a man who stripped three women naked and locked them in a warehouse. The women didn't consider escape, and built a friendship inside that place. They held and comforted one another, whispering gentle words as they created their own world. One of the lines went something like this: 'They did not believe themselves imprisoned.' Written as if the women's bodies were sacred objects, as far removed from violence as possible. Whenever the man returned, the illusion shattered. He kicked those serene women, drawing out screams and forcing them to their knees. Once he'd done what he wanted, as much as he wanted, he left, locking the warehouse behind him. And so the women caressed each other's bodies once more. That section made Sujin laugh out loud. But it was a later part that she'd found really hilarious. At the end of the novel, the man is mercilessly beaten by some guys down an alleyway. As his ribs shatter and his legs break, he thinks of how he longs to be back in the warehouse. Sujin burst out laughing again. Then a strange emotion came bubbling up inside her. She felt the tears would flow any second. Sujin took a long, deep breath and left the library. At two o'clock, there'd been a special lecture by a famous translator. It was already four. Sujin had no interest in such things. But she'd been contacted three times already asking her to attend the drinks afterwards, and so, reluctantly, Sujin dragged herself along.

The translator was a man. He was well-known, even having won a translation award in Japan, and Anjin was his home town. Sujin arrived to find a much bigger event than she'd anticipated. Only scholarship students like Sujin, and those with top grades, had been invited.

Jina was there. As was Hyeongyu. And the guy, too.

She hadn't wanted to sit anywhere near the guy, but there was only one available seat. Sujin was forced to sit opposite him. It also happened to be right by the translator. The seat was still empty—everyone had presumably thought it'd be awkward sitting next to him. Sujin and the guy ignored each other. The guy was sitting next to Hyeongyu.

Sujin looked around and suddenly felt angry at Hyeongyu. Beside the translator, beside the professor; that was where Ryu Hyeongyu was sitting. A man who knew his privileges all too well. Her head began to ache and a pain shot across her whole body as if she'd been beaten. She leant back in her chair and briefly scanned the other students. Apart from Hyeongyu, the guy, and two male students sitting opposite, the rest were girls. Jina's eyes glistened as she watched the translator. The translator felt her gaze, but didn't look over in her direction. He was exchanging unfunny jokes with the professor. Then, he began talking about an old girlfriend from Anjin.

'Then one day she dumped me completely. I'll never go through the likes of that again.'

The translator said the girl had been sexy.

'I feel a bit bad saying this in front of so many women, but I'm sure you'll understand the expression from a literary mindset. She had a kind of sex appeal that would eat men alive.'

The girls laughed. The professor nodded and poured the translator another drink.

'But not long after I won the award in Japan, she contacted me. I couldn't believe it. She wasn't the kind to get back in touch with the ex-boyfriends she'd dumped. Guys, you understand me, right? Your first love. I put aside all other plans to see her. Actually, we met up in Anjin. It felt weird seeing her. I could see her from behind, and I slowly walked over. It wasn't until I sat down that I saw her face. I'd been overwhelmed with so much expectation and intrigue. I took a sip of water and slowly raised my head. Then I met her gaze.'

The translator burst out laughing.

'How was she?' the professor asked.

'Really disappointing, to be honest. She looked so old. Oh, I shouldn't say that, should I? Girls? You know what I mean, right? What I mean is that—I'd always had an image of how she'd end up looking, but she was so different to what I'd envisaged. She'd put on a load of weight, and really had aged terribly. And you know the unbelievable thing?'

No one replied. The translator went on.

'She asked me for work. She wanted help getting her feet off the ground, no matter how small the job. Wow, what a feeling. For the woman who'd played me the whole time we were dating to stoop so low.'

The translator laughed out loud again. He downed the

drink the professor had poured him. For the first time, he returned the girls' gazes.

'Don't let yourselves go,' he said, in a joking tone.

Kim Jina was the first one to laugh. The girls next to her chuckled alongside. Right, he'd asked for the benefit of the doubt for his 'literary expression', after all. Sujin felt her insides knot. Her lower regions throbbed, just as they had after she left the hospital. Everyone was laughing. The guy was laughing, too. Louder than anyone else. It was then.

'I'm sorry I'm late.'

Lee Kanghyun arrived alongside an English Literature professor. She was the only female professor in her department, and Lee Kanghyun's supervisor. It was she who'd organized the translator's special lecture. Sujin and the other students rose to greet the professor. Everyone naturally shifted down seats. The professors sat together with the translator, and Sujin sat by Hyeongyu.

The professor tapped the translator—*tuk*—on the back and said, 'Have you started lecturing already?'

If Sujin had known the translator would be teaching at Anjin University from the following term, and a few years later appointed associate professor of the English Literature department, she could've read the situation. And if she'd known the English professor had been the translator's sunbae when they were undergraduates, she would've fully grasped what was going on. The event had been set up with the translator's professorial appointment in mind, to sound out in detail what they could each seek to gain from the relationship. Sujin wasn't able to pick up the adults' respective interests, but she did come back realizing one important thing. After some time had passed, she understood that this realization had been identical to the puzzle between the professors.

'What have you been talking about?' Lee Kanghyun asked.

'Just this and that,' the translator replied. 'I was actually about to talk about my new book coming out. You came at just the right time.'

The English professor nodded and smiled.

'Well, I'm sure whatever you were saying, you were giving the students some helpful advice.'

Sujin wanted to go home. She wanted to see Yuri.

Then, beside her she heard the guy whispering to Hyeongyu, calling him older brother, or hyung.

'Hyung, shall I pour us a drink?'

'Hm, not sure I should.' Hyeongyu spoke with ease.

In a pleading voice, the guy continued, 'Come on, hyung. Don't be like that, have one more.'

Hyeongyu smiled. Sujin turned her head towards him. She watched the guy's hands as they poured drink into Hyeongyu's glass. He held the soju bottle reverently in both hands. Those two hands, meekly overlapping one another, as if declaring they would never do a thing without Hyeongyu's permission.

Sujin gazed at Hyeongyu's profile. That handsome, chiselled face. Then she realized. That's right, you'd never tear this guy's clothes off without his permission.

She remembered the novel she'd read. Sujin's mind was overrun with the man's dreams as he was beaten, longing to return to the warehouse. I'm going back. I'll go back. To where I can do what I want; where I can do what I want, as much as I want. But it was only in his mind. In the end, he fell to his knees and begged the men.

Spare me.

Please, stop.

Spare me, please!

How have I only just realized? The guy was always stuck at Hyeongyu's side. And to Hyeongyu's mates. He carried the bags of Hyeongyu's female friends and bought them coffee. And now, as he poured Hyeongyu's drink, pestering him to have just one more, he kept a constant eye and ear on the conversation taking place between the translator and professors. What they were discussing, which students they thought highly of, what kind of applicants they'd be focusing on recruiting in future; he gathered and stored these conversations greedily in his ears. How have I only just realized? What she'd been feeling up until that point wasn't guilt. She wasn't suffering because of the surgery. It wasn't a sense of shame from the mistake she'd made that night.

It was hatred.

A mistake? All right. We can call it a mistake as much as you want.

But why me?

Why did *I* have to be your mistake? You made a mistake with me and went freely on your way; but how come it doesn't end there for *my* body? Why is my body in pain? Why does my body have to split and wrench because of your mistake? Sujin was out of control with rage. She was in pain, terrified that rumours would spread, and had gone through so much without being able to tell a soul; yet you call it a mistake? You wouldn't make that kind of mistake with guys like Hyeongyu, would you? Must know you can't mess with him. Or the translator, or the professors; you'll be sitting before them as the nice, well-behaved student. And what do you think of while you do it? The warehouse? How you long to be in the warehouse, where you can make mistakes and no one cares; where you can make mistakes and not a single problem comes of it?

Am I the warehouse?

I want to trample him, Sujin thought. Bring him to his knees before me, fuck him up so badly he won't even be able to look at me, won't be able to lay a single finger on me.

Sujin's hatred didn't stop. What do I need to do to crush you? What exactly is it, that thing you obey? The thing you believe you must never cross. Sujin slowly turned her head.

She saw Hyeongyu's side profile. The handsome, chiselled face.

This is exactly the thing you fear.

I need to control this person. Just then, Hyeongyu turned to look at Sujin. Hyeongyu looked flustered when he noticed Sujin staring at him. Sujin didn't avert her gaze. The face that guy wanted, and therefore feared; she gazed on and on at it. All right, I'll play by your rules. Like a proper man. I'll be even more man than men.

Yeah, it's fine as long as I'm not a woman.

That's how I'll trample you. That moment, her pain completely vanished.

Sujin felt nothing in her lower regions. She looked on at the people present with an expression fuller of expectation than she'd ever had. Then, she stared long and hard at the guy's hand, which hovered meekly once again over Hyeongyu's glass; just the thought of snapping Kim Donghee's pale feeble fingers put her at ease.

That was long ago.

Once Sujin had started dating Hyeongyu, Donghee could no longer look her in the eye. He glanced at her like someone who'd committed a sin. The Donghee who'd once send her weighty smiles now acted as if he'd never known her. Sujin made Donghee suffer. She only hung out with the guys he was good friends with. When Hyeongyu said he was going to meet Donghee, she came up with some excuse to stop him going. If there was a girl he was interested in, she'd set her up with one of Hyeongyu's friends instead. But that wasn't enough to satisfy her. That couldn't be called revenge. It was nothing more than a childish game.

Then Kim Jina started that rumour. Donghee and Sujin were seeing each other.

At first, it'd sent Sujin into a huge panic. How had Kim Jina found out? What did I let slip? She felt a chill creep over her.

Sujin had actually met Donghee in a café near the bus stop. It hadn't been planned. She'd been on her way to Palhyun. It was a hot day. The sun was blazing. She'd only recently started dating Hyeongyu. Her heart raced, and she had butterflies. Hyeongyu was at the English hagwon. He'd messaged saying he'd come and see her off once he'd finished. She'd arrived in plenty of time for the bus, so thought she'd grab a coffee nearby. When she stepped inside the café, there was Kim Donghee.

Sujin ignored him.

She'd only ever run into him when other people were around; this was the first time it'd been just the two of them. Sujin acted as if she hadn't seen him, but her heart felt like it might burst out of her chest. *What if he acknowledges me?* Recently, she'd heard Donghee had asked if Hyeongyu could get him some part-time work in the administration office. Sujin had stopped him. She hadn't directly said not to help Donghee. She'd simply asked him to help out someone else in their year instead.

Sujin dropped it into conversation. 'Actually, there was someone else I thought you could help...'

It was someone worse off than Donghee, who was working two kitchen jobs alongside their studies. Sujin never said, 'Don't help Donghee.' She just went to great lengths to explain how difficult the other student's circumstances were. After some deliberation, Hyeongyu connected Sujin's friend with the administration office job, and told Donghee he'd find him something else. Lately, Donghee hadn't been turning up at department gatherings.

What if he suddenly starts harassing me?

Chest pounding, Sujin bought her coffee and immediately left the café. She messaged Hyeongyu asking when he'd be arriving. Sujin could clearly feel Donghee's gaze boring into her. She'd escaped the situation. That was all. *Jina had seen that?*

Sujin was shaking. *What if everyone found out?* But she soon pulled herself together. *Let's use this situation to my advantage.* Sujin was 'another person' now. There was no need to worry what Kim Donghee and Kim Jina thought.

Sujin waited patiently. Then, when she was told about the rumour again, she burst into tears.

Sujin cried and told her friends she'd heard even more horrible rumours elsewhere.

Yang Sujin's dating Kim Donghee, not Ryu Hyeongyu.

No, Yang Sujin and Kim Donghee are just friends with benefits.

Yang Sujin is two-timing Ryu Hyeongyu and Kim Donghee.

Afterwards, the rumours inflated by themselves. Exactly what Sujin had been waiting for. Sujin could act like the perfect victim. After all, she knew what it was like more than anyone else! Sujin spread her own gossip. Inside the sham rumours, she stealthily portrayed Donghee as her oppressor. Then people would think, though misunderstood, Donghee actually was that kind of person. Rumours like that were worst for the girl. Aware of that, Sujin dived right into the rumours' centre. She adjusted the focus to return to the person who'd started the awful thing: Kim Jina. Sujin even told people they were from the same village.

'Jina's family were better off than mine. Her parents weren't bad people, but sometimes they slagged off my mum.'

That was enough. People believed Jina had started the rumours out of jealousy. Jina had probably never received more attention than back then. Horrible dress sense. That pretentious way of speaking. People talked like they knew Jina so well. Sujin made people feel that way by letting things slip here and there. 'She took part in bullying me once at primary school. It scarred me.' Rumours naturally spread. Kim Jina is so immature. Kim Jina is a liar. Kim Jina is a gossip.

Donghee quietly held his breath as if nothing was happening. Donghee was clever. He was probably frustrated. Probably wanted to stand in front of everyone and say, 'I slept with Yang Sujin!' But that would be a second attack on Sujin, and no one would take him seriously. If Sujin hadn't been dating Hyeongyu, and if she therefore hadn't been a central figure, that reality would have been a complete revelation. And then Sujin would have been trampled all over. But that wasn't the case. If Donghee did as much as open his mouth, Sujin knew she could totally destroy him. If that were to ever happen, Sujin was going to call Donghee a liar. Otherwise she'd disclose that he'd raped her. In either case, Sujin had the upper hand.

Sujin had Hyeongyu, and she had others. Whenever she was excluding and disparaging Donghee, she followed the men's rules perfectly; but when asking for protection, she became a woman again. If she wanted to ask for help or claim something was unfair, there was nothing more effective than a woman's tears. Penetrating people's hearts. Appearing weak; in need of protection. Shed tears from a chagrined face and declare your fear of being hurt, and people's hearts open right up. Guys, especially, would do anything to show they were different from those simple-minded men. So they instantly bowed their heads at the woman's request. That was how Jina and Donghee were pushed out of the department completely. Sujin had thought that was the end.

Then she found out Donghee and Jina were dating. Sujin saw Donghee affectionately rubbing Jina's shoulders. She saw Jina smile as she walked over to him.

'Those two deserve each other,' people said.

Sujin said she didn't care. Whatever.

Why me?

I was just a careless mistake; but why not Jina? Why are you treating her differently? Sujin's heart filled with hatred once again. Then she knew. This wasn't something easily let go of or resolved. Her heart was already well on its way to festering. Hatred releasing a vile stench and devouring her heart. She hated Jina. She hated her more than anyone. Sujin cursed Jina over and over. Stupid bitch. Liar. Liar. That year, Jina left Anjin and Donghee enlisted. Then Yuri died.

That was all long ago.

'Welcome,' the part-time barista called towards the door.

It was then that Sujin, who'd been standing at the counter retracing old events, was brought back to the present. A long while had passed. She took a sip of cold water. Her husband's words stuck in her memory. You haven't changed. That's right. Sujin hadn't changed. Her heart still festered as it had back then. Was her husband trying to leave her? When they'd first started dating, she'd put her guard up again and again. But it'd been twelve years now. Hyeongyu was a good husband. It was difficult not to love someone like him. Sujin realized something scared her even more than the thought he might know some horrible secret. That eventually, she'd lose him. What good is truth? The truth is nothing more than a naked display of how grotesque I am. Can't I just keep living as if nothing ever happened? Nothing at all.

A customer stood in front of the counter. Sujin slowly raised her head. A familiar face was before her. That face— the reason why lately she was constantly reminded of things she wanted to ignore. That chagrined face. You've been like that ever since you were young. But you never happened to me. You never existed.

Then Jina spoke. 'Ha Yuri's diary. You have it, don't you?'

12

Jina

'STAY AWAY FROM CHUNJA'S GIRL. Those lot are no good,' Grandma would say.

When I was young, those were the words I hated hearing most. Nothing else bothered me; whether I was being scolded for not cleaning my room, or berated for my falling grades. But I couldn't stand Sujin being bad-mouthed. Gossip about Sujin felt like a dig at me.

How times change.

'What are you talking about?' Sujin stared at me and asked.

I'd originally planned to sound things out. Tana didn't want me going to see Sujin. I think it'd be better if you went to the Support Centre first, she said. After much deliberation, however, I knew I needed to find the diary first. But the truth was, my body ached to see Sujin. In truth, I missed her. I wanted to know. How would Sujin react when I brought up the diary? And now, she was looking at me differently. I was certain; Sujin definitely knows. I tried pushing my speculation further.

'Yuri's landlady told me. You sorted out her things. She told me you took her diary.'

Sujin slightly furrowed her brow. 'So what?'

Gotcha.

'There's something I want to check. Let me see Yuri's diary.'

'I don't have it.'

Then Sujin turned away from the counter. She asked the part-timer to watch the floor, before walking out round the back of the building. She didn't say a thing to me; she didn't seem to care whether I was there or not. I controlled my anger. Up until this point I'd just been dragged into things by Sujin. I didn't want to have to endure any more. I followed Sujin behind the building. Stepping out through the door, I was a little taken aback. There were multiple alleys connecting with other buildings, sprawling like spiderwebs. It felt somewhat familiar. Undergraduate meetups would always be held at places around backstreets like these. Bars and restaurants in this kind of deserted area were cheap and generous; perfect for departmental gatherings. But this street looked especially familiar. Where have I seen this place before?

But that wasn't where my attention should have been right then. I grabbed Sujin by the shoulders. She slapped my hands away.

Coldly, I asked, 'Why are you so angry?'

Sujin crossed her arms. She continued to stare into me, and asked why I was suddenly so interested in Yuri. 'You weren't even close with her.'

I looked into Sujin's eyes. That old, familiar gaze. Okay, let's cut the bullshit.

'Yuri was being harassed by someone,' I replied.

'And?'

'She must've written about them.'

Sujin laughed. 'What is it you're doing right now?'

I held my breath for a moment. I spoke again. 'Cut it out and just show me. I know you have it.'

'I don't,' Sujin said to me stiffly. 'You're a joke. Seriously, what are you doing? Did Ha Yuri appear as a ghost last night in your dream or something? Is she feeling bitter? Has she asked you to avenge her?'

'Yeah, she asked me to avenge her. She feels extremely bitter,' I replied, icily. At that, Sujin shut her mouth.

Resolutely, I added, 'It wasn't me who started the rumours about your husband and Ha Yuri.'

'Right, fine. You already told me. What's that got to do with this?'

'It was you who wrote the Twitter post, wasn't it?'

I could tell from Sujin's stare that she was sick of me.

Firmly, I insisted to her, 'I'm not a liar.'

'I said fine!' Sujin shouted. 'Fine!'

My emotions bubbled over, and I raised my voice. 'Why are you so angry? If it's not true, why get so mad? If there's nothing in it, why not show me? What gives you the right? Did Ha Yuri say she'd leave the diary to you? She didn't, did she? And what do you care about Ha Yuri? It's not as if you two were friends, either.'

Sujin kept her mouth shut. I didn't back down.

'Show me. I know you have it. If you don't let me see it, I'll tell. I'll tell everyone something weird happened. I'll spread rumours everywhere. I'm that kind of person, just like you said! I'll be a real creep. I'll tell people you're hiding something and that's why you took Yuri's things. The reason's obvious. The rumours about Hyeongyu sunbae and Yuri were true. If they weren't, then why did the two of you go and clear out her room? Did you not think people would find it strange? I'll tell people. That you were afraid the truth would come out and so you hid everything!'

'Watch your mouth.'

'Let me see it, then.' I gasped for breath before continuing. 'She was being harassed! I know. There were numbers on the diary, right? I know what they mean. All I need to do is check. Show me and that'll be the end of it! If it's really nothing to do with you, then why can't I see?'

I kept talking by myself. The words I'd been holding inside my head came pouring out at random.

'You're a woman. Women need to understand each other on things like this. We have to! You can't treat another human being like that. Vacuum cleaner?! People deserve a name at least a little better than that!'

Sujin unfolded her arms. She took a step towards me. Then she spoke.

'Fuck that.'

Sujin turned around and walked ahead. It was unbearable. I squeezed my forearm tightly in my hand. The pain made it a little easier to endure. I'm still okay. I can put up with a bit more. Sujin took five steps forward, and suddenly stopped. She turned around and strode towards me. Face to face, eye to eye. Then, coarsely, she spoke.

'Stupid bitch.'

'What did you say?'

'What is it you're doing here?'

Before I could say a thing, Sujin came at me.

'Can't treat another human being like that? Came up with some nice words there. Give it up already. Stop dragging up the dead! Think you're something now, do you? Think you're some kind of women's rights activist just because you've been in the newspaper and done a few interviews? Don't make me laugh. Think I wouldn't see through it? You *are* a liar. Another human being? Women should understand each other? Think I'd believe that? Shall I tell you the truth? You came here just to screw me over. You've waited a long time for this. The poor kid from Palhyun. Chunja's daughter. The kid you used to hang around with. The girl who sat all on her lonesome if you didn't play with her, because she had no friends. You're a nasty bitch. You always have been. When you wanted to play, you'd come over and sweet-talk me, then saunter off again once you were bored. The way you used to throw tantrums when people told you not to play with me was exactly the same. Did you think I wouldn't know? You wanted to be special. You felt proud of being friends with the poor kid no one else would play with. But what to do? You studied so very hard, and even though you acted like you'd become another person, you ended up at the same university as me. And I even got better grades than you. You think I wasn't watching you? Did you think I wouldn't notice you always leering at me? That I wouldn't notice you checking out what I was wearing, reading, who my friends were, what classes I went to? But once I started dating my husband, you must've realized you could never win. How about I spell it out for you? Did you think I wouldn't notice you following my husband to every department gathering, and studying the room just so you could get close to him? But my husband had zero interest in you. Still doesn't know your name or who you are. That's all you are.

'But now you drag my husband into it? If you can't have something, you want to make sure no one can, am I right?'

Sujin started to press her finger into the top of my ribcage.

'You always thought you were better than me. That was how you confirmed your own existence. Having someone beneath you was always proof you were an okay person. But bet you didn't know what to do once the person you'd always looked down on was above you. You didn't have the guts or the ability to steal my husband, either. That's why you started studying to transfer unis. If nothing else, you wanted to be well above me when it came to academia, no? And then what? What's so great about going to Seoul? No one envies you. Only you thought that was important! And what did you get out of it? You're nothing. You're nothing more than a snivelling woman who met a guy, who then slapped her up.

'How about I tell you exactly what I think? A woman who was actually smart wouldn't go round getting slapped around like you. I can sympathize with the guy. I know just how much you rile up and provoke people! You're literally nothing, and still you think you're all that? That's why you came to talk to me. To tell me my husband was a weirdo. That my happiness was all lies.

'You really are a pathetic bitch.

'And you think you're all that, do you? The only one who pities you is yourself. That's what you do best. You're just using Ha Yuri. Getting attention talking about gender equality, saying you're a courageous woman, a domestic violence victim—must make your heart beat out of its chest. You probably feel like you're doing something proper, something great. Women like you are so full of jealousy you dig around other people's lives. What is it you have? Who do you think you are? Ha Yuri? What do you know about her? Do you know what it was to be friends with her? You never looked at her once the whole time we were at uni. You thought you were better than her. You looked down on her more than anyone else. You treated her as less than human. You thought you were different from her. So you know what happened to Yuri—and what? Think that means you know everything about her? That you understand her?

'Just tell the truth. You're jealous of me. You hate me having things, you hate that I'm better than you, that my life's better than yours. You'll die before you acknowledge that, and so it's driving you out of your mind! Just admit it! Don't confuse your problem with something actually important. You want to do all this just to feel like you're doing something meaningful? You couldn't have stooped any lower.'

'That's enough,' I said.

Sujin went on. 'No, let me spell it out. You're the kind of bitch that deserves to be knocked around. I've asked you so many times already. What is it you're doing here? I'll ask again. What is it you're doing here? What are you going round Anjin doing?

'Makes you mad, right? Want to tell everyone you're the victim? That you were assaulted, that he's the bad guy. You went to great efforts telling people in Seoul, but no one bought it. Your colleague stabbed you in the back and you were treated like a gold digger. You're a failure. That's why you ran away to Anjin. Made an excuse to escape here. I don't care who's saying whatever on Twitter, or what you think happened to a girl who died eleven years ago, it's none of your business. You've come all the way here to run away from everything, and act like the perfect victim so you can pull at people's heartstrings. You think that if you do something here, people will think you were in the right. But you're a coward. You've run away from the one person you needed to face, stooping so low as to dig up dirt on other people. I don't think you're a victim.'

'I said that's enough!'

'No! I'll make it even clearer. You deserve to be beaten up, and always will do. You're a liar. You'll live your life being slapped around by whoever.'

It was then.

I punched Sujin in the face. My body shook and I was so repulsed it was like my insides had turned upside down. Sujin cupped her face and groaned. I was trembling. I wanted to hit her again. I wanted to grab her by the hair and shout as I hurled her to the floor.

It's your fault. I said, it's your fault!

What did I just do?

This isn't me.

I rushed over to Sujin. She shouted at me to back off. There was a red mark on her cheek.

'Go on! Do it then!' Sujin screamed at me.

My hand shook as I approached Sujin once again.

Sujin shoved my shoulders with both hands and screeched, 'Show me what you've got! Go on, show me what you've got!'

A huge resounding echo filled the alley. I remembered Lee Jinsub's face when he hit me. In the alleyway, moments of being trampled into the ground. I'm an affectionate person.

I'm a good person deep down!

It was then. That familiar alleyway merged with my memory, and a particular scene rose to my mind. An old recollection came sprinting towards me.

Evening moved into night. Winter. The final department meetup. 8th December. The moment I saw everyone in the restaurant, the disheartening moment I saw Yang Sujin and Hyeongyu sunbae and turned back around; that moment I was so embarrassed I couldn't speak, filled with uncontrollable rage; the moment Yuri ran out from the alley.

'Jina-ya!'

I hated Yuri calling my name.

'Listen, can you help me with something?'

Yuri scanned around, an uneasy look on her face. She seemed afraid someone might discover her.

Irritated, I asked what she wanted. Yuri moved towards me, as if about to open up about something. That's when I heard the voice.

'Yuri-ya!'

A man's voice coming from the other end of the alley. It was familiar. One I'd definitely heard somewhere before. The guy's shadow hung faintly beneath the light of the street lamp. A tall, tall, tall guy. Just then, Yuri turned around as if to ask for help. I frowned. Guess in the end the last person I'll see is you, then, Yuri.

I spat coldly at her, 'You can't get away from here, can you?'

Then I turned around. Yuri kept calling my name.

I didn't look back.

Yuri called to me again.

'Jina-ya?'

'Jina-ya, help me.'

I kept my gaze forward as I walked on. And I left that place completely behind.

'That's the kind of bitch you are,' Sujin said.

13

Kanghyun

LEE KANGHYUN STEEPS some black tea in hot water. She's tired. The student who's just left is twenty years old. One of her sunbaes sexually assaulted her; he groped her breasts and put his hands down her pants while she was drunk, she said. She reported it to the women's centre, and an unofficial agreement was reached. Originally, she'd pushed for the male student's expulsion. His parents pleaded and chaos ensued. They offered the girl a settlement equivalent to around a term's tuition, and made a verbal promise that he would take the next term off.

He didn't, of course.

Lee Kanghyun is tired. This kind of thing happens several times a year. Girls come to Lee Kanghyun in floods of tears. They believe she'll help them.

'I don't want to be in his classes,' the female student says. 'Please make it so I don't have to see him.'

Yeah right. Lee Kanghyun rubs the student's back sympathetically. She bursts into tears.

'Move that sunbae to another class. Every time I see him, I'm reminded. I'm scared.'

After a long bout of the girl's crying, Lee Kanghyun slowly explains that, unfortunately, it's not up to her. The student, face resentful, looks at Lee Kanghyun. I don't have the energy for this. But Lee Kanghyun doesn't let her true feelings show. She would never say she's taking the male student's side. Instead, she says this: You dealt with it all by yourself. It takes a lot of courage to fight like you have. I have so much respect for you. But shouldn't a true woman of this day and age accept the allotted punishment and then discuss how to improve things in future?

She really doesn't have the energy for this. Why drink alone with the guy? Why drink until you black out? Do you really trust others that much? And a man, at that? It was you who went and trusted him; why are you relying on someone else to deal with it? Did you really believe he was just going to see you home? Naturally, she never says any of this. Lee Kanghyun is well aware you can't say such things. But she can't understand. You drink. The guy says he'll see you home. You go with it. Why? It only got to that stage because you went along with him. Didn't think oppa would do such a thing? It's exhausting. Unbearably exhausting.

Whenever something like this happens, there's always another professor who says, 'Unbelievable, these young guys…' He opens his mouth like one man sternly criticizing another, before ending with, 'They haven't learnt self-control yet, that's why.'

Bullshit. She loathed the argument that it was just as difficult for guys trying to control their hard-ons as it was for the girls crying over how they'd trusted oppa. The problem doesn't come from being unable to control one's urges. It comes from believing it's okay not to control one's urges. But she doesn't say anything.

Kim Donghee, stupid son of a bitch.

She laughs.

Pacify them enough and the female students relent. They give up. It's important to let them know, as much as you can, that they're the victor. Just as you'd talk to a young child that's been badly bullied. 'But you made it through. In the end, you're the winner.'

You showed that guy you're not to be messed with! I have great respect for you. I'll do everything to make sure something like this never happens again. But I can't move the classes around. I'll have a word and see what I can do about next term. There's nothing I can do right away, however. If you're really finding it difficult, how about not attending that class? I'll talk to your lecturer. At around that point, the student realizes: Lee Kanghyun isn't going to help her. There are ways of moving Lee Kanghyun into action, of course. You can make the issue public, but that requires announcing to the whole world you're a sexual assault victim, and then enduring an exhausting and convoluted process. And so they're afraid, and end up letting it go. Knowing nothing was ever properly resolved, they begin to fester from within; every day brings nightmares and extreme distress; they become thin as a rake from the emotions they have no release from—that's none of Lee Kanghyun's business, though. But today, as the student was leaving, she said something that grated on Lee Kanghyun's nerves.

'Everyone tried to stop me, saying you wouldn't help, but I believed you'd protect me.'

Not my business. Much more important to Lee Kanghyun was protecting the department's image.

But there are, of course, students who won't let it go. Like Kim Eyoung.

Kim Donghee, stupid son of a bitch.

She laughs.

Lee Kanghyun had known something like this would happen sooner or later. She'd known Kim Donghee was the type from the moment she saw him. He thinks he's different, but he's just your typical man. Thinks only of self-promotion. Ambitious, a try-hard. What makes people like him unique is incredibly simple. Loyalty to hierarchical structures: matches the world to that framework. Kim Donghee draws a clear line between the people to butter up and those to disregard. Who Kim Donghee gives highest priority to depends on the occasion. No matter where he is, he forms an instant ranking. Always thinks he's in control of the world. Even fancies himself a feminist. He once wrote a column for the university paper saying how he respects women. That they turn dark violence into light. How he loathes those who beat and harass women. But that he worries that somewhere within him is the potential to be like that, too.

'If it weren't for women, I wouldn't have known the real face of the world. Women always help me live as another person.'

Lee Kanghyun laughs. Even in a column on women's rights, he goes to great pains to show what an egalitarian he is. However, it isn't only Kim Donghee who thinks that way, and so Lee Kanghyun decides to let it go. The men in the university want to be known as feminists even more than the women do. They know what looks good and so nab the label for themselves.

Male professors who discuss feminism are seen as progressives who pay attention *even* to women's rights; but if female professors do the same, they're 'feminazis' who can't see the bigger picture. You couldn't deny that Kim Donghee was smart. And so people are pretty well fooled by him. Nice Kim Donghee, earnest Kim Donghee, oh, persevering Kim Donghee, capable Kim Donghee. But he'd never reached Lee Kanghyun. She'd distrusted him from the very beginning. Lee Kanghyun doesn't trust men. She doesn't trust women, of course, either. They're all exhausting. Lee Kanghyun has no interest in anyone apart from herself.

Lee Kanghyun's father thought her selfish for not marrying. She gets married, then he calls her cold-hearted for not having a baby. For the love of God, Abeoji. Then what does that make Umma? She killed two of my older sisters in her womb. Lee Kanghyun almost wasn't born. She was the third daughter, and the fifth girl her mother conceived. Lee Kanghyun survived, thanks to the doctor's warning that if her mother had yet another abortion, she might not be able to get pregnant again. And she was given a man's name. Lee Kanghyun. Only then would she have a younger brother. But there were no younger siblings. At that point, her mother was already thirty-four years old. And she'd contracted an illness;

an STI. A virus her father picked up somewhere had invaded her mother's womb. It wasn't lethal. But her mother was never once properly examined.

'What is there to examine when I can't even have a son?'

When Lee Kanghyun's uncle had an affair and his wife left home, sending the family into turmoil, her mother cursed her sister-in-law.

'Men just can't help it sometimes. What a song and dance over nothing! Nothing! Nothing!'

The virus—that wasn't nothing—contorted her pelvis and destroyed her womb. Lee Kanghyun doesn't feel for her mother. But how does a person whose existence has been denied since birth carry on living? Lee Kanghyun focused exclusively on herself, so she could feel whole without needing anyone else. She was the only and most important thing in the world. However, in reality, she came up against numerous barriers. When the time came to go to university, Lee Kanghyun said she was going to Seoul, and her father tried to shave off her hair. Then, when she said she was going to Anjin University's law school, he told her to get an arranged marriage instead. Abeoji was the one holding the purse strings, and so she met him halfway. She said she'd study English literature, work as an instructor after graduating, then marry within three years. The year Lee Kanghyun graduated, she immediately submitted her application for postgrad, and got a studio flat with the money she'd saved. Hagwon teaching, private tutoring, translation: if the work paid, she took it. Her supervisor—a woman and Seoul National University graduate—took her female pupils, who'd just started to increase in number, under her wing. However, trust-no-one Lee Kanghyun soon realized her supervisor just wanted to *look* as if she was taking special care of the female students. Her supervisor liked men. Male hoobaes who'd graduated from the same university as her. Men at Anjin University with whom she could form groups, build power, and establish new connections. People called her Anjin University's very first feminist professor, but, well, Lee Kanghyun didn't think of her supervisor as a woman. Her supervisor was even more of a man than the men were. She would never relinquish her seat to one of Anjin University's female pupils. It was the same for her fellow faculty members. There was no way she'd give the room next door to some weakling of no help to her. And so when the Eurasia Cultural Content department was formed, sooner rather than later, Lee Kanghyun cut ties with the English Literature department. When in 2005, with one of the English Literature department professors approaching retirement, her supervisor brought in the translator, the girls—who'd styled their hair every morning with her supervisor's perm as their model—couldn't hide their confusion.

Even so, it wasn't as if Lee Kanghyun had been on her supervisor's bad side. The two had never once clashed, privately or publicly. Lee Kanghyun knew precisely what her supervisor desired. Right now I'm working as a professor at a local university, but one day I'll return to Seoul! Those bastards who pushed aside someone as qualified as me. Men! Lee Kanghyun detected her supervisor's rage. Whilst her friends would cluelessly gather round her supervisor at drinks events, Lee Kanghyun knowingly pushed forward the next male students who'd slipped to the back. Her supervisor could hold her drink better than the guys, even. Obscenities? Her speciality was making the male students dance at the noraebang. Professor or not, guys didn't sell smiles easily in front of women. Lee Kanghyun searched out enthusiastic guys for it. Political correctness? Give that to the dogs. At one gathering, Lee Kanghyun's drunken supervisor slapped the behind—*tuk*—of the male student beside her, shouting, 'Give us a song, will ya?'

The student blushed in humiliation. Lee Kanghyun sat back and watched. You're humiliated? Kid, women go through this every moment of their lives. Judged since birth on whether we're pretty or not; given a thump on the back if we spread our legs when we sit; get bad grades and we're told if we're not going to be a doctor or a public prosecutor, to study for the civil service exam; when our little brother doesn't listen to us we're told we should have been their older brother; raise our voice and we're hysterical; when we get married it's all over, we're told. No, we end up telling ourselves. Once I get married it's all over. I'm no longer a member of the family.

And I don't have a name. Guys, kids, suck it up. You have to go through it at least once in your life. It won't kill you.

However, don't think that was Lee Kanghyun's desire for revenge—she sat the female students next to the male professors, too. Lovely, pretty, clever female students. Flower-like girls.

Giiirls! You're on your own now.

And like so, Lee Kanghyun quietly searches out her professors' wants, and gets what she wants in return. Acting like she wasn't lusting after a position; acting, when given work, like she was carrying it out without complaint; act, act, act; acting like a kind, obedient girl; acting like she wasn't competitive; act, act, act. Then one day, people started calling Lee Kanghyun a feminist. She snickered to herself. I'm a what now? Not a feminazi, but a pure feminist? Sure, why not? Lee Kanghyun thought it suited her perfectly. Exactly the kind of independent woman men like. The kind of feminist who, though unmarried, would never be against it; who doesn't interfere in 'men's things', but pays her equal share when the bill comes around; who doesn't get mad at lewd talk or jokes that border on sexual harassment; who has the common sense not to join when the guys move on to a second bar; who knows to point out how recent women's movements have gone too far, that there are more important things to focus on. A feminist who practises the kind of feminism they permit! More than anything else, they like the fact she teaches *Jane Eyre*.

'It really is a wonderful novel. I don't read the work of writers these days. There's no progression.'

They really just don't have an eye for contemporary literature; but she doesn't let her real feelings show. It's true that *Jane Eyre* is an impressive book. And Lee Kanghyun has no interest in contemporary novels, either. Reading recent literature won't get her promoted. 2004. The Eurasia Cultural Content department was about to be formed, and there was havoc. A fierce battle of wits, weighing up new and old rice bowls. Skipping over to the new bowls felt like a waste of all that hard work, but holding on to the old bowls brought uncertainty over when one's own turn would come around. Under everyone's watch, Lee Kanghyun meets with the dean. Meets with her supervisor. Her sunbaes. Think tanks. Researchers. She moves over to the Eurasia Cultural Content department and becomes the principal's general secretary. This can't be. Everyone was speechless. How did Lee Kanghyun talk them all into it? A forty-something woman; and she's not even good-looking. Whose breath stinks, too? Of course, they don't have a clue. *While you lot were debating whether or not to join for the second round, I had the sense to slip out once the bitching about university bureaucracy had begun, and made a list of everything the staff and professors responsible for this bureaucracy wanted.* Money didn't solve everything. Lee Kanghyun isn't rich. At times like these, she uses her father. Her father, who has a close relationship with Anjin's central figure, Ryu Hyeongwoong; her father, who spent his whole life working as a civil servant and building up connections in the city. Abeoji, one of the Philosophy professors is hoping to become principal next year. Abeoji, the Education department professor is running for superintendent. Had no luck when it came to having a son, but won't give up on having luck with his children. *Abeoji, oh, my abeoji!*

The Seoulite professor in the ECC department says the students here are innocent, not like in the city. They don't have big aspirations, and they look happy to me, he says. Lee Kanghyun reckons he won't last long. Thinking jibang kids don't aspire to anything. Thinking these almost twenty-year-old kids could feel content just because they'd only ever lived outside of Seoul. You only need to hear what he said next to appreciate his impoverished sense of imagination.

'If I'd have known, I would have brought my wife and kid with me. But I've got a boy and bringing a son to the jibang is a bit, you know.'

This zealous professor can't understand why the students grow more and more hostile towards him. He worries the students aren't able to keep up with his lessons. Is he handing out too many high-level assignments? Is he too harsh with grades? He's never once shown regional discrimination during class. He thinks himself innocent. I never let it show! I'm an egalitarian! Eventually, his lecture feedback hits rock bottom and he reveals his true self. 'If I'm honest, I think the kids are a bit stupid.'

The following year, Lee Kanghyun becomes associate professor before he does. He criticizes Lee Kanghyun. Acting like it's just friendly criticism, he judges her. A successful non-scholar?! Lee Kanghyun is associate professor, regardless. He still doesn't understand. Anjin kids aren't stupid. They recognize someone crushing their aspirations faster than anyone else. It's the same as killing two older sisters in the womb before being born yourself. Why do you think Anjin University kids are treated well by Anjin people? Why do you think it's difficult for people from Seoul or from other jibang universities to get a position here? Defending their territory? Old-boy connections? Regionalism? Not enough. Not enough imagination. Because people in Anjin have stunted their own children's aspirations. Those who crush aspiration do so because they've had their aspiration crushed by someone else. Thought it would bloom again; but once it's been severed, it's too late. Think they can't break into universities in the capital simply because of skill? Not enough. Not enough imagination.

Sometimes, all the kids in Anjin look like girls.

Just then, Kim Donghee enters her line of vision. A man whose aspiration has been perfectly stunted. Closing in; his goal to become number one. Unlike her supervisor, Lee Kanghyun didn't make her male students sing. Yet Kim Donghee was the type to get up and sing of his own accord. Once the song was over, he sidled up to her and whispered, 'Seonsaengnim, I respect you.'

Respect? Don't make me laugh. A student needs to know how to despise their teachers. The ones who throw around the word respect like that are the ones who want to exploit its power. As if he knows Lee Kanghyun, as if he's somehow similar to her, Kim Donghee sends her messages on the sly. Lee Kanghyun looks blankly at him. Obsessive, acknowledgment-craving bastards like him are easy to crush. Don't acknowledge them. You're incompetent, You're useless, You're unnecessary, You're not the same as me. Then Kim Donghee crawls in of his own accord. I'll do whatever it takes. Whatever. That moment, for the first time in a long while, Lee Kanghyun feels humanlike emotion. It's what she feels whenever she sees something squirming to survive. But she soon recovers her composure. When she was young and that feeling surged up, she went out and found a partner for the night. Who says women don't date out of sexual appetite? Lee Kanghyun has never gone out with a guy she didn't want to sleep with. The small number of brief flings she's had were purely about sex.

But with age, that shrivelled away, too. Fiddling with herself in the research room was much more pleasurable. Yet every year several female students came to find her and ruined her mood.

Why would you trust them?

Why would you follow them?

Why!

That's why they all think they can just kill you! But Lee Kanghyun pats them on the shoulder. The department's image is more important than anything. Eurasia Cultural Content department. Almost twelve years old, highest graduate employment rate across the humanities division—it mustn't get out that something shameful took place in this young department, so full of life. And under the watch of feminist Lee Kanghyun at that.

Kim Donghee finally hunts her down. He shouts.

'You can't just leave me like this.'

Speaking as if he was dangling a sword over her head or something. Stupid son of a bitch. Coherent and precise, Lee Kanghyun recited the words she'd prepared.

Listen here, when did I ever coerce you? Tell me when. Each time you helped me, you wrote up the document yourself and stamped your seal on it. Did I force you to stamp it? You did it all by yourself. And what were all those documents for? To show that you'd received appropriate remuneration for the work you did. Where is it you think your research funding comes from? How do you think you managed to get your own office? Where do you think your scholarships and research funding all came from? How do you think you ended up with key roles in the projects? And how many think tanks did I connect you with? Did you or did you not receive money from them? You did. My work is one project, which is just one piece of a business. You think any of the work you were involved in was ever included in my individual papers or research results? Look here. What do you think all this is? Is that how you saw your work?

You wanted it, too. You did it because you wanted to; what are you kicking off for now?

At the now blue-lipped Kim Donghee, Lee Kanghyun strikes one final blow.

And another thing; do you know how many girls come to see me each year? I'm like a Catholic priest giving confession. Do you seriously think your name hasn't come up at least once?

At the end of her stealthily cast fishing line, Kim Donghee quivers. No surprises there.

Lee Kanghyun tells Kim Donghee she'll move his classes to another college, and so to sit quiet. She makes it very clear that she's gone through a lot in order to specially arrange for this. Perceptive Kim Donghee understands immediately. If Kim Donghee has any virtue, it's this. From now on, Kim Donghee will remain faithfully at Lee Kanghyun's side.

Once Kim Donghee had left, for the next few days, out of nowhere Lee Kanghyun felt her libido surge. There was no outlet for it. Her husband offered her no release. An itch-like feeling deep inside her. Her husband had no clue where to touch her and always simply roamed around the entrance. Husband. What a strange word. Do I really have a husband? Sometimes she wonders how she ever ended up here. Ambition? Greed? A longing for recognition? All part of it; but that wasn't it exactly. There was some kind of other sensation that had kept pulling and pulling her up, all the way here. What was it? For the first time in a while, in a really long while, Lee Kanghyun becomes emotional. One day, she was granted permission to be born, and from then on she'd kept growing older. Hang on, how old was she again? She keeps forgetting her own age. No, it feels like she's still a baby. A baby, who knows nothing, and so has done nothing. A baby, waiting for someone to tell her she can do anything she sets her mind to. But no one ever did. From birth, right into her fifties, not one person recognized that Lee Kanghyun was waiting. It was only Lee Kanghyun who felt it thoroughly: I'm alive, I'm here right now. However, she quickly pulls herself out of her feelings. She didn't want to whine about how childhood trauma had decided her life and the like. And she never had. Until now, she'd been the one to push herself. She suddenly realizes the reason. To survive. Simply to survive. Man or woman, if someone gets in the way of her survival, she ruthlessly pushes them aside and leaps upwards. And she'll continue to do so, as long as necessary.

Kim Eyoung puts up handwritten posters.

Twenty years old. Chose all-out war over surrender. It suddenly occurs to Lee Kanghyun that Kim Eyoung hadn't come to see her. Just then, she recalls the words of the female student who'd just left.

'Everyone tried to stop me, saying you wouldn't help, but I believed you'd protect me.'

Everyone had tried to stop her. The girls. The girls she'd sent away. The girls whose names and faces she didn't remember. The girls who'd stupidly followed oppa, clung on to love, got hurt, and whined about it. Those girls had got together and said something, it seemed. I can't be bothered. I really can't be bothered. Things will probably get messy. Someone from the student committee will come see me, and then from the university paper, and if things go wrong it'll go to the press. Just because a man rubbed your back. Lee Kanghyun frowns. She types at her mental calculator and tries hard to determine the most advantageous solution.

Kim Eyoung is indeed an Anjin girl. She'll do whatever it takes to survive. Kim Eyoung and Kim Donghee. Lee Kanghyun holds a gulp of now stone-cold tea in her mouth and quietly weighs the situation. She counts the female humanities professors. She counts the male professors who'll back her. She goes through all the cover-ups she can think of from other departments. Kim Eyoung won't back down, regardless. Just like Lee Kanghyun never backed down, and rose all the way here. Lee Kanghyun identifies with Kim Eyoung. That's right, she's much like that kid. Then maybe it'd be more effective to add fuel to the fire, instead. Lee Kanghyun will be the one to gain a name out of it, after all. I just have to create the story. I'll say I kept silent to protect the privacy of the girls I sent away. All I need to say is that, from now on, I can no longer sit back and watch. On the other hand, let's think of what I can get if I keep Kim Donghee in my clutches. The university won't want to acknowledge a scandal like this, after all. In particular, if a rumour like this gets out about the humanities department, it'll impact the image of our partner enterprises. Let's be logical about this. Which side is it? Which side do I seek to gain most from? The further she falls into her thoughts, the more pleasure Lee Kanghyun feels. Her privates twitch like an aquatic plant. She sets down her teacup and stands before the mirror. Much like she always does when making an important decision, she puts strength into her lips and whispers: Okay, smile. A stench wafts from her mouth.

14

Jina

S UJIN ALWAYS USED to go round with her square rucksack
slung off one shoulder. At school, Song Boyoung hated
that. Said she was copying the annoying unnies. The older
girls wandering the streets clutching their handbags. The ones
who made eyes at the boys and showed off their legs. Ugh,
that girl's *so* annoying.

A long time has passed, and many of those memories have
vanished. Only a few things are clear. No one said hi to Sujin
when she got to school in the mornings. If Sujin said hello,
no one responded, and no one turned to look. Song Boyoung
made an example of Sujin: don't do as I say, and you'll all
end up like her.

I was picked on sometimes, too. If only she'd consistently
hated me like she had Sujin. As long as I acted right, Song
Boyoung soon forgave and played with me. One day she'd
play with me, the next she'd ignore me; she'd play with me
for two days, then ignore me for four. In the morning she
played with me, and ignored me in the afternoon; she'd play
with me all day then ignore me on the way home. I cried a

246

lot. I was nine. That experience stayed in my heart for a long time. Maybe that was why it became so important for people to like me. The act of submitting to someone's authority, the self-hatred of never having once stood up to it; maybe, in the end, that was what ruined me.

Why did no one help us?

We grew close so naturally. Two girls bobbing together like an island in the classroom. On my way home one day, I ran into Sujin. We walked home together. By the time we'd woven through the alley, we were holding hands.

After school, we strolled the rice levees together, and went on the swings in the playground. Thanks to that, Song Boyoung's tyranny at school rolled right off my back. If we could just endure those four, five hours each day, we were free. Song Boyoung couldn't control us outside the classroom. We found great delight in deceiving her. No matter how hard you try, you won't tear us apart. Time was passing. I believed we could stay like this forever.

It wasn't that Song Boyoung hadn't realized. She'd let us grow close.

Autumn.

We met in the fields. Cosmos flowers bloomed on the wayside. We walked the path single file. We picked flowers and made each other rings. We ran ahead and spun back around; we laughed a while then held hands. We held hands—until we heard that voice.

'Jina-ya?'

We turned. Song Boyoung was standing before us.

'What are you two doing?'

I should've ignored her. I should've kept holding Sujin's hand. What could be so scary about a nine-year-old little girl?

I was scared.

Guess no one will talk to me at school tomorrow. Everyone will make fun of me. How long will it be this time? One week? A month? More than that, I feared who Song Boyoung would choose. Her method of breaking up best friends was simple: make one the outcast. Cosy up to the other and become their friend. Me or Sujin, who will it be?

I'm still trying hard to forget that day.

Why couldn't you just leave us alone? You didn't like Sujin and me; you always picked on us. Why did you hate us being together so much? Why?

Song Boyoung gestured to me. 'Jina-ya, come here.'

For a few seconds, I stood exactly where I was. Then Song Boyoung stretched out her two hands.

'Come here. It's okay.'

I went to stand beside Song Boyoung. Sujin held on to my hand as I walked ahead. She squeezed tight and wouldn't let go. I slapped that hand away. I didn't look back. Song Boyoung took my hand, and I stepped forward without a single look at Sujin. Like that, we distanced ourselves from her. Then, I heard footsteps. Sujin was following us. Song Boyoung laughed.

'Quick, run! Chunja's girl's following us!'

At those words, Sujin stopped in her tracks.

Chunja's girl. Poor thing. That kid whose situation will never get better, for whom life will never change.

You want to know what happened? What I did?

Jina-ya? Jina-ya?

Sujin called my name. I didn't look back. I walked with my eyes set on the distant setting sun. The gentle breeze was still within my palm. The scent of the cosmos flowers I'd felt until just a moment before remained in my body. But I paid attention to none of it. All that was in my eyes was the sun's rays, heavy as they sank. It was the only thing before me, all that was coming for me. I forgot the smell of the voice that clung to my body.

I opened my eyes inside the bedcovers. My limbs were heavy. I hadn't been outside in two days. Tana was at work. I hadn't told her what'd happened when I saw Sujin. Tana hadn't asked, either. She seemed to be doing her best not to. I lay in bed all day. I didn't get out of bed the next day, either. I heard Tana sigh; I pretended I hadn't heard. Tana stripped back the duvet.

'Just forget it all,' she said.

I faintly nodded my head. And I was still in bed now. Three-thirty in the afternoon. I shifted my body. After all, it seemed very inconsiderate of me when my friend was putting me up. Should I make dinner? I pushed back the duvet again and stood up, but my legs trembled. I could hear my ringtone from the living room. Huh, why's my phone there?

I laughed. It was Tana. She'd chucked my phone into the living room in the desperate hope it would force me to crawl out of bed. I walked slowly out of the bedroom and checked who it was.

Kang Seungyoung—the guy the pianist had put me in touch with.

Motionless, I looked down at the number, and pressed the call button. Once, and then again. He picked up. A deep, husky voice. As I was about to mention Yuri's name, I realized I needed to take a shower and have something to eat.

After that year, the nightmare stopped. Song Boyoung moved to another school. When she left, the children hugged one another and cried. I don't think it was fake. Song Boyoung had understood the importance of friendship more than anyone else. To some, she truly had been a good friend. And so she knew the cruelty of taking that friendship away. As we moved up a year and our teachers changed, the school's atmosphere changed little by little, too. It was the countryside, after all. When kids from the village picked on and bullied one another, things only got ugly between the adults. As we moved up the years, the number of classes and the number of students shrunk.

That atmosphere was further cemented in middle school. More kids had to go home to help with chores after school than went to hagwon, and some were looking for jobs. From an early stage, we were divided into those who studied, and those who were searching for work. Once Song Boyoung moved schools, Sujin and I grew close again. We were part of the studying group. I got decent grades, and so my parents had high expectations. Sujin just about managed to keep up with me, but lacked aspiration. Every day, Sujin said how she wanted to go to college and get a job ASAP to help her grandma. The two of us were close.

We never once spoke about what had happened in the fields. If we talked about it, we believed the relationship we'd just about managed to piece back together would come tumbling down again. But in not discussing it, we were also pretending it'd never happened. We were close. However, Sujin was a burden. I'd done something terrible to Sujin, and so whenever I saw her, I felt guilt.

I cut off contact with Sujin once I went to high school. When she wrote letters, I didn't reply, and when she called, I didn't answer. When I came back to Palhyun I just stayed at home. At first, I felt guilty. But later, I really hated the idea of seeing her. I didn't have the mental space. I wasn't getting the grades I needed, and whenever I saw my parents they pressurized me. I'm doing my best, I'm at my limit—what more can I do? By chance, I saw Sujin out a few times. I didn't acknowledge her. I got angry. When I saw Sujin, it felt like I was still stuck in Palhyun, and I couldn't bear it. No matter how hard I tried, the things I pined for remained beyond my grasp; meanwhile, the one person I wanted to free myself of pined for me.

What really riled me up was her grandmother. Sujin was Chunja's daughter, her grades were bad, she wasn't even pretty—why did her grandma dote on her so much? All my parents did was sigh and ask why I couldn't do better, yet

Sujin's grandmother seemed to love her granddaughter just as she was. How was that possible? That grandmother was Chunja-ne, after all. The Chunja-ne my own grandmother constantly ridiculed and looked down upon. Sujin's face glowed as she walked around the neighbourhood arm in arm with Chunja-ne. That expression brimming with confidence, never doubting she would be loved no matter what.

I hated looking at that face.

Because it reminded me my own was full of darkness.

It was Christmas Eve, and for the first time in a while, Sujin called me. It was the day I first went to church with Tana. And, for the first time in a while, I answered the phone. Probably not expecting me to pick up, Sujin's voice was tinged with panic as it greeted me. Even so, she seemed pleased. Glad, enthusiastic. Jina-ya, merry Christmas. Sujin greeted me as if nothing had ever happened. Merry Christmas, Jina-ya. That's right. I'm your only friend, after all. That was when I realized. Unlike my grades, unlike my parents, my relationship with Sujin was something I could control. I didn't answer the phone when I didn't feel like it. I picked up when I did. I met up with her when I felt like it, and didn't see her when I didn't. My seventeenth Christmas Eve, and on the other end of the line was the one person I could treat however I pleased.

In the fields. That day, I knew Song Boyoung would choose me. In truth, I'd taken a step before she'd even called my name.

That's the kind of bitch you are.

Yeah, you're right. And that was why on Christmas Eve, I said to you, 'I don't want to be friends with you.

I'm going to become another person. So don't contact me anymore.'

That moment, a beautiful chorus resounded.

Yeah, that's the kind of bitch I am.

'Kim Jina-ssi?'

I was lost in thought when a voice called to me. I raised my head. A man was standing in front of me. Kang Seungyoung. Yet one more guy who'd known Yuri. Around 1.65m tall with a sturdy physique, like the pianist had said. He reached out to shake my hand. I could feel calluses on his palm. Partly because of the robust energy he gave off, he looked like someone whose job was physical.

'I hear you're writing a novel,' he said as he sat down.

I smiled naturally. In telling a continuous string of lies, I began to believe I really was writing a book. He studied me. I held his gaze. Step by step, I explained, just as I had prepared. Yuri was the inspiration for my novel, and it seemed she'd been going through a difficult time before she died. As well as her suicide attempt, I said there were a few things I'd been wondering about, and asked him to share anything he knew.

'Then Yuri can be at rest, too,' I said.

Kang Seungyoung stared blankly in my direction. It was obvious he didn't believe me. I let my gaze slip down. I'd been so shocked when I'd looked him up online, just like the pianist had warned me. I'd heard of him before, too. Knowing the kind of person Kang Seungyoung was, I'd been even more insistent on going to see Sujin that day.

And so I spoke exactly as a novelist would. Yes, Yuri had met this guy. He must've given her advice. For sure. Yuri had, without doubt, been dealing with a serious issue. However, after my shouting match with Sujin the other day, I'd wanted to forget all about it, just as Tana had advised me. Sujin was right. What'd Yuri got to do with me? But then this guy Kang Seungyoung had replied to my message, and now I was here. Why have I come to meet this man? I haven't dealt properly with my own problem yet. I can't do this anymore. Should I just end it all? Was it the same for you? It must've been horrible. How could it not, when you'd been surrounded by all those dirty relationships? Was that why you'd wanted to die? What had you wanted my help with? Yuri-ya?

'I don't believe you. You're not writing a novel, are you?' Kang Seungyoung asked.

I laughed awkwardly and looked at the man before me. The expression on his face was cold. He took a sip of coffee and then spoke.

'I work as a personal trainer. I wake up at five a.m., do a simple workout, then clock in at six. I work until ten at night. I do personal training as well as orientations for new members, so I'm very busy. I end up monitoring the gymgoers' progress. Most people come to lose weight. The InBody results come out similar. High body fat percentage and low muscle mass. Their physical strength isn't good either, naturally. They get out of breath just walking twenty minutes on the treadmill. If you have high body fat, it's good to start with cardio. Slow walking or cycling are most effective—exercise that doesn't put too much pressure on the joints. Training that doesn't need equipment, like crunches and push-ups, helps too. Then you gradually increase the intensity, and do more muscle-building exercises. We also recommend adjusting your diet. Actually, exercise has a knock-on effect. To lose weight, diet is most important. Ready meals, greasy food, late-night snacking, alcohol; you need to give it all up. You have to centre your meals around vegetables and protein. Eating hansik is good, too. But it's not easy. You have to go for work dinners, you want to snack, you want to drink café mochas covered in cream. But if you don't make adjustments, the weight won't come off. For my personal training clients, I create a slightly more detailed workout plan. What's important is that it takes time. You won't see the results you want in just one or two months. It takes at least three, but you can need up to six months or a year. I emphasize that heavily. At the beginning, everyone works hard at it. They come to the gym faithfully for a week or two. If you ask them, they're adjusting what they eat properly as well. They have hansik for breakfast and lunch, then salad for dinner. But most of them crumble. In the middle of the night, they get hungry. They had a certain amount they used to eat, but that's suddenly reduced and so their body jolts. In the end, dieting is a battle of perseverance. Overcoming that isn't easy. Three months on, it's difficult to find them. A few do remain. People still persevering. What do you think the difference is between those who remain and those who give up?' he asked me, and took a sip of coffee.

I thought a while, then replied. 'I'm not sure. Is it the ones who lack perseverance that give up?'

He smiled. 'That's basically right. But what exactly is perseverance? Something you're born with? To a certain extent, yes. There are people born with more patience. But patience shows itself when there's a reason. That's what I think.'

He finished speaking and looked at me. He'd spoken at great length, but I didn't get the feeling he was trying to patronize me. Bit by bit, I listened attentively to what he had to say.

'You need a goal. A goal for change. I don't think women saying they want to lose weight to get a boyfriend is a bad thing. Losing weight for yourself is a good thing, too, but I think the former goal is just as worthy of respect. It's much more feasible than saying, "I'll get slim within a year for myself." The more specific the goal, the better. In one month, I'll lose X inches from my waist; in three months I'll get down to a size 55. If you come up with a concrete goal, you'll work hard to keep renewing it. It needs to be pressing in order for you to do it, of course. If it's something I really want, I'll do anything to achieve it. I want to change, I want to be different from how I am now. It's about deciding a new goal to achieve every month or two, then ticking it off.'

He drank some more coffee. The cup was almost empty.

'Yuri wanted to change,' he said. I sat still.

'I attend a meeting once a week. They say the exact same thing there. That you need a goal. A goal to live well, a goal to change, a goal to no longer let the past rule over you. The perpetrators are the ones who did wrong; why is it the victims who have to suffer in hiding? It's not enough to enjoy all the things you missed out on. We need to be even happier, enjoy life even more. We, too, have the right to a goal.'

He stood up from his seat and got some water from the fountain. He placed a glass in front of me.

'I began my volunteer work after Yuri died. Until then, all I'd thought of was dying. It was also then that I started working out. Until that point, I'd just lived off part-time work. I've told this so many times now, it feels like someone else's story. Anyway. I'd never seen anything through to the end before. I collected all the compensation money and financial support in my bank account and chipped away at it little by little. That money was ridiculous. I got it because I was entitled to it, of course, but when I saw it there I wanted to die. Is this all I'm worth? I thought. Even though I didn't think you should determine a person's value that way, when I saw the money, I saw myself like that. Naturally, the financial support stopped. A lot of time had passed. But because the money had been cut off, I got angry and wanted to die again. It felt like people weren't interested in me anymore.'

He wiped his palm on his lap. Then he asked me, 'Are you really writing a novel?'

'No,' I replied, and immediately smiled. I felt a weight fly off me. He was different to what I'd imagined. I thought he'd be depressed, aggressive. Yet Kang Seungyoung came across as someone really healthy. A person who wants to share his health.

Kang Seungyoung.

From the ages of nine to eleven, he was routinely raped by his uncle. Kang Seungyoung is the same age as me. Three years ago, he'd released a book talking about his experience. He volunteers at the Anjin Sexual Violence Support Centre.

Various press outlets interviewed him, and recently he appeared in a documentary at an independent film festival. I got his contact details from the support centre. His reply to my message asking about Yuri read:

Sure, there have always been some things I've wanted to say about Yuri.

He continued speaking, 'Then what makes you interested in Yuri?'

I hesitated, before responding, 'We were in the same year at uni.'

'Okay.'

'The last time I saw her, she asked for my help.'

'I see.'

'But I just walked away.'

He didn't say anything. Neither did I. Silence. Slowly, he began to talk again.

'After the interviews, some people claimed I'd only done it because I still needed the attention. "Think it's something to brag about?" they asked. They were right. We need attention. Because there's a horrendous lack of it. No one's interested in why the appeal failed in court, or the punishment my uncle received. What people are interested in is my pain. How much it hurt, what he did to cause the pain. It's similar to watching a fight. Everyone concentrates on who hits who where, and who falls first. No one's interested in why they came to blows, or what happened to them afterwards. And then yet others were like, he's a man, not a woman, how is that even possible? Does he have some kind of issue? What they're saying is that things like this don't happen to guys.'

I sat in silence. I understood why Yuri had spoken to this man.

'Yuri was the first,' Kang Seungyoung said.

'I'd never told anyone my story before. Thinking about it, after meeting Yuri, things started to slowly improve. It was also the first time I'd ever given advice. It was the first time I believed I had value. That's why I feel indebted to her. We met twice. We went for a meal, had a cup of tea, and talked for around seven hours. I knew the moment I saw her. I'd been hounded so much by those emotions myself, and could see it in her face. A face that longs so much for somebody's touch, but is full of so much fear. I'd always been like that, too. I craved the love of others, but once I'd finally grabbed onto someone, I was overwhelmed by anxiety. Fear I might lose them. I don't deserve this kind of love—maybe someone up above is having their fun with me. Is this happiness going to be taken away? That anxiety prevents you maintaining the relationship—because the other person can see it. And you can't date someone who's also anxious. No one could put up with me. I wanted to die. I could see the same in Yuri's face. She had the rage of someone who'd been consistently violated. But I don't think Yuri ever once let out her anger. You're angry without realizing. You're afraid that the moment you let that rage explode out, you really will be left all alone.'

'Did Yuri tell you she was being harassed?'

'It wasn't harassment.'

I listened. Kang Seungyoung continued.

'It was rape. She said she kept having sex even though she didn't want it. When she said no, he only came nearer, ignoring what she said, and forced her into it. That was what made her unwell. Yuri was on the brink of stage 1 cervical cancer. Physically, she was really suffering. The pain continued day after day. But the guy ignored her appeals. He closed in on her, claiming she was lying just to get attention.'

I clasped my two hands together.

'Did she say who the guy was?'

'No, that I don't know. She said he was in the same department, though.'

I swallowed. Hyeongyu sunbae. Maybe it was true. I remembered Sujin's shouting. You just want to screw me over, you just can't accept me.

'Did she say why she didn't report him?' I asked.

'Thinking back on it, the situation had been a bit vague. It hadn't started out as coercion. Yuri had thought they were dating. But when they met up, it was nothing but sex. She'd once told him she wanted to go out for lunch, and apparently he'd laughed in her face. Why would I do that with you? he said. From that point on, Yuri had wanted to stop seeing him. But she'd probably never once told anyone no. She half-heartedly ran away and avoided his messages and calls. That seemed to be when his attitude changed. He became violent, coercive. Then he'd suddenly be kind. He'd pick up Yuri's heart and drop it again, doing exactly as he pleased with her. Yuri thought that even if she did report him, no one would believe her. She told me her nickname had been vacuum cleaner.'

'Did she expect everyone to take the guy's side?' I asked.

Kang Seungyoung nodded his head. 'Yes, she did say that.'

Of course everyone would side with Hyeongyu sunbae. No one would've believed Yuri.

'Yuri did ask for help in her own way. She went to see one of the female teachers in the department who she thought was trustworthy. She taught a lot of feminism classes, and so Yuri said she trusted her. But apparently, straight away she asked Yuri if she'd led him on. She told her to stop kicking up a fuss all over some guy she was seeing and to leave.'

Kang Seungyoung gave a bitter smile. So she'd gone to Lee Kanghyun, then. I would've done the same. There was no women's centre at the uni back then. Even if she had gone to the police, who knows whether they would've conducted a proper investigation. She'd gone to Lee Kanghyun for advice. If it'd been Hyeongyu sunbae, people wouldn't have easily accepted her assertion. Of course, there's a chance it would've been properly resolved. There was certainly the possibility. But Yuri had been deceived far too much in her life to believe that.

'Seems no one helped her, then.'

I blushed as I spoke. I remembered telling him just a moment before that I'd ignored Yuri's cry for help. Sure, I could claim I hadn't known what it was Yuri had wanted help with. But I knew. I'd guessed the problem. If not that, then why ask someone she barely knew like me?

But why did it have to be me? Suffering humiliation, having your private life disclosed, being misunderstood. Even if you can put up with all of that, if people won't believe you, you end up not wanting to tell a soul. I also wanted to give up. No, I have given up. I guess that's why I'm here in Anjin.

'And that's why she thought only of dying instead. And she

was a student. She had no money. Getting laser eye surgery like most students her age wasn't even on her radar. I get it. Yuri was a difficult person to be around. She was a lot, and fell for anyone who showed her even a bit of kindness. I went ahead and told her: that's not loneliness, it's anger. You're mad, and that's why you want to die. That was how it always had been for me.'

I took a sip of water to quench my thirst. I waited for him to speak. 'I feel like I've freed myself from a lot of this stuff, but it's still difficult to talk about.'

'Of course.' I waited; he went on.

'I was nine years old. I'd been left behind by my parents who'd passed away. No one could help me. My uncle would always say to me, if you owe someone something you have to pay them back. How are you going to repay me? It was two years before I was taken to A&E and the doctors reported it. Those two years completely changed me. I became another person.'

I smiled. He'd made three attempts on his own life, and survived each time. In an interview, he'd said: Aside from when I felt the urge to die, I've lived a happy life. There were people who cared for me, things I wanted to eat, plenty I wanted to buy. Wanting to die, it was a feeling that appeared on impulse. It wasn't as if I was sad and depressed day after day. I enjoyed my life. That urge rose up very occasionally. I let the past, which would rear its head out of nowhere, destroy and dominate my happy day-to-day life. I don't want to let my uncle control me anymore. I won't be controlled.

'I told her my story. It was the first time I'd told anyone.

I said that, right? She listened intently to me. I told her how a photo taken of me in hospital was used as evidence. I told her to gather evidence, too. Evidence that it had taken place against her will. She said she'd been told the same thing at the sexual violence support centre. They'd also told her to collect evidence. It was unsurprising. I told her there might be other victims, too. That she should find them. She said there was already another victim she knew of.'

I raised my head. There'd been another? What did this mean? The story was heading in a direction I couldn't handle.

'Who?'

Kang Seungyoung shook his head. 'She just said it was a friend. Someone in the same year as her, but that they wouldn't help her, regardless.'

'Why not?' I barely managed to ask the question, my throat dry.

'Yuri said they'd never want to speak about it. Said she didn't want to tell them. She didn't want that friend finding out. Then she suddenly criticized herself. Called herself pathetic, a disgrace. That she was an idiot for letting it happen, even though she'd known. Of course she'd suspected and had been cautious around him, but he was good to her and so she'd let her guard down, she said. He can't be that bad, can he? Surely he'd had his reasons? That was how she saw it. I don't know what she meant. It seems there'd been some story between her and the guy. But she didn't tell me. She was probably protecting the victim. I think with Yuri, she made it seem like she was revealing everything, without ever saying the one really important thing. Anyway, she said this friend was dating someone who no one would ever cross, so she was safe. Said he was a guy with influence. I don't know. I didn't know the situation, so took it at face value. That was it. I've always regretted that I didn't help more. I think to myself: if I'd just been a little more proactive, maybe things would've been different. Maybe Yuri would still be with us now. Maybe she would've been with me at the time of the accident. Organizing the evidence to report him, or opening up her heart. Anyway. If nothing else, she wouldn't have been alone. So I thought long and hard. Who had that guy been? The son of a professor or someone connected to the university? Was that what had made it difficult for Yuri? I wanted to find out. But Yuri died, and without the person concerned I couldn't do a thing. So I was glad when you got in touch. I want to help, even now.'

Then, cautiously, he asked me, 'Do you happen to know who it was?'

I'd been holding my breath for a while now.

A girl in our department dating someone you'd never cross. It could only be one person. I clasped the cup in my hand. My body trembled.

Was it you?

You too?

'It can't be,' I whispered. My body continued to quake. I squeezed the cup even tighter. That happened? To you, too?

'But she looked unsure. Yuri kept saying she didn't know if anyone would believe her. The last time I saw her it was the beginning of December, and she said she'd gathered all the evidence she could. She'd written down everything she could remember, got her treatment records, but was always anxious whether it'd be enough.'

'Was she worried people wouldn't believe her?' I felt like I was about to cry.

'Yes, and she said that when she met up with him, it didn't feel like rape. I said that was a misunderstanding and she cried. She said she really did see it like that. And she wasn't confident the records would be effective. She'd kept them, intending to report him, but then maybe someone would say she was inviting rape. It was possible—it wasn't as if the guy had appeared out of nowhere, attacked her and then run off. Quasi-rape is difficult to prove. I really hate that word. Apparently the guy's attitude had been the same. You never once made it clear you didn't want it. Even if you did, when did you really mean it, though? He was like that. Exactly the same.'

I held my face in my hands. I suddenly regretted coming here. No, there's no way. I'm being overly sensitive again. I'm thinking weird thoughts again. That voice returned. You don't want to accept me. That's why you want to screw me over! Yeah, it's true. I envied you. I envied, hated you. That's also why this doesn't make sense. No, it can't be.

'And my uncle,' Kang Seungyoung said, 'each time he made me write a letter.'

I lowered my hands and looked at him. That sturdy, flawless build. Maybe that's why he works out? To never go through that again. Of course, both he and I know. There's no one who deserves to be taken advantage of. But it happens. There are clearly those who think they can get away with treating people like that. Escaping the hitlist of evil; doing everything possible not to enter that line of vision. It'll be okay as long as I get stronger. Ages nine to eleven. This young boy no one protected. Small, fragile. Maybe he'd resented his own body. If I'd been a little stronger, just a tiny bit stronger, enough to defend myself. Why? Why do I always make it my fault? I've done nothing wrong. Is it my fault it always feels like I've been ruined?

'The letters' contents were simple. I wanted to have relations with my uncle. I was beaten by my uncle because I'd been bad. Everything is my fault.'

I sat in silence. How is he able to talk about something like this with such composure? That was all he knew about Yuri, he said. He appeared genuinely saddened by her death. After all, he was probably the one guy who hadn't seen Yuri as a sex object. Had Yuri felt comforted by him? Or had she witnessed an even darker future? Regardless, it's clear Yuri had been trying hard to get out of her situation. Announced she wanted to die, kept records, got counselling. What else had she done? Yuri.

Yuri. And then Sujin.

It can't be—but the stories lined up too much. Even made-up stories in novels have their background in reality. Sujin and Yuri. Maybe, because of him, the two of them had become friends. But there was no way Sujin would've actively involved herself in Yuri's situation once she'd started dating Hyeongyu sunbae. She would've wanted to pretend it'd never happened. A clean page of a sketchpad. A ruined picture torn to shreds;

a white sheet ready to start afresh. Then what had Yuri been trying to do? She must've wondered about potential other victims. Right, she must've been searching for them.

Another person. Not Yuri or Sujin, but another person.

Just then, Kang Seungyoung seemed to remember something. 'Oh, thinking about it, there was one thing the guy always used to say to Yuri.'

'What was that?' I asked. My voice, nervy, came out thinly as it trembled.

'Yuri told me that whenever she cried, or looked to be struggling, he'd say: Don't take this the wrong way. You have a victim complex.'

I sat perfectly still. I didn't say a thing. I couldn't think. I couldn't do anything. My body shook. In truth, I'd been shaking all along. Now I know. Now I understand perfectly.

Kang Seungyoung, his voice panicked, asked, 'Kim Jina-ssi, are you okay? You don't look so good.'

I rose from my seat. I was going to be sick. I ran out of the café. There was a telephone pole; in front of it, I threw up the contents that had risen in my throat. The coffee I'd poured into my empty stomach came flowing out just as it was.

In truth, I had always known it could've been this. But I hadn't wanted to think about it. That sheet of paper had been torn up. It hadn't happened to me.

It never happened to me.

*

You were angry back then. A summer's day, hazy from the scorching heat. You got so angry when I said I'd seen you. At the time, thinking I'd misspoken, I panicked and felt guilty. So even when you put me through all that, I just sat back and took it. I felt it was something I had to endure. Because long ago, I'd coolly cast you aside. I thought you were getting your revenge. Why hadn't I been able to see it any other way? That in reality you'd been afraid. How hadn't it crossed my mind that you'd been petrified a terrible truth would be exposed?

Then, you appeared before me; suddenly, in the street. But it looked as if you'd been waiting for me. You asked for my help. Not because we'd spoken to each other a few times. Not because you'd been walking past and seen me by chance. You'd been waiting a long while to ask me. It was a problem you could discuss only with me.

Kim Jina is a liar.

There's only one person who'd say that. I'd known from the beginning. I'd known, but I'd ignored it—in case it really had been true. I didn't want to face it again. I wanted to live with it perfectly forgotten. Because you'd never been in my life; because it could be no other way. The clean piece of paper. The torn-up white sketchbook. I'd wanted to draw a new picture. I can't. In truth, I'd simply painted over with each and every colour to hide the image beneath. But I knew. That as long as I didn't look properly at the picture below, the recoating would do nothing but spoil the paper even more. I can't pretend it never happened. Because it did happen to me.

To you, and you; and then another person.

You're a liar.

This was what Donghee had said to me the day we broke up.

15

Sujin

S UJIN HEARD THE SOUND of running water as she entered
the flat. It was coming from the bathroom. Her husband
hadn't told her he'd be home early. Sujin didn't want to go into
the bedroom. Her right cheek still stung from where Jina had
slapped her three days before. Whenever Sujin looked in the
mirror—though she knew it was only her imagination—her
face was hardening like a rock.

Another human being.

Sujin thought she could hear Jina's voice. You're a joke.
Actually, Sujin hadn't said everything she'd wanted to. Should've
said way worse. However, she did wonder if she could've
actually said any more. That day, Sujin came home, put an
ice pack on her face, and stared a while at her desk drawer.
At the far back corner was Yuri's diary. She hadn't looked at
it once in eleven years. She'd had plenty of opportunities to
get rid of it. She and her husband had moved three times, and
spring-cleaned whenever the seasons changed. They'd replaced
their furniture twice, and so she'd changed desks twice, too.
Each time, Sujin moved Yuri's diary to a new location. Her

husband doesn't know she has it. He hasn't brought Yuri's name up once since they cleared out her room. Back then, he'd looked satisfied, like he'd performed his duty. Just like he had whenever he'd helped a hoobae whose family situation was difficult, or lent money to a friend, no strings attached. Believing everything over, he had peace of mind.

Long ago, the day Hyeongyu told Sujin he liked her, he'd said, 'I think you're afraid of people.'

This was what he said to her then. He'd stay by her side. He'd be with her always. Sweet, affectionate words. He was commanding and full of confidence. Seeming not to think there was the minutest chance Sujin would ever refuse him. He chose her. With that, his world was complete. Then what about Sujin's world? If he decided to leave her side, would Sujin have to silently accept that, too? But Sujin didn't think too deeply about it at the time. She didn't go out of her way to say it'd been her who'd first wanted something between them. Internally, she'd wondered at how easily things had happened, and clutched as fast as she could at this good luck right before her eyes. That was how she believed she'd held on tight until now—good fortune.

He came out of the bathroom; heat radiated from him.

'You're home?' he asked her, drying his hair with the towel.

She couldn't look at her husband. How can someone treat another human being like that? Kim Jina had been wrong. People do all kinds of shit to one another. Sujin had long since held that reality close to her chest. She'd been mistaken in thinking Donghee had been ousted from the department.

Donghee hadn't turned up at department gatherings because he'd been studying. People, no matter who they are, always think the world centres around them. Sujin, not wanting to become the target of gossip, had believed that if she put Donghee on the spot, he'd panic. But Donghee simply hadn't associated with other undergraduates not up to his standards. Even before his military service, Donghee had been chasing after graduate school society events and the like, laying out his future. He'd remained unmoved even when Sujin got in the way of his working student scholarship, or when she spread rumours about his relationship with Kim Jina.

It was true Donghee could no longer treat Sujin as a pushover. However, that was all there was to it. Sujin couldn't crush Donghee. He hadn't been crushed—he was seemingly unaware Sujin had attacked him at all. When he returned from the army, he was appointed department student president, dated one of the new students, got the best grades across all of the humanities department, was awarded a scholarship and went on to graduate school. And he kept in touch with Hyeongyu. Hyung, what are you up to? Hyung, are you free today? Hyung, shall we go for a drink? To Hyeongyu, Donghee was an affable, clever hoobae. When from time to time she learnt the two had met up for a drink, Sujin was overcome by fear. Maybe they're talking about something else? Or what if those two know something?

Once, she'd slipped it into conversation: had Hyeongyu ever talked with Donghee about her?

'Donghee, talk about you?' Hyeongyu replied. 'Oh, you two are in the same year, aren't you?'

He said Donghee had never talked about Sujin, but he had asked about her once.

'Hyung, everything going well with your girlfriend?'

To Donghee, Sujin was nothing more than Hyeongyu's girlfriend. To be precise, he had that much respect for her. It was as if Donghee had no memory of the—to quote his own words—'mistake' he'd made with Sujin. How can Donghee keep in touch with Hyeongyu like it's nothing? Because he believes he's done nothing to Sujin. Or maybe he knows what he's done and doesn't care. No matter what had gone on between him and Sujin, it wasn't worth not meeting up with this hyung he so respected. Sujin couldn't tell Hyeongyu not to see Donghee—not because she feared Hyeongyu would discover her secret, but because at times, it felt like he was no different from Donghee. If Hyeongyu thinks so much of Donghee, if he can care so much about someone like him, then in the end isn't Hyeongyu just the same? Such suspicions made her think of Yuri.

Yuri's diary. Endless **o**s and **x**s. Jina said Yuri was being harassed—the exact same thought Sujin had the moment she saw that diary. A thought she'd buried as soon as it entered her mind. Sujin loved Hyeongyu. Hyeongyu was the best man in her life, and so she loved him. He was the most brilliant person in her life, and so she loved him. No, Sujin didn't believe she could love anyone more than she loved Hyeongyu. Her love froze when she met Hyeongyu, but then continued to expand. Just like the cell that one day began to stir, the next day opened up its hands, and then the following day stretched out its legs, before forming the face of a living child; an organism that

273

keeps on growing even after it's born. Sujin's love for Hyeongyu lived and moved; it didn't stop growing. But there was just one thing. The faces of Yuri and Donghee that overlapped with his—they tortured her. She could've given Hyeongyu all her love. She could have given all of herself. Those faces, however, stunted her courage. Really think you can trust him? A whole twelve years. All that time. Whenever she was in a bad way, Sujin had thought of death. It wasn't that she'd wanted to die; she wished Donghee would die. A car accident, stabbing—she prayed for a cruel death. Like how Yuri, holding Sujin's secret, had disappeared, and could therefore no longer question Sujin. She wished Donghee would disappear, too. Then maybe Sujin would be completely happy.

'What's wrong?' her husband asked.

Sujin raised her head. Endless questions hovered on her lips. She needed to choose. Spit out all those questions, and she'd come to see a different future. Ask nothing, and life would continue just as it is now. As if nothing had happened; as if she didn't remember.

'It's nothing,' she replied.

She was about to get up from the dining table when her husband spoke. 'What do you mean, nothing?'

She turned her head; her husband was looking at her bitterly.

'It's really nothing?' he asked.

Her husband sighed. He moved towards the table and sat in front of her. His face was resolute, like he'd made a decision.

There were times Sujin had wondered why people always left her. Umma, Jina. And now her husband, too. Of course, more had stuck by her. Her grandma, her friends. And until now, her husband. Throughout her life, more had handled her with care than pointed the knife, but she couldn't cope with any more little scratches. Sujin was happy. She'd been happy without her mum, and even when Jina left her. Even after Donghee did that to her and slunk off, she managed to make it through. Sujin wasn't someone gripped by misery. Misery had only caused her to waver briefly. Yet with each crisis of misery, she forgets all the happy times. Because each time, she hears a voice. A warning: everything you've enjoyed until now, it was all fake, it'll all vanish. Don't let your walls down.

'You make me uneasy,' said her husband.

Sujin was instantly hurt. No matter how hard she tried to retain her composure, words like these hurt her. Uneasy? *And you don't think I feel that way?*

'Why's that?' Sujin asked.

'Why do you think?'

Sujin jumped up from her seat. He was acting like Sujin had done something wrong. Telling her to work it out for herself, to say how she'd wronged him. Sujin didn't want to continue the conversation any further. Let's leave it. Surely in a few days we'll have moved on to something else. But Sujin couldn't hold it in.

'Did you not consider it might be you who's the problem?' she answered. 'Never thought that you might make *me* uncomfortable?'

'*Do* I make you uncomfortable?'

A conversation like a repeat sign at the end of a piece of sheet music. Again, she thought: let's leave it, this conversation is pointless.

She replied, 'Yeah, you make me uncomfortable.' Her tone was spiky. 'I'm dying here I'm so uncomfortable, and you won't tell me what the problem is, won't explain why you're acting like that, and just come and go like a lodger. What exactly is the problem? If you don't tell someone how can they know?'

'Yeah, how can they know if you don't tell them?'

He parroted her. Then he shut his mouth. Sujin was lost for words. He'd turned her heart inside out, and yet still hadn't told her a thing. Sujin got up from the dining table. She was heading towards the bedroom when he opened his mouth again.

'Why won't you be honest about wanting a baby?'

Sujin stopped in her tracks, no idea what she was supposed to say. But she soon gathered her thoughts, and replied, slowly.

'What are you talking about? I told you, I don't care.'

He looked at Sujin. 'Did you think I wouldn't know?'

Sujin said nothing. Her mind went blank. She wanted the conversation over. She wanted to go to bed and sleep, to wake up in the morning as if nothing had happened; have breakfast with her husband, go to the café, have a good day. What is it you know?

'I know how you've been secretly watching the nursery kids.'

Sujin didn't respond.

'I know how you go on our friends' pages every day and look at pictures of their children. I know how you search baby clothes online whenever you have time at the café. And I know how you go to the department store and hold the baby shoes in your hands.'

Sujin was going to speak, but didn't. Nothing she said would make him understand. Hyeongyu and Sujin's baby. A situation she wanted, with the person she wanted; a future she created for herself. Yeah, Sujin did want a baby. Maybe it was just her hormones. Maybe her maternal instincts were kicking in as she got older. But part of her also didn't want a child. She couldn't trust what was going on in her own head. And thinking of children triggered thoughts of Yuri's diary, making her uneasy. Can I cope with having his baby? Will I be able to trust my own child? And so when she learnt it would be difficult for Hyeongyu to have children, she'd been secretly relieved. She had honestly felt a weight lift off her. Yet Sujin doubted all her own thoughts. Wanting a baby, not wanting a baby; she believed it was all connected to what had happened twelve years before. Because she'd gone through with the procedure, it felt like this time it was her choice to want a child. Because she'd gone through with the procedure, it also felt like this time it was her choice to not want a child. Because of what had happened, it felt like she no longer knew what she really wanted. And so she scrutinized: children's pictures, voices. Did she really want one? But she only grew more unsure, more confused. There was one thing, however; one clear fact: she didn't want to talk about children with him. She didn't want to hurt him. If she said she wanted a baby, he'd blame himself and fall into despair. If she said she didn't want a baby, he'd resent himself, believing it his fault she'd given up on it. She didn't want either scenario. But it was difficult to explain all these emotions to him. So she chose to stay quiet.

And she'd continued to keep her mouth shut. He looked at her with a sad, numb expression.

'Look here, you never tell me anything,' he said. 'You've always been like that. You thought I wouldn't know you don't trust me? You've always expected my feelings to change. Think I wouldn't know you were uncomfortable, that you doubted me? But Sujin-ah, it's okay to feel bitter. Feel as bitter as you want. Only then can you move on. This is our life. Not our own respective lives, but the life we're living together. Even so, I waited. I was waiting for you to bring it up, for you to be able to talk about it. You think I've lived life being showered with nothing but praise, don't you? That I've got everything I ever wanted? But what I dreamt most of was you. For you to trust me completely. I always thought that if you could only trust me as much as I love you, if you could just do that, then I could do anything. I thought that, at some point, things would change.'

His speech was slow and considered. Sujin could barely speak. Her voice was raspy.

'So you're saying nothing's changed,' she said.

He gazed blankly at her. This person she loved—how could she explain that the reason she'd said nothing was because she hadn't wanted to hurt him? I've always wanted to give you everything, I've lived 'our life' since the moment I met you—how could she say all this?

He spoke. 'Ha Yuri's diary—I know you've had it all this time.'

The two looked at one another. For a very long time, Sujin had doubted. Doubt had spread all over like the veins of a leaf. But she'd always known: that holding on tight to this thread of doubt *was* Sujin. If she let go of that doubt and the same thing were to happen again, she'd sink into despair and wouldn't be able to pick herself up this time. A deep, bitter scar remained, but Sujin had made it through. She'd survived. The likes of Kim Donghee couldn't dominate her life. There was only one thing Sujin feared.

Ryu Hyeongyu. He whom she longs to give everything. If you turn away from me, my dear, then I will not be able to cope.

16

Marianne, the Mariannes

F AR, FAR AWAY in a novel set somewhere down south, the woman who'd written it said: the wordless man listened only to the stories of others. People said he was a source of comfort for them. But what he really wants is to return to his friend. To return to that other wordless person he loves, trusts, longs for. Pick fruit and sweet things, and walk familiar paths as the day draws to a close. They held each other's stories to their chests.

We were wordless.

We were Marianne.

I remember the first time I read *Jane Eyre*. A story of bravery. I lent the book to Sujin. When Sujin returned it to me, we talked about courage. We never once doubted that we, too, would become Jane Eyres.

Sujin didn't ask why I'd called her. She watched me enter from where she was sitting and gently nodded her head. I sat opposite Sujin. I thanked her for coming. We sat like that for a moment.

For a few days I'd debated: whether it was right to tell Sujin, what the point of it was. They say truth speaks for itself, but that's a cliché. Sharing the truth would be a weight off my chest—so perhaps it was mere moaning. If simply to ease my own mind, it bore no connection to telling the truth.

At first, I'd planned to say nothing. So much time had gone by. As Kang Seungyoung had said, we don't have to be controlled by the past. He's right. But what if the past isn't over? What if I'm walking upon a stopped clock?

I thought of Lee Jinsub. Yet another past patched over my own. After he hit me, he always grew depressed. He wanted forgiveness; to lessen his guilt. He bought gifts. He gave me bags, clothes, necklaces, none of which I could afford myself. He couldn't afford them, either. I believed he did it out of genuine remorse. And so I took them. That's a lie; I coveted those items, too. When I thought of how he'd hurt me, I didn't think twice about accepting them. It was a trap. As the violence continued, so did the presents. And I didn't pay anything towards our dates. Sometimes I selected the gifts I wanted. If he showed reluctance, I made sarcastic remarks. Can't do this for me after you hit me like that? You're so cheap. Cheap. You have no right to hit me.

At some point, the apology gifts became advance payment. I said it was out of fear that I hadn't reported him. Yes. I was afraid of people, of women, telling me how despicable it was to report him when I'd already been adequately compensated. I feared being told I'd lowered and sold myself as a woman. And so I was scared no one would help me. Cheap. I was cheap. He isn't controlling me. It's my own memory.

*

The moment I saw Sujin this time, too, I was overwhelmed by disgust. Past, future, and everything I'd planned to say in that moment—all of it disgusted me. But I had to say it.

Fasten the first button wrong and the rest follow suit, they say. I don't think that's right. You only need to undo the button and refasten it. Of course, you can make another mistake. But then you only need to do the button up once more. Kang Seungyoung's advice was this: life can always be started over, changes can always be made.

But what if I'd lived believing I was buttoned up correctly when I wasn't? Without realizing where I'd gone wrong? If I've been putting the buttons in all the wrong holes? Or what if all along I'd just been pretending I didn't know?

Then Kang Seungyoung would say: face it head-on. Keep on ignoring it and the buttons will stay fastened wrong, until one day you can cope no longer. He'd never say there was no hope. But what he would say is that the longer you ignore something, the longer you have to endure it.

And so I had to tell Sujin. I wasn't looking for a response or for her agreement. I was saying what I should have said long ago; that was where the first button had gone wrong. It wasn't about me needing the other person to know. It was exactly that: an incorrectly fastened button. The truth, made visible through its lopsided clothing.

'I was twenty,' I began. Sujin stared; I held her gaze.

'I'd been with my boyfriend about a week when we went

on our first trip together. To the western coast. We ate grilled mussels and went to a hotel. I'm sure some people would ask how I hadn't seen it coming, but I honestly hadn't. It felt no different to going away with my female friends. Of course, I wasn't stupid enough not to realize what happens between a guy and a girl when they're alone. But I never considered I'd have sex. I saw myself as different from other people. I knew it would happen sometime, but not right away. I believed my boyfriend would think the same; I was dating him, after all. I automatically assumed everyone thought like me. My boyfriend hid it well. We chatted. About uni life, jobs, our parents, food—everyday conversation. Then as soon as we got to the room, there was a switch.

'As if he'd been waiting all that time—as if it was a given— he started trying to remove my clothes. I panicked. And then he said to me, "You came here because you wanted it, no?"

'I told him I hadn't. But I wasn't able to say it with confidence; it was true that I'd chosen to come there with him.

'But then my boyfriend said, "Okay, all right."

'He threw himself on the bed and said, "For some reason I thought you'd be really cool, but guess you're just another naïve country girl."

'You know I'm from the countryside. Those words don't bother me now, but back then, I hated it. Who doesn't want to be more sophisticated? I'd always dreamt of being a strong career woman. Those cool girls, I wanted to be like them, and believed I would. Those words hurt me. The atmosphere turned cold. He looked even angrier. He'd said it was all right but he looked extremely unhappy. I became uneasy. All I'd done was say no to something I didn't want, how could he not understand that? I thought maybe I'd done something wrong. Maybe I'd caused a misunderstanding between us. Seeing him look so certain, surely he must have got some kind of signal from me, and I'd led him on without realizing.

'I sat there perched on the bed, and as if he was really disappointed, my boyfriend said, "I'm pretty upset you see me as that kind of guy. I thought I'd been respectful of you, but I guess you must think I'm a piece of shit now."

'I suddenly felt really bad. No way, I thought. I was worried I'd hurt his feelings. What if I lost him over this? I've never told this to anyone. Not even Tana. You're the first one I'm telling. I was afraid—that people would call me a girl desperately clinging onto love, afraid of being discarded; that I was an embarrassment to women. I'd seen what happened to Yuri. I'd seen how the endless words directed at her had eaten her up. Do you remember?

'How they called Yuri a humiliation to women. How women like her weren't worth protecting, that they didn't deserve help. Though they criticized guys for talking about women's private lives, they left them to it when it came to slagging off Yuri. Women's rights weren't for her. All she'd wanted was to be loved; she hadn't known that she only had to love herself. Remember?

'I bitched about Yuri in the same way, too. Back then, I didn't know. I didn't know that in wanting to be seen as a good person I was leaving myself open to being mistreated.

'We were lying quietly on the bed, and about ten minutes had passed. Then my boyfriend got on top of me. I put my hand on his chest and pushed him slightly away, as a signal to back off. But I'd already lost my resolve, and was flustered, so I couldn't firmly refuse. How could I do anything when I hadn't fully grasped the situation at hand? He gripped my wrist tight. It hurt. I told him to let go and tried to move my hand. Sujin-ah, until then I hadn't realized a man's strength. I'd never been hit by a boy. I had no idea that when a guy hits you, it's as if your body is being squashed to pieces like a lump of tofu. I believed that if I resisted, if I resisted with all my strength, if a guy cornered me, that I could always get away. He was tall. He almost completely crushed me. Even with all my strength I couldn't overpower him. I stopped resisting. There was no way out of the situation anyway, and I even felt guilty—what else could I have done? I didn't sleep a wink after. What had I just done? What'd happened? I believed I really was a naïve country girl. What did I think this was? Shouldn't I know how to have a no-strings-attached fling with a guy? I was blowing this out of proportion. I didn't know how I was supposed to take it. This carried on for four months.'

Sujin said nothing. I took a sip of water before continuing.

'I wanted to look good. I lost my real beliefs to the me who wanted to look good in front of others. But I thought this was what a relationship was. I didn't feel as if I loved or was loved, but I thought the only important thing was having someone at my side. He tried it on with me when I really didn't want to as well. Even on days when I'd very clearly said "no". When I was on my period, when I was unwell. He got what he wanted from me. And I used to think I'd wanted it, too. I wanted it; that's why we're together. It wasn't as if a mugger had appeared in a dark alley holding a knife and told me to remove my clothes. Or that I'd resisted within an inch of my life and he still hadn't backed down. I didn't want to admit I was being dragged along against my will. That would've been shameful. How could there still be women so spineless in this day and age—and how could that woman be me? I didn't want to be seen like that. This isn't the Joseon Dynasty, I told myself, I'm a modern woman, a woman who does what she wants. Sex is nothing, it's nothing. It's nothing. It's meaningless. But I wasn't okay. Sometimes I cried. After I'd been forced against my will, I cried, not understanding what was happening. My life, my body; I couldn't believe that I wasn't in control of any of it. And so I couldn't tell anyone. I couldn't even trust myself—how was anyone else supposed to believe me? My boyfriend looked at me, mystified. He really couldn't understand. He seemed to have no clue why I was acting like this or what the problem was. He said, in a concerned tone of voice, that I was the one with the problem.'

Sujin and I maintained eye contact the whole time. When we were young, we would walk the rice fields together. The fields were vast—so vast we thought our hearts would burst. At dusk the world was coloured every warm shade of red. The air breathed in the last heat of the day, radiating the gentle scent of the afternoon sunlight. We filled our lungs with the breeze and ran to the end of the levee. The crimson-dyed evening was tender, a smile brimming with love.

Thinking of my childhood always brought back these moments. Young girls bursting with goodwill and expectation.

We spoke little. We were wordless. We didn't need to say anything; the world's story was within us. The sun trembled as we stretched out our hands. Back then, I believed: that we could do anything we wanted. If I could return to only one moment in time, without hesitation, I'd choose then. I'd go back, hold Sujin's hand, and run. We'd link arms, stroll around the village, and scoff at whatever anyone said. We'd put fruit and sweets in each other's hands, and walk the endless levees on and on. For that opportunity, I would give anything.

I spoke once more. 'This is what Donghee said to me: Don't take this the wrong way. You have a victim complex.'

The first buttonhole.

But that wasn't what I'd really wanted to tell Sujin. I held my breath. Sujin was silent. I called out to her.

'Sujin-ah.'

Sujin replied. 'Yeah?'

I had one reason for being there. There was something I'd really wanted to say. I smiled at you—your face familiar, like an old memory. Even if you say you can't accept it, it's okay; I'm not doing this to unload my own heart. Not to unburden myself of the truth. It's something I must say to you—that's why. There's no meaning in you accepting it, no need for you to understand. But it means something to me. This is me acknowledging something that happened between us, something I did. You want to know what happened? What I did? This is my real story. My first buttonhole. This is what

I really wanted from Kim Donghee, from Lee Jinsub. The words I needed them to say. The words I never once heard. The words I never once said to you. Those words were always in my heart.

I spoke.

    'Sujin-ah, I'm sorry for leaving you there that day.'

I'm really sorry.

PART 3

17

And, to Eyoung

Tʜɪs ɪs ᴛʜᴇ ꜰɪɴᴀʟ ᴘᴀʀᴛ of the story.

A few days later, Sujin called me. We met up and she handed over Yuri's diary. She told me many things—about what'd happened to her.

Not long after, I heard Sujin and her husband had separated. Apparently a misunderstanding on Sujin's side had turned things sour. Stories like this spread in a flash. People whispered about what a big mistake Sujin had made.

Sujin hadn't spoken about Hyeongyu sunbae that day. And so I had no choice but to guess what had happened to her based on what people said. Within those rumours, Sujin was a character from a legend. The wife who defied the warning not to look her husband in the eye. The girl who ignored advice not to wonder as to his true face. The naïve woman who stupidly fell for the words of the unnies green with envy. Late one night, she held a candle over his face. A single drop of wax fell on her husband's wings and awakened the curse of the gods. Why did you have to go rummaging around? You should've listened to me when I told you not to look. Foolish girl. Abandoning love after being tricked by something like that? Why couldn't you trust his love? That's right. She was foolish right until the story's end. Ignored the warnings, drank the potion and fell into an eternal sleep. In sight of the gods. That's right. She drank the potion right in front of everyone's eyes. I won't be at the mercy of the spells you cast any longer. You lot didn't order this death. It was I who chose the eternal slumber.

We convince ourselves the choice was our own so we can ignore that we are tied to fate. However, perhaps in the end—standing before fate—the one thing we can do is choose. For a long time, the scene where the husband returns and wakes her from her sleep was the only one I remembered.

I wish Sujin happiness. Whatever choice she makes, it'll be for her; a choice made of her own volition. I'm not saying this to prove I wish her the best—that day, she told me herself.

Once Sujin had finished speaking, I let her know my plan. She nodded her head in earnest, and said, if it helped, I could use her story, too. I asked if she was really okay with it; she said that she wasn't. That she really didn't feel good about it. She was concerned people would bad-mouth her family. But Sujin said that, if needed, she would step up. After all, if it had to be done, it had to be done.

'Lately, for the first time in my life I feel like I'm living on correct time,' Sujin said. I had no idea what she meant, and so just listened. Until now, Sujin said, she'd always believed she'd made a choice, but in truth, she was just convincing herself she was holding the key. I entered through this door, and therefore I can open it. But in fact, the key she was holding was a fake; it opened no door. She'd been trying to console herself, she said. But Sujin said that now was different. It's not only keys that open doors.

'Whatever I do, I'll be fine. Things could go to shit, of course. But even then, I'll be okay.'

That moment, I knew: Sujin really would be okay. And maybe I'll never know the whole story. Little rumours, hidden slander, secret revelations written on pieces of paper will travel here and there; but they won't tell you anything. Because we'll never be friends again and share what's truly on our minds. It's funny, those kinds of things you just know. Regardless of anything else, when it comes to that type of thing, I know. This thing I can have faith in; recalling Sujin's words that day, there's something I feel optimistic about. I'm happy I have that memory.

And we really never saw each other again after that. I still haven't heard news of her—by that, I mean about what happened with Hyeongyu sunbae.

If you were to ask how much time has passed, I wonder.

I don't want to talk about how long has passed since that day until this moment, until now.

This is the real final part to the story.

It took place from winter that year to the following spring. I moved out of my place in Seoul and came down to Anjin.

I got a job at a small travel agent and once a month I'd visit my parents in Palhyun. At the end-of-year holidays, when I tried to help cook, my mum scolded me. The kitchen's tiny enough as it is, stop getting in my way and go watch TV or something, Umma said.

'You really don't need my help?' I asked.

She clearly wondered what I was on about. Tactfully, I spoke again.

'Maybe you want help but just aren't saying.'

Umma looked at me, bewildered, and said, 'Since when did I not say anything? I told you to go away.'

Then she told me to take the recycling out. 'You can help with that.'

Buy some ice cream while you're at it, she said. I stepped outside through the door. Snow fell in mighty flakes.

Around when the cold winter air began to gently ease, I went with Tana on a trip to Osaka. We visited Arashiyama, an area dense with bamboo groves. We walked out through the grove and bought some fresh cream Swiss roll sold at the entrance; it was set atop green bamboo leaves.

When I returned, I sent Lee Jinsub a message. I said I'd no intention of talking to him right away, and maybe never would—but that this didn't mean I had nothing to say. I told him I'd contact him once I'd finished what I was working on and gathered my thoughts, and so not to try and talk to me in the meantime.

And, I added, 'Don't think this is over.'

Suddenly, I understood. It finally felt like I was living on correct time.

He didn't reply.

I carried on what I'd been doing. First, I read Yuri's diary in detail. Kang Seungyoung and the pianist—I searched out everyone who'd known Yuri and wrote down all they remembered. I made voice recordings, too. I compared the testimonies, including my own, against the diary. There were still plenty of parts requiring guesswork, but there were some for which the truth was incontestable. Someone had seen a bruise on Yuri's wrist the day after she'd marked in her diary. At a department drinks gathering, someone had witnessed Yuri see Donghee and run. Someone had also seen Yuri and Donghee sitting and talking together, and someone had seen her cry in front of him. Someone had seen Donghee lose his temper at Yuri, too.

But that was all long ago; the memories would lack credibility and reliability as evidence. I wanted to find something indisputable. I kept talking to people, and tried to form a picture of what had happened with as little emotion as possible. Hardly anyone recalled exact dates, but some remembered the general time period. I matched up their eyewitness accounts with Yuri's diary. The period in which someone had seen Yuri avoiding Donghee overlapped with when she'd been going to the hospital for some time. When Yuri was seen crying, or with Donghee, the diary was filled with crosses. In this way, I organized the contents of the eyewitness testimonies, compared this against Yuri's diary, and drew up a timeline. The once-hazy image then grew clear. So much was unveiled—like how most people, rather than not knowing what was happening to Yuri, simply hadn't cared.

I noted down the last time I'd seen Yuri, too. 8th December. The day before—7th December—Yuri had scored a cross. It was the final mark on the calendar.

As if restoring an ancient artefact, I dug up dates and events from the past into the present. As the blurred outline grew a distinct form, I could see a singular picture. I grew certain that the notebook was a record of when Yuri had sex against her will. I felt like I could move onto the next stage.

And so now I could search out clearer evidence. I could probably get the Sexual Violence Support Centre consultation records, as well as testimony from the gynaecology and obstetrics doctor who'd examined Yuri, and from Lee Kanghyun, the professor Yuri had no doubt gone to see.

I wasn't the victim, nor was I the police or the prosecution—I wasn't certain things would make it that far, given the victim, Yuri, wasn't there to give testimony. But revealing what had happened between Yuri and Kim Donghee wasn't the only purpose of restoring the diary. That was just one piece; parts of Yuri scattered in all directions. The original state of those worn fragments, split and strewn; its complete form unknown. I was piecing it together.

Spring.

*

I stepped through the entrance to Anjin University, and cherry blossoms sprinkled white over my head. I breathed in the scent. This was the smell of Anjin I remembered. The fishy stench of the lake; walks on rainy days. I would shove my feet half into my green-smeared trainers, and walk on and on all the way here—to see those petals fallen to the ground under the weight of the raindrops. Walking that spongy, white path; it erased that stale odour attached to my body. What happened? Which memories still remain?

I headed towards the humanities grounds. As she'd said over the phone the day before, Kim Eyoung was putting up hand-written posters on the walls. I walked over to her.

I told Kim Eyoung the words I'd prepared. About Yuri and me. And about the other friend, whose name I couldn't reveal, but who, if Kim Eyoung wanted, would testify. About women; about a few possibilities that may or may not be achieved through women's testimonies. And about yet other women, who, looking at those possibilities, may or may not get the courage to stand.

Kim Eyoung received Yuri's diary with cautious hands. She carefully turned its pages—this is the moment the story began. Yes. An obvious conclusion. I'm like the cliché of the story. Isn't it so? A person you could meet anywhere. Something that could happen anywhere. An event neither remarkable nor impressive. A person who'd always existed. This is my method. Much like writing somebody endless letters, burying oneself into books, recording everything that had happened one by one; doing anything and everything I could.

However, from time to time, all those things become fabrication—not when I speak of what I went through, but when I write down what I did. I write, over and over, several versions of my memories. A cliché only goes as far as closing the door and stepping out. No one knows what's needed to open a closed door, or to close a door once more. And so I write in your name.

Your story: the one you wanted to tell everyone, yet that no one could read. Within your story, we stand together in the narrow alleyway. Dim light falls to the ground, and a long shadow presses down on your shoulders. You call my name, but I turn back around. I walk away.

Jina-ya?

Jina-ya? Help me.

I look ahead as I walk. I'm imagining the huge rice fields before me, that place vast, so vast I thought my heart might burst. To tear off your voice that clung to my body. To forget that my body was already sodden with the stench of the water, emitting its stale odour.

But at some point, my heart changes. I turn back around. You stand before me. I look at you and walk. Because in that story, I'm a person you could meet anywhere. Someone who went through the kind of thing that happens all the time, someone neither remarkable nor impressive, the kind of person who has always been there. It has to be this way. That's why within this story, at the conclusion I say the words that naturally flow out; the reply most obvious.

*

'Yuri-ya, what is it?'

Twenty years old.
　Eyes shining bright.

But that's not how the story ends. The person to end this story is you. The person at the start of the whole story, who opened back up an old future. And maybe this is where the real story begins. Because in the final chapter of the story, the moment everything came to an end, the person to respond is you. That's right. Now it's your turn.

18

Yuri

Date: 15th December 2006

ACCIDENT & EMERGENCY
PATIENT PERSONAL BELONGINGS BAG

Registration number: 19049

Patient name: Ha Yuri

List of belongings: bag, purse, student ID card, makeup bag, papers (documents—specified as school assignment)

Recipient: None (discard)

✚ Anjin University Hospital

Final Assignment
Content Creation Practice
15th December 2006

Title: Another Person

Eurasia Cultural Content Department
Class of 2005, Ha Yuri

AUTHOR'S NOTE

I won't set myself limits; I live each day in that expectation.

Rest in peace, Yuri.